DONOVAN
DYNASTY

A DONOVAN DYNASTY NOVEL

AC ARTHUR

FOREWORD

Dear Reader,

It's that time again! I so love jumping back into the world of the Donovans again. It's like being home.

Roark Donovan came onto the scene in DANE. He's one of the UK Donovans who're finally ready to have their stories told. By the end of this book you'll have another look at Ridge and Suri and the always lovable Aunt Birdie. Tamika Rayder came into Roark's life at a moment they both needed healing and closure. To have them fall in love at this volatile time was a task, but I believe it's what they both needed. There're a few other Donovan favorites in this book. I hope you'll enjoy catching up with them.

Happy Reading,

ac

PART I

"No one ever told me that grief felt so like fear."
—*C.S. Lewis*

CHAPTER 1

Hyde Park, London

For as long as he lived and as many breaths as he'd be blessed to take, she'd always be the love of his life.

The worship space in Bolton Park Baptist Church overflowed with people who'd come to pay their respects. Their presence added a mixture of heavy perfumes and colognes that, combined with the strong, sweet aroma of the many flowers occupying the space, had Roark Donovan closing a fist over his mouth as he coughed. The couple who'd just walked past, shook his hand and whispered words meant to comfort. All Roark could think was that they must've had some sort of competition going for which one could have the most offensive scent.

He was already tired of standing, and he was definitely tired of saying "thank you," "we appreciate it" and "yes, we'll let you know if we need anything." The latter particularly rubbed him the wrong way, because nobody in this room could give him the one thing he needed.

His mother.

At some point, the clergy filed into the room. Two men cloaked in robes standing just behind the pastor, who adjusted the microphone on the podium before speaking.

Roark had no idea what was said. He sat when they were directed to do so, and as part of the family, was not asked to stand again. When the choir stood, there was singing, clapping and crying. He'd heard more crying in the past two weeks than he ever wanted to hear again. As if on cue, Suri bent down, burying her face in her hands as she cried even harder.

His heart ached for his sister, and when he put his hand on her back, rubbing in small circles, he wished like hell that single act could take all the hurt and sorrow from her. It couldn't, he knew that, but hearing her cry, knowing she suffered and being helpless to stop any of it, was just another part of this nightmare.

Ridge sat stoically on Roark's other side, his fists tight and resting on his thighs. Roark's younger brother wore a black suit almost identical to Roark's but for the style of their jackets. Their shirts were white, ties a blood-orange color that was their mother's favorite hue. Suri wore a cream-colored dress with an orange belt and matching shoes. The three children of Maxine Donovan paid homage to the woman who loved and raised them.

Roark was pulled from his thoughts when the pastor stood in front of him. He looked up and listened to what was being said, nodded and then reached for Suri's hand. She gripped his hand in return, and he recalled the way she used to do that when she was little and he'd hold her hand as they'd crossed the street. At thirty years old, she was ten years younger than him and still much shorter, which he noted when they both stood.

The funeral director was giving instructions for what would happen next, who'd go where and how they'd continue with the day, but all Roark could think about was that this was almost over. The time he had with his mother close by was almost done, and his chest felt like it was collapsing with that thought.

Disregarding what was being said, he released Suri's hand and stepped away from the first row of seats, where he'd been standing. He walked with steps that felt heavy and labored toward the rose-gold-colored casket and placed both his palms on top. Dropping his head and closing his eyes, he hoped she could feel him, hoped she knew how much he loved and appreciated her for all the sacrifices she'd made for him and his siblings. She'd been everything to him, and now, he wasn't sure what he'd be without her.

Hands rubbed his back this time, one from the left side and another from the right. Suri rested her head on his arm, still crying, quietly now. Ridge stood close, and the moment Roark heard his brother sniffle, warm tears ran down Roark's face.

"Who cooked this macaroni and cheese with this awful, crumbly mess on top?"

Bridgette "Birdie" Donovan was not happy today.

Or any other day, for that matter. Roark tried not to pay too much attention to her whenever she was around. Today, he especially didn't feel like dealing with her bristling candor, nonstop complaints, or burning insults. In short, he just didn't feel like Aunt Birdie.

"Come over here and get me another plate, and leave that

mess in the pan. Better yet, take it back into the kitchen—nobody needs to see that catastrophe." His aunt was talking to Jade, his cousin Linc's wife, who was five months pregnant and still as beautiful as ever in a knee-length black dress.

Roark immediately pushed his chair back and stood. He picked up the plate Aunt Birdie had referred to. "I'll get you another plate." He hadn't been able to hide the crispness in his tone and wasn't really interested in how his aunt felt about it.

Aunt Birdie was the only girl and youngest child of Roark's great-grandparents, Rowan and Adeline Donovan. She was ninety-two years old, had no children and had never married. She'd also never worked a day in her life. Thanks to her inheritance from her parents and the increasing worth of her shares in Donovan Oilwell, she never had to. She owned a house in her hometown of Beaumont, Texas but spent most of her time traveling or harassing the staff at the Donovan family-owned Camelot Resort on Sansonique, their private Caribbean island.

For the last two weeks, she'd been in London, staying at the flat Roark had rented for Suri after the fire had destroyed a good portion of his parents' Hyde Park home. To keep Suri from locking their great-aunt in a closet, Ridge had agreed to stay there with them temporarily. Jade touched Roark's arm in silent thanks as he walked past her, and he did everything he could to muster up at least a partial smile in response. "Sit down, you've been on your feet since eight this morning," he told her.

Jade and Linc were from Las Vegas, but two years ago, Linc had moved his wife and twin twelve-year-old daughters to Paris, where he'd opened his new casino called the Odyssey.

"I'm fine, just trying to make sure this goes as smoothly as possible." Jade lifted a hand and tucked her long, dark hair back behind an ear. "I know this isn't easy."

"Shouldn't have had this get-together." Aunt Birdie rolled her eyes as she looked around the room. "People've been dropping by all week, smiling in our faces like they knew Maxine personally. Some of them probably only knew how much money she had after Gabe died."

Roark chaffed at the mention of his father, who'd died when he was seventeen. "It's polite."

"It's a nuisance," Aunt Birdie snapped. "And I thought you were getting me another plate."

After a brief sigh, Roark didn't even bother to comment, but turned away from Jade and walked toward the kitchen of the hall they'd rented for the repast. Forty-five minutes ago, he'd left his mother's body at the cemetery, where she'd rest forever.

There were one hundred fifty people in the main hall, sitting at tables topped with white linen cloths. A buffet was set up with enough food to feed double the amount of people who'd received special invitations to the family repast. Roark had wanted to return home. There he could continue working with the fire investigation officer at the London Fire Brigade on the cause of the fire that had torn through his parents' home, killing his mother as she'd slept.

"Excuse me, sir. Can I help you?"

The starkly spoken question brought his focus back to the present, and Roark blinked before shaking his head. "Sorry. Yes. Could you fix another plate for my aunt, without macaroni and cheese, please?"

The woman, dressed in black pants and a white chef's jacket, smiled and took the plate he'd extended to her. "Certainly. I'll bring it to your table, Mr. Donovan."

He was Mr. Donovan. He had been since that rainy

Saturday twenty-three years ago, when he'd stood graveside, watching as his aunts and uncles laid long-stemmed roses on top of his father dusky gray casket. Today, he'd set five long-stemmed orange roses on his mother's casket—one for each member of their family. She'd always called them her 'heart'. Even after his father had passed away, his mother had continued to love Gabriel Donovan. Now, the two of them would be together again. Roark swallowed hard and took a deep breath. The release was shaky as he fought back tears. Clenching his fingers into fists at his side, he insisted he was done crying, at least for today.

Remembering to thank the staff member and once again smile, Roark turned away from her. In the main hall once again, he looked around at the many people either sitting at tables or standing in small groups talking. A good number of them were family, Donovans who'd come from as far as Las Vegas, Nevada, and from his mother's side, the Walters, who were mainly from the UK. Also, in the mix were business associates who'd worked at Donovan Oilwell UK, the branch of the family company Roark's father had run until his death. The company Roark and Ridge had been running up until two years ago, when Roark had branched off to create a new arm of the Donovan dynasty. Roark had teamed up with his cousin Dane to bring Donovan Oilwell UK into the 21st century by expanding into the clean-air market with a focus on fostering sustainable cities. From that collaboration, Donovan International had been born.

New businesses, new family members—everything was changing.

But change was good. His mother had always told him that. Without change, life became stagnant, boring.

Roark felt like his life was over.

Until a little body slammed into his calves, and the arms that went with said body wrapped around his knees.

"Whoa." Roark looked down to see the top of a head full of dark brown curls. "Slow down there, buddy."

His warning was followed by giggles, and when the little boy looked up at him, Roark couldn't help but chuckle too. He also couldn't resist picking the toddler up and holding him close.

New life. Maxine had loved kids and had never missed an opportunity to tell her children how many grandchildren she'd wanted. In the past few years, she'd slacked off a bit on saying this to Roark because of his divorce, but he knew she'd still felt the same. She'd wanted a house full of grandchildren, who'd be the fifth generation of Donovans. As Roark nuzzled a chubby cheek, he closed his eyes with the pang of disappointment that his mother would never be granted that wish.

The feeling wasn't allowed to fester, as from the other side, another toddler had latched onto him. Now, Roark chuckled harder before bending down to scoop the second smiling kiddo into his arms.

"Good catch." Noelle Remington smiled as she walked up to him and crossed her arms over her chest. "You look pretty comfortable with those two."

"I'm not upset they found me." In fact, their laughing eyes and cheerful voices—even though he couldn't understand their child-like gibberish—gave a sprinkle of joy on this otherwise bleak day. "They were running around so much at the flat last night that I only saw them in a blur."

Noelle was his cousin Brock's wife and Jade's sister. Brock and Noelle ran Linc's Gramercy II casino in St. Michael's, Maryland. The set of twins Roark held in his arms were their children, Bradyn and Natasha.

"They don't call them the 'terrible twos' for nothing," Noelle quipped. "But kids look good on you."

They felt good too, a fact that only brought back the pain Roark was becoming all too accustomed to. "We don't have any little children here. Well, now we have your sister's twins, Torian and Tamala, but they're not children. I know, because they told me so a few months ago when I took them to a fashion show in Paris."

In contrast to her sister, Noelle wore her hair in a short, curly style that closely resembled her children's except for her bright blond color. She also wore a black dress with black pumps and large diamond stud earrings. "Yes, my nieces are really growing up. I didn't see them that often when they were living in the States, and now that they're all the way across the pond, I'll see them even less." She smiled when Bradyn reached out to her, and she lifted him from Roark's hold. After kissing his chubby cheek, Noelle returned her attention to Roark. "I just wish this visit could've been for a better reason. I'm so sorry for your loss, Roark. I know we're far away, but if there's anything you need that Brock and I can help you with—"

Roark knew how that sentence would end, and he cut her off with a shake of his head. "I know. Our family's always been tight-knit, even when thousands of miles apart. But we'll get through this—Ridge and Suri and I." He'd said those words a lot in the past two weeks. He'd even sat with his brother and sister trying to convince them that those words were true. But inside, Roark wasn't so sure.

"And Aunt Birdie. I heard her telling Uncle Bernard and Uncle Albert that she wasn't leaving until she knew the three of you were alright. She said your parents would've wanted it that way."

"I don't know about that," Roark added with another

shake of his head. "Aunt Birdie and my mum had their moments."

"Aunt Birdie has moments with everyone," Noelle replied and then reached out to rub her hand over her daughter's head. "Are you getting sleepy, sunshine?"

Roark looked down at Natasha, who'd rested her head on his shoulder and stuck her first finger into her mouth. He hadn't noticed she'd stopped giggling, but had instead allowed himself to languish in the warmth of her against him. "I can bring her over to your table." He wasn't going to let her carry them both across the crowded room, even though he'd seen how easily Noelle handled both the toddlers in the past few days.

"Thanks. We brought their car seats inside, so she can nap in there until we leave."

There were six family tables set up and positioned toward the front of the room. Brock, Uncle Albert and Uncle Bernard were sitting at one when Roark and Noelle approached.

"It's nap time," Noelle said, and Brock immediately stood to take Natasha from Roark.

"Thanks, man," Brock told him.

"No problem." It wasn't a problem to hold two of his youngest family members, or to watch their sweet faces as they were set into the seats and given cups of milk.

"How you holding up?" Uncle Bernard asked.

Roark nodded. "I'm good," he lied.

"He's steady, like Gabe was," Uncle Albert said.

Albert and Bernard were technically Roark's cousins, as their father and Roark's grandfather were brothers, but they were senior members of the family and as such were given the respect of a title before their names. Just as Linc's daughters called Roark "Uncle Roark." Respect was something branded into the minds of all the Donovan children from day one.

Uncle Bernard agreed with a nod. "And smart too. I've seen the financial reports from Donovan International. You and Dane are building something great there." That was said with the pride of a Senior Donovan, for the son he'd just gotten to know in the past couple of years, and for Roark, whom they'd all kept tabs on since his father's death.

"Thanks, Uncle Bernard. We've been working really hard on developing innovative techniques, and we're starting to see some success." Those words were easy for Roark to say. Business had always been easy for Roark.

"Carrying on the legacy, that's what it's all about," Uncle Albert added. "I've got grandkids, Bernard's got grandkids. Our children are all married and branching off into their businesses. That's what our great-grandfather wanted. It's what Gabe and Maxine wanted. The three of you have to carry on for them. You have to keep the family going here."

"Yes, sir," Roark replied, accepting yet another responsibility to carry. He felt his phone vibrating in his pocket and immediately reached for it. "I should take this," he said with an absent glance at the screen.

Uncle Albert stood, clapping a hand on Roark's arm. "Don't let everything be about business, Roark. Enjoy your family while you can."

Because tomorrow wasn't promised.

Uncle Albert hadn't said those last words, but Roark knew how the saying ended. He knew, because his mother had said it often after his father's death. Just as she'd been sure to keep their small family as close to her as she possibly could, until she couldn't anymore.

"I will, Uncle Albert. I promise." But Roark didn't know how far that promise was going to go. Right now, he couldn't see past his grief to do much more than handle the most mundane of business tasks, let alone think about how he was going to keep his family together. And by the time he'd gotten out of the main hall and into the foyer of the building, his phone had stopped ringing.

"Hey, Roark."

After swiping the screen to see the call had come from a number he didn't recognize, Roark looked up at the sound of his name. He pushed his phone back into his pocket and walked across the room to where Linc and his other cousin Cade were standing.

Cade was on the phone with his back turned to them, but Linc reached out and clapped a hand onto Roark's shoulder when he was close. "He's on the phone with Investigator McGee. They went back over the scene this morning, using the dogs to see if they can identify an accelerant."

Linc and Cade also wore black suits, white shirts and orange ties. In fact, every member of the family had been asked to wear something in that color scheme in honor of Maxine. As he thought of that now, he recalled Jade and Noelle had been wearing a wrist corsage made with the same orange roses that adorned his mother's casket.

"Why didn't he call me? I specifically told him to call me with any developments," Roark said when Linc's words registered in his mind.

Linc let his hand fall from Roark's shoulder as he nodded. "And we told him not to bother you with it today. The only reason I'm telling you now is because they think they found something."

Roark didn't like that there'd been a concerted effort to not tell him what was going on with his mother's case, but wasn't going to argue that point here today. Besides, Cade was an FBI agent; he could obviously get more information than Roark would be privy to, even though Cade's specialty was profiling and not fire investigation.

Cade turned to them, tucking his phone into his pocket. "Gasoline," he told them with a solemn look.

Linc smirked. "Not very original."

Rage clawed at Roark. "In the house. How did someone get into the house and pour enough gasoline around to torch the entire second floor? There's a top-notch security system that wasn't disturbed in any way."

"Yeah, I know." Cade showed no outward reaction, but Roark knew that was because he was in work mode. "McGee's gonna continue his investigation, but it looks like he may be turning it over to the homicide detectives at some point."

Cade's words were bland, and Linc followed them with a concerned look, while Roark felt like exploding. Anger poured into every crevice of his body, inching out the grief that had taken up permanent residence since the night he'd received the call that had changed his life.

"I've got some contacts within the MPD too." Cade may have worked primarily in the US, but he knew the ins and outs of all the law enforcement agencies over here such as the Metropolitan Police Department. "I'll be on the phone with them first thing tomorrow to see if he can stick his nose in before McGee finishes with his report."

Cade had also gotten the autopsy report expedited. Roark's fists were balled so tight the muscles in his arms began to ache.

Linc slid a hand into the front pocket of his pants. "Have you talked to Ridge and Suri about all this?"

"No. I don't want to worry them." Roark ignored the fact that he was keeping info from his siblings, the same way he'd just been angry about Cade and Linc keeping info from him.

"The media isn't going to give a damn about worrying any of us. The fire being in such a prestigious neighborhood, not to mention the resulting death of one of the wealthiest women in London, has already been receiving front-page coverage. Tabloids are just beginning to dig into whatever they can find on Aunt Maxine, going back to when she and Uncle Gabe first moved into that house. This won't be our secret for long."

Roark knew Linc was right. He knew he should talk to Ridge and Suri, but he couldn't. How was he supposed to tell his brother and sister that their mother had been murdered?

CHAPTER 2

*T*hree days later, Roark was once again at his office, sitting behind his desk. With one ankle propped on his knee, he leaned back in the chair and stared out the window. As Donovan International's CEO, he had a large office on the top floor of the glass-and-steel building they owned on the South Bank of the River Thames.

He'd been here since seven this morning, had reluctantly attended an R&D meeting at ten-thirty, had lunch at one and now at three-fifteen was avoiding the mountain of paperwork that had accumulated during his two-week absence. No matter how hard he tried, getting his mind to focus on his job wasn't working. He knew he had things to do, and was acutely aware the initial three to five years in a new business were crucial. While this wasn't his first turn at running a company, He needed to remain focused, to stay on top of everything so he could spot potential problems before they got out of control.

Right now, all he could see were the heavy gray clouds that had been hanging around all day. Glancing down, he saw the shined top of one wing-tip shoe and the black sock he wore beneath charcoal-gray slacks. His left hand rested on his thigh, while his right elbow was propped on the desk. With every breath he took, he was reminded that his mother was no longer here on this earth with him. That she'd been taken away by someone who'd wanted her dead.

That was a hard pill to swallow and each time he tried, it left a bitter and nasty taste in his mouth. The desk phone chimed, and Roark turned quickly to stare at it. It chimed again, a little red light toward the edge of the phone's screen blinking with the sound. His assistant usually answered and screened his calls, but she wouldn't answer this one, because it was on his personal line. Every executive in the company had a personal line for family and clients they'd speak to no matter what was going on. His family knew the best way to reach him was his cell, and since he'd already established he wasn't in the mood to do anymore work, he just watched the red light continue to blink.

Years of his father teaching him about good customer service, being a good listener to their clients and accessible to the extent that it didn't interfere with his family life had Roark cursing before reaching out to grab the handset. "Hello." One word spoken in a solemn tone that he hoped let whoever was on the other line know he didn't want to talk.

"Hello, Roark."

He sat up in his chair slowly, dropping his leg down until his foot stomped the floor. "Katrina?"

"I called your old number, and some guy answered." She gave a little chuckle. "Then I was transferred to the operator, and she told me you no longer worked in that office, that you'd moved on to another business venture. She gave me the number, since you didn't bother to tell me about the change."

Facing his desk now, Roark rested both elbows on the desk blotter. "I haven't seen or heard from you in four years."

"We were married for three and a half years."

"And you left that marriage because I no longer made you happy. I took that to mean you had no intention of keeping in touch." At the time, Roark had taken the words in the very short note Katrina had left him to mean a number of things.

"Even in the end, you couldn't muster up the strength to care." Her tone was always accusatory.

He pinched the bridge of his nose and contemplated asking her what the hell that was supposed to mean, but too much time had passed and now he simply didn't care. The marriage was over, and he had no intention of taking that dive again. "Is that why you tracked me down?" His temples throbbed and he hoped like hell her answer would be no. Because if Roark didn't want to work, he definitely didn't want to talk to his ex-wife about the demise of their marriage.

The quick intake of breath being released with a loud huff was a sign she didn't like his question. She was probably running her fingers through her hair too. That's what she did when she was frustrated. Why that memory of all things slapped at his already bad mood, he didn't know.

"I wanted to express my condolences. I read about the fire and Maxine's death."

"Thank you.," The response came as if he were still on autopilot.

"How are Ridge and Suri holding up?"

"They're fine."

"Right," she snapped. "Because you're taking care of them. And nobody needs to take care of you, because you're Roark Gideon Donovan. You're the strongest, most dependable, most—"

"I'm at work, Katrina." He'd interrupted her because he

didn't need to hear what his ex thought of him. Not today. "I appreciate your call, but we're all handling this as best we can."

She sighed. "I don't want to fight with you, Roark."

He couldn't tell if that were true or not, so he just didn't respond.

"Did all of your family come? I know Maxine loved to see your father's side of the family more than her own. She hated that you guys were the only Donovans in London." Katrina was from Toronto. He'd met her when he'd been there on a business trip. For a couple of months, they'd done the long-distance thing but he'd quickly tired of that and had asked her to move to London. She'd accepted, and he'd leased her a flat for a year before they were married.

"All of them couldn't come, but enough did. It was great seeing them." It had actually been really nice to have so much family so close by for a few days. Suri had loved being around all the children.

"I would've come too. If you'd called to let me know what was going on."

"You made your loss of interest in me and my family pretty clear four years ago." His words were filled with hurt and disdain, even though he hadn't felt anything for Katrina in a very long time.

"And now I'm making it known that I wish I would've been told the woman who'd once been my mother-in-law was dead. Damn, Roark you don't have to be such an insufferable ass all the time."

"I have to be who I am." And in doing so, that did make him insufferable most of the time. He was already aware of that fact. How many times had he had to be the bad guy with Ridge and Suri? How many times had they hated something he'd done or said in regard to a decision they'd made? But that hadn't mattered; Roark did what he thought his father would've done in the same circumstances. He took care of his family the way he'd always done, and he didn't give a damn who disagreed with that.

"I wanted to be there, Roark. Can't you understand that, at least? I would've liked to have been there to see her one last time."

"It was a closed casket." Because her body had been burned too badly for any other option.

She made another sound that he knew meant she was getting tired of this conversation. That was fine—he was too. "Tell, Ridge and Suri how sorry I am that she's gone." She took a quick breath. "And sorry that they're stuck with you."

The line disconnected before he could respond, and Roark slowly placed the headset back on the base. He wasn't giving Ridge and Suri that message, just as he wasn't going to acknowledge how much the disappointed sound of Katrina's voice reiterated how he'd failed at being a good husband. Not only had he failed with her, the marriage hadn't produced any children either, both facts he knew had saddened his mother.

The Next Day

"The last will and testament of Maxine Luraye Donovan states as follows." Francois Favre had been the family attorney since before Roark was born. His lean frame sat hunched over a large dark wood desk. Wire-rimmed glasses were perched midway down the length of his nose, and his long fingers shook slightly as they held onto the papers he now read from.

Roark sat in the middle guest chair across from Francois, his elbows resting on the arms of the chair, his gaze aimed at the solicitor. Per their usual seating arrangement, which was more than a little strange, Ridge was on one side of him and Suri was on the other. They were the only ones summoned to this meeting with the solicitor, but Aunt Birdie sat on the green-and-burgundy paisley print couch across the room. She'd insisted on coming, and while Roark could've put his foot down and staunchly refused, he hadn't had the energy to turn away one of his oldest relatives.

"I nominate and appoint Roark G. Donovan as Personal Representative," Francois continued.

That fact was of surprise to no one, especially not Roark. He'd been running his mother's house as if he were the head of the household since he was twenty-five, and before then—in the years between his father's passing and Roark coming of age—Francois had handled all the legal stuff for Maxine. Other attorneys at the large firm where Francois worked took care of Donovan Oilwell legal business. Once Roark had finished college and taken over the company, he'd made sure all the firm's attorneys reported directly to him with everything involving his mother and the oil well.

Francois went on for another twenty minutes, going over every detail of the thirty-page will, and nobody said a word. But the silence didn't last long. "Now," Francois continued. "You'll recall in the first few pages where the expenses were discussed. It was your mother's wish that funeral and burial expenses be paid as soon after her death as reasonably convenient."

"Everything was paid upfront," Roark interrupted.

Francois' cool gray eyes peered over the top of his glasses. "As evidenced by the copies of the funeral director and the cemetery's bill you provided."

Roark caught the tendrils of annoyance in the solicitor's comment, but he didn't care. He wanted to get this over with quickly. "Then there should be no need to discuss those expenses at this time."

"Let him do what he's getting paid to do," Aunt Birdie added.

Suri reached between the two chairs to touch Roark's arm, and when he looked over to her, it was to see her giving him a "calm down, it's almost over" nod. He took a deep breath and released it slowly while Francois turned his attention to another stack of papers.

"The insurance company is prepared to immediately release the funds from the policy it held. The check will need to be added to the estate to be processed. Then it may be disbursed in equal amounts to Ridge, Suri and, of course, Roark." Francois nodded at each one of them as he said their names.

Ridge shifted in his chair. "We don't need that money."

"You may do with it what you wish, sir," Francois told him with a nod. "But I must add that in light of the murder investigation, what you do with that money may become—"

Suri dropped her hand from Roark's arm. "Murder investigation?"

Francois stopped speaking and glanced at Suri, then to Roark. When Roark didn't immediately speak, Francois huffed. "The autopsy report stated cause of death as homicide. That means someone killed your mother." His tone was brisk and without any emotion.

Roark wanted to reach out and grab him by his scrawny neck.

Suri was immediately out of her chair. "What?"

Ridge sat forward. "Wait a minute, why are we just hearing about this?"

"Because I didn't want to tell you until we had more information." Roark knew the moment the words were out that all eyes would turn to him, but he wasn't prepared for how heated those glares would be.

Even Aunt Birdie stood from where she'd been seated and made her way over to stand right behind his chair. "You knew, and you didn't tell any of us," she said. "You'd better have a damn good reason why."

Suri was shaking her head. "There is no good reason. You had no right!" Her voice went from almost cracking with grief to yelling with rage in about three seconds, and Ridge got up and moved next to her.

"We're entitled to any and all information regarding our mum, Roark. You should've told us." Ridge wasn't any happier than Suri was at this moment—which Roark had expected—but he wasn't yelling. At least not yet.

"I didn't want to upset you more than was necessary." It was the only excuse he had.

Roark hated the pain etched on his siblings' faces. Ridge had the darker complexion of their father, his long locs pulled and twisted into some intricate design that left them hanging neatly down his back. He was only an inch shorter than Roark and stood with an arm around Suri's shoulder.

Suri leaned into Ridge, her arms folded across her chest. She was the mirror-image of their mother, except her flair for making a bold fashion statement no matter what she wore and her love of makeup. Today, her hair was styled in a very neat bun, her lips were ruby-red, and the black-and-white checkered pantsuit she wore fit her small frame perfectly.

"This has been extremely difficult for all of us. I wanted to get all the facts first before I came to you with this." He still believed that had been the right move, even though the two of them were staring at him as if his words had floated into oblivion.

Aunt Birdie poked him in the shoulder. "Well, cat's outta the bag now. Tell us what you know."

Roark glanced over his shoulder at his aunt and met her steady gaze. She wore black today as well, with some type of silver wrap. Her gray-streaked hair was styled and hung straight to her jaw. "From the start, the firefighters believed the fire was intentionally set. But they have to follow protocols in their investigation, so we did the next best thing and had the autopsy expedited." He was still leaving out bits and pieces, but he suspected they just wanted him to get to the point.

"Who is 'we'?" Ridge asked.

Roark met his brother's gaze. "Cade, Linc and I."

"Oh, so our cousins get to know what's going on with our mum's death, but we don't." Ridge didn't hold back the heat in his tone, and Roark couldn't really say he blamed him.

That didn't mean he wasn't going to hold steady to his reasoning. "Yes. You know that as an FBI agent, Cade has access to people who can dig into things quickly and quietly. Linc was there the day the Station Officer from the Fire Brigade shared some of their preliminary findings, so he was automatically in the loop."

"And you couldn't pick up a phone and call us? We couldn't be looped in?" Suri shook her head, her lips thinning as Roark knew she was doing her best not to cuss him out in front of Aunt Birdie.

"Not a smart move," Aunt Birdie said. "But what's done is done. What did the report say?"

Roark stood then. He was tired of everyone looking down on him as if he were in the hot seat. Well, he technically was, but he didn't have to act like it. "She was alive when the fire was started." He said those words quickly, because no matter how many times he'd read them, or saw the typed words on the report in his mind, he still hadn't come to terms with them. "There was smoke in her lungs." He cleared his throat and pushed on. "There was a drug in her system."

"A drug?" Suri asked.

"Succinylcholine. It's like a powerful muscle relaxant. So, she laid in her bed, wide awake, while her room and the ones closest to her were set on fire." There, he'd said it out loud. Somebody had killed his mother, and Roark had no idea why.

Tears were already running down Suri's face as Ridge held her closer, his lips drawn in a tight line. Even Aunt Birdie was silent.

Francois hadn't spoken in the last few minutes but now walked around his desk and came to stand in front of them. "A detective by the name of Gibbons, who works in the Major Investigation Unit of the Metropolitan Police Department, called the office yesterday. As I'm not in the criminal division of our firm, I didn't take the call, but the message was passed on to me because of our appointment today. The detective wishes to speak to each of you about your mother's death. You are, of course, not advised to talk to anyone without legal counsel." Again, the solicitor's words were delivered in a very dour tone as he folded his hands in front of him.

"Oh, my stars. They're suspects." Aunt Birdie stepped closer to Francois. "You're saying my nephews and niece are suspected of killing their mother? Of drugging her and burning her in her bed? I've never heard anything more preposterous in my life. We're Donovans! We're dedicated to family above all else. You and this detective are out of your damn minds!"

Roark moved to place a hand on his aunt's shoulder. "It's okay, Aunt Birdie. I'll handle this." He didn't look back at Ridge and Suri. He kept his hand on his aunt and stared

Francois directly in the eye. "We'll make statements regarding our whereabouts at the time of the fire, and that's it. I'll contact Edward Burrows in your criminal department, and he can have those statements notarized and submit them to the detective. That'll be the extent of our cooperation with the MPD."

Francois acknowledged Roark's words with a stiff nod.

"As for the will and the estate, send me, my brother and sister a copy. We'll handle whatever's necessary and let you know if we have any difficulty. Now, we're leaving." Roark guided Aunt Birdie toward the door, hoping his siblings would follow.

They did, and once outside the solicitor's office, they watched as Roark helped Aunt Birdie into the back seat of the car waiting at the curb for them.

"We're not finished." Suri wasn't going to let this go easily. "I'm beyond pissed at you for keeping this from us, and I know you have more answers than what you just gave in there."

"She's right," Ridge added. "We'll meet at your place tonight to discuss."

Roark only nodded his agreement. There was no use in arguing with them on the street. He wasn't going to apologize for doing what he'd thought was right to protect them. He'd been doing so all their lives and he wasn't going to stop now, no matter how bent out of shape they were about it.

CHAPTER 3

Painswick
Gloucestershire, England

"*D*ammit!" Tamika ran to the stove, pulled on oven mitts and moved the large pot of sauce to one of the back burners. She turned off the burner she'd had on high heat—hence the reason her meatballs and sauce were bubbling. Well, that wasn't the only reason. If she hadn't been focusing on the right words to put in the text message she was sending, she would've remembered to keep her mind on her food.

While the mitts were on, she pulled open the over door and eased the shelf out midway. She almost sighed as the aroma of the fresh bread hit her nostrils. It needed a few more minutes to get that golden brown on top, and then she could take it out. After putting it back and closing the oven, she moved to the counter and picked up her phone.

Of course, there was no response yet. It was silly to think

he would've responded so soon. Especially since he'd been ignoring her for the last week.

"She won't eat a thing," Tuppence, the housekeeper said when she entered the kitchen. "For weeks, I used money from the house account to pay for one of those meal services. She never ate any of it."

Because the food was probably nasty.

Tamika didn't say that aloud and she went to the stove so Tuppence couldn't see the face she made to go with her thoughts. "My mother taught me how to cook. My grandmother taught her. She'll eat this spaghetti and meatballs. It was my Dad's favorite."

Again, she left out what she was really thinking. Her mother was going to eat this spaghetti, even if Tamika had to stuff each forkful into her mouth.

Sandra Rayder had lost forty pounds in the last year so that her once-toned build now appeared gaunt and wiry. Legs that used to walk unflinchingly on five-inch heels barely held her small frame upright when Tamika had insisted she get out of bed and walk into the bathroom for her shower. Her mother wasn't sick, at least not physically. Sandra was heartbroken and depressed, and while Tamika knew she couldn't feed her mother out of either of those conditions, she was hopeful that leaving her apartment in Alexandria, Virginia to come to the English countryside would make a difference.

Tamika was still trying to convince herself that was her main reason for coming here.

"Thank you for all your hard work, Tuppence. I'm glad she's had you this past year."

Tuppence, the five-foot-tall woman with low-cut gray curls on her head, umber complexion and robust demeanor, had kept this house going for the last fifteen years Tamika's parents had owned it. The lovely four-bedroom cottage situated in the Golden Valley area of town had been a twentieth wedding anniversary present from Tamika's father to her mother. Up until last year, the Rayders had come once a year for three weeks to vacation here. The remaining time, the rooms had been rented, the money going into the Rayders' retirement fund. That, in addition to the money from her father's pension and life insurance, was what her mother was living off.

"It's my job." Her tone was curt as always, and heavily tinged with a British accent. "It's also good that you came. She needs you." *And you should've been here before now.* Those were the words Tuppence left out.

It didn't matter whether they were stated or implied, Tamika already knew, and she'd berated herself enough for that knowledge. But there'd been a much more important reason for her to remain in Alexandria after her mother had decided to leave.

"How long will you stay?" The housekeeper's movements were as brisk as her tone. Every part of the large, country-themed kitchen was hers, and everything she did was to highlight that fact. Like now—she opened a cabinet and pulled out the colander Tamika was going to need in about five minutes when it was time to remove the noodles from the boiling water.

"Not sure yet." It was a lie, but then again, it wasn't. She accepted the metal colander and switched off the burner beneath the pot of boiling water.

Tamika had been meaning to visit her mother in the last year but hadn't found the time. She should've made the time and perhaps she would have if she'd known how serious her mother's condition was. Luckily for them both, the insurance company where Tamika worked had decided she needed a very long vacation—or rather, a permanent one.

"You should make the time to be with her. Your father's death hit her hard. Never seen two people so much in love." Tuppence picked up a cloth, went to the sink and turned on the water to wet it. She moved to the counters, wiping them down with a vicious and efficient rhythm. All the while telling Tamika exactly what she thought, without having to be asked. "It's hard when a part of you is gone. I know, because my Jon left me ten years ago." "Oh, I'm sorry, Tuppence. I didn't know your husband passed away." To be honest, Tamika didn't know a lot about the woman, because she wasn't as in love with this place as her parents had been. This was only the third time she'd been to England.

Tuppence shook her head. "That fool's not dead. He left me for a young spit of a girl, and I hope he rots in the bowels of hell for it. Still, in those first few months he was gone, I missed him horribly."

Tamika turned her head from the steam rising up from the noodles she'd just emptied into the colander and gawked at Tuppence. "You missed him after he left you?"

The housekeeper shrugged. "Sounds silly, but there it is. Love works in all kinds of ways nobody understands. Anyway, your mother is missing her husband, her best friend."

"She's staying in her bedroom all day and night, not eating, not talking to anyone but you. That's not healthy." And it was scary.

Tuppence continued to shuffle about. "No. It's not. But it's part of the process."

"What process is that?"

"The grieving process. Everybody goes through it differently."

Tamika rinsed the noodles and went back to the stove to

dump them into the pot with the meatballs and sauce. The last thing she wanted to hear about was the grieving process. Her father had died in a fire at his office thirteen months ago. She wasn't grieving, she was pissed off.

"You're in denial," Tuppence said.

"I'm trying to fix this dinner so Mama and I can watch *Black Panther*. I can't believe she's never seen it before."

Tuppence didn't say another word as she continued to clean the kitchen. The silence was golden, and Tamika finished mixing the food. She eased the bread out of the oven and buttered the top before slicing it and added those slices to a small woven bowl.

Tuppence came up behind her, reached around and set two plates on the counter before walking away, still not saying anything else. Tamika filled the plates with the spaghetti and meatballs. She transferred the two plates to a tray with the bowl of bread and then went to the refrigerator to grab the chunk of parmesan she'd picked up at the market. When she turned around, she bumped into Tuppence, who had one hand propped on her hip, the other holding the cheese grater out to her. Tamika accepted it with a stiff smile and then added a generous hill of grated cheese on top of each plate. When she turned to put the cheese back, Tuppence moved around her, adding two napkins, knives and forks to the tray.

When Tamika went to the cabinet, she removed two green-colored glasses.

"She likes lemonade. I make it fresh every other day. Scoop out some of the lemons and add to her glass." Those were the last words Tuppence said before she left the kitchen.

Tamika shook her head and chuckled; Tuppence was the surly grandmother nobody in the family wanted to piss off, but that's exactly what Tamika had managed to do, and she'd only been in Painswick for a week.

. . .

Two Hours Later

With more sadness than she thought she could ever feel again, Tamika watched as her mother reached out a hand to grab the butter-yellow-colored duvet and matching sheet.

Sandra lay back against the many pillows and pulled the covers over her slowly, as if every movement was a tremendous effort. "Thank you for cooking, MiMi."

The sound of the nickname her parents had given her warmed Tamika to her soul and made her think back to happier times. But those times were gone, and the present was a persistent problem. She'd moved the tray with their empty dishes on it a while ago but had remained sitting on the opposite side of the bed from her mother while they'd watched the movie. "It's no problem, Mama. You know I love cooking. It soothes the mind, just like you and Granny used to say." Tamika wished her mother would've said it earlier today. She wished her mother would say anything more than the few polite words she'd been tossing at her and Tuppence.

Sandra adjusted the covers, pulling them up to her neck this time, and nestled down in the bed. Tamika tried not to dwell on the fact that her mother had lost so much weight her pajamas were a couple of sizes too big, so the sleeves were rolled over several times to rest a few inches above her wrist. Her hair surrounded her face in limp strands that, while clean, had no style and no other evidence of care. That was a stark contrast to the woman Sandra used to be. The woman whose hair had once been thick and long, hanging down to her shoulders, styled perfectly thanks to Ms. Evelyn at the beauty salon she'd gone to since Sandra was a teenager. Tamika recalled spending many Saturday mornings in the basement beauty salon, playing with the other little girls whose mothers swore by Evelyn Beauchamp's blessed styling skills. It wasn't until Tamika turned fifteen—the age Sandra had deemed appropriate for her to get a relaxer—that she'd finally been able to climb into Ms. Evelyn's chair.

"You know, it's still pretty early. We could watch another movie. Tuppence has all the latest DVDs in the main sitting room. She said guests like to have a good selection of movies to watch, considering she only subscribes to satellite service with basic channels to help keep costs down. When the guests take a movie, there's a small rental fee incorporated into their final bill, so the cost of purchasing the DVDs levels out. She's got a good head for business." And Tamika was talking a lot, a habit she'd had since she was eighteen months old and had said her first word, "some."

Her mother said she'd waddled around the house for weeks after that fine day begging for "some" of everything she saw—applesauce, marshmallows, her father's cigar and even her mother's body lotion. The thought made Tamika smile.

"Why don't I go down to see if she has *Claudine*? I know that's one of your favorites."

"No!" Sandra said the word so loudly and with such vehemence, Tamika jerked back and blinked at the woman who otherwise appeared frail and weak. "That was the movie your father took me to see on our first date." Those words were spoken in a softer tone as Sandra stared up at the coffered ceiling.

Tamika had forgotten that was the reason the movie was her mother's favorite. She wouldn't have suggested it if she'd remembered, and now she was even more irritated with herself. The whole reason for coming in here with her mother tonight was to help Sandra snap out of whatever mood she'd been in, and so far, Tamika was doing a horrible job. "We can watch something else. I know Tuppence has lots of older movies, because she believes they're what movie-making was really all about. Just name anything you want to see, and I'll—"

"I don't want to watch any more movies," Sandra said. "I just want to rest. I'm so tired."

"Mama, you've been in bed all day." And she wasn't sick. Tamika had no idea how a person could lay in bed for so long without being down with a high fever or in some other type of physical discomfort.

"I'm comfortable here."

"Why don't we take a walk? You can show me the canal pathway. I know it's one of your favorite spots here, but Tuppence said you haven't been out walking yet. Let's go together."

"No." Not a shout like before, but just as final.

Tamika closed her eyes and tried to come up with the right words. As close as she and her mother used to be, she didn't have a clue how to get through to her now.

"None of this is the same without him."

She barely heard her mother's words in the hushed tone, but her eyes opened and she stared down at Sandra once more. Her mother's cinnamon-brown skin tone, which Tamika had proudly inherited, appeared a little ashen, her lips drawn. High cheekbones were now the dominant feature of a face Tamika had always thought was the most beautiful she'd ever seen.

"I came here because I wanted to be closer to him, but he's not here."

"No," Tamika whispered. "He's not here, Mama." And for that, Tamika was sorrier than she could ever explain.

"He's gone." Sandra's voice cracked on that last word, and Tamika felt a sharp pang in her chest. "Gone for real."

Death was pretty final, but Tamika knew better than to remind her mother of that fact. Instead, she eased over on the bed and put her hand on top of her mother's. "I'm here, Mama. I'm right here with you in the house you and Daddy loved so much."

Sandra closed her eyes. She made no effort to take Tamika's hand in return, or to hug her daughter, or any other motion that might give both of them some semblance of relief. "I want to sleep now," her mother said. "I just want to sleep."

CHAPTER 4

Dynasty Manor
Gloucestershire, England

Nestled in the heart of the Cotswolds—that was how his mother had always described Dynasty Manor. Roark drove through the open iron gates, tires crunching along the gravel path that lead to the front doors of the seventeenth-century estate. His father had purchased this property as an investment thirty years ago but hadn't had time to visit frequently. It was run as a B&B, with eight luxury suites and a private clubhouse available for rent. One of his mother's favorite hobbies was interior design. The Hyde Park house where Roark and his siblings had grown up was impeccably designed and redesigned every five years because Maxine had known how quickly trends changed. The year after she'd applied a redesign to the Hyde Park property, she'd visit Dynasty Manor for two weeks, redesigning the rooms here as well.

Roark parked his car and walked inside. He was greeted by Geoff, the concierge he'd spoken to on the phone.

"Good morning, Mr. Donovan. As I stated on the telephone, I'm honored to accommodate you for as long as you like." Geoff was a short man who stood like a trained soldier, shoulders back, chin up. His rheumy eyes remained focused on Roark.

"Thank you." Roark extended his hand and shook when Geoff accepted it.

"There are empty tables at the back of the Garden Breakfast room. Lily will show you the way. Will you need a workstation set up?"

Roark shook his head as he looked around. He'd never been to the manor before had never had the time or the need to get away from his life until now. "Not necessary. This won't be a long meeting."

"Very well, sir. I'll take care of your bags."

Geoff introduced Roark to Lily, a pretty brunette who chatted about the flowers and the cool summer air while they walked. Once in the breakfast room, he sat at a booth, his back against the velvet-studded seat, his gaze focused on the entryway. He wanted to see her when she walked in, wanted to take his time and assess everything about her before she joined him at the table. Before she said what she had to say about his mother.

Tamika Rayder, that was her name. She'd been calling him since the funeral last week, and yesterday, she'd sent him the first text message.

When he was settled at the table, Roark pulled his phone out of his pocket and pulled up the thread of messages from Ms. Rayder.

Mr. Roark Donovan, my name is Tamika Rayder and I need to speak to you regarding a private family matter.

Roark had ignored that message because her name wasn't familiar, and at that point he hadn't realized the phone number was the same as the one that had called him at least twice a day for the past six days. Then, around ten last night, the next text came.

I realize you may be wondering who I am and why I continue to reach out to you, but I think you'll be very interested in seeing this letter your mother wrote to my father last year...three days before his death.

That, the last part, had stopped Roark cold. He'd just stepped out of the shower and had held the towel around his waist in one hand, his phone in the other. He'd read the message again and then five more times before he'd responded.

If this is some type of joke, I'll have you arrested and jailed.

She hadn't responded until five this morning. The pinging sound of his phone notifying him of a new message had woken him from the light sleep he'd been struggling through.

I don't have time to joke. I just want answers and you will too. I'm in Painswick but I can come to London to meet with you.

After rubbing his eyes and reading the message again, he'd replied: *We'll meet in Painswick.*

He'd provided the place and the time and now waited for her arrival. Waited and wondered who the hell Tamika Rayder was and how she or her father knew his mother.

What he knew so far was that she was prompt. At exactly eleven-thirty, she walked into the breakfast room and immediately met his gaze. That was how he knew it was her, because while Roark had never seen her before, he was certain she'd seen him. At least a picture of him. All she had to do was visit the website for Donovan Oilwell or Donovan International. And why would she have done that? Because Maxine Donovan, as the wife of a Donovan and heir to one of the largest corporations in the country, was well-known in

London. If Ms. Rayder was bold enough to reach out to him via phone and text messages, she would've done her research the minute she'd seen his mother's name on a letter. Finding his personal cell phone number would have taken a lot more effort.

He watched her walk toward him. Confident steps, taken in high-heel black shoes, black pants, black-and-white print blouse, a chunky necklace that hung to the center of her bodice. Her hair was past her shoulders, dark, straight and silky. She carried a purse, its thin strap over her right shoulder, and she smiled when a server almost bumped into her. When the server mumbled her apologies, Ms. Rayder replied, "No worries. I'll hurry and move out of your way."

"Congenial" and "cheerful" were words he might use to describe her so far.

"Mr. Donovan," she said when she finally stood close enough to him. "I'm Tamika Rayder."

Roark didn't smile. He met her gaze and inhaled slowly but didn't react to the sweet scent she'd brought with her. "Where's the letter?"

She tilted her head, her mouth turning down in a frown that disappeared seconds later. "Well, okay then, we'll get right down to business." With a hand on the back of the chair, she pulled it out and took a seat across from him. She hooked her purse on the side of the chair beside her and signaled to the server to request a glass of water. "My father's name was Lemuel Rayder. He was the fire chief in Alexandria, Virginia."

So, she was American. He could tell by her accent, but he'd learned long ago not to make quick assumptions. In business, as well as in life generally, Roark was a slow thinker and a contemplative reactor. "You're a long way from home. Are you sure you're just following up on a letter?"

Her water arrived, and she immediately picked up the glass to take a sip. Then another as she sat back in the chair, staring at him over the rim. "I'm not a stranger here. My parents loved Painswick."

He watched her lips while she talked and ignored the way her fingers gripped the glass and her arm lowered it to the table. Her lipstick was a dark crimson color that didn't seem to be too much and he shouldn't have cared if it was. Yet, he couldn't stop staring at her. "It's still a long way to come for a letter." He finally tore his gaze away from her mouth, finding her eyes once more. "Where is it?"

"Don't you want to know what it says that would make me come all this way to speak to you?"

"We've already settled how far you've come, and I can read."

She smiled. It was a slow movement, each side of her mouth lifting until the smile was not only an alluring distraction but also added a light to her chestnut-colored eyes. "I'm betting you can also be a little friendlier. I mean, you run not one, but two multi-million-dollar companies. You can't possibly be this borderline rude with your business associates. Perhaps you just don't like women who call you repeatedly and leave cryptic text messages, things I can totally understand. But still, you could at least have something to drink and try to be cordial."

"I've never been called borderline rude." But he could definitely see why she was the first to bring that character flaw to his attention. "Look, now's not a good time for my family. If you really have something my mum sent, I'd like to see what it's about."

She reached into her purse and pulled out an envelope. When he didn't say another word, she set the envelope on the table and pushed it until it was right next to his hand.

Orange , or another very light citrus fragrance mixed with something more floral—that was what her scent was. Soft, a tad sweet and sensual, very sensual.

Roark felt his brow furrow and reached for the envelope. He pulled out the letter and began to read, going through what read like a pen-pal style of correspondence.

Haven't seen you in years—hope all is well. It's nice to know we all turned out to be upstanding adults, even when nobody thought we would.

There was a smiley face drawn after that sentence, the circle of the face not closed completely, the way his mother used to do. Forty-year-old Roark still remembered how his mother drew, probably because whenever she'd written his and his siblings' names on their gifts for Christmas, she'd drawn either a smiley face, a heart or a Santa face beside it.

His chest tightened as he continued to read.

I wonder sometimes. Do you? It's been a really long time, but then some days it doesn't seem like that long ago. It was probably silly of me to write to you, but we were once close and as we get older, I think more and more about our time together.

The letter ended there with her name signed, the slash from the "x" longer than the rest of the letters. It was his mother's signature.

Roark folded the letter again and put it back in the envelope. "You said your father died."

She nodded. "Three days after he received this letter."

"How do you know when he received it?"

"My father was very organized, to the point he had an accordion folder with dates where he filed his business mail. I found this in there."

"Because he didn't want your mother to see it."

"They weren't having an affair." Her tone was adamant, and he was given a glimpse of the fire buried beneath the softness.

"My mother was a widow, but I'm assuming you already knew that."

She shifted slightly in her chair—trying to regain her composure, he figured. "Why would you assume I knew anything about your mother?"

"Because you didn't come all this way just to visit the place your parents loved. You found this letter, saw my mum's name and return address and wanted to find out who she was. A simple Google search would've provided enough preliminary information. But not my private cell number. The fact that you have that tells me you did some digging, very deep digging. The logical next question is why? If not an affair you want to keep your mother from finding out about, then what?"

"I want to know how exactly they knew each other."

He noted she didn't address his comments about her digging to find his number. He'd let it pass, for now. "Why is that important if you don't believe it was an affair?"

"Timing. This letter arrives, and from what I can tell after going through everything my father owned in his work and home office, it was the only letter he'd ever received from your mother. And three days later, he's dead."

"But he died in the US. My mother hasn't been to the States in years."

"Perhaps she knows someone else in the States. Perhaps she was planning a trip to see my father."

Roark had had enough. He shook his head. "I don't know what you're trying to get at, and this letter means nothing to me. So, I'll bid you a good day, Ms. Rayder." He stood and was about to walk away when she grabbed his arm. There wasn't a bolt of heat, or even a pinch of shock, but there was something, he thought as he looked down at her fingers on the dark sleeve of his suit jacket.

"I believe this letter's connected to my father's death," she said, looking up at him with enough sincerity and banked passion in her eyes to have his mind warring with his body for a few seconds.

"I disagree." He eased his arm out of her grasp. "Don't call me again."

To her credit, she didn't try to stop him again. She didn't speak another word. He didn't turn back to see what she was doing, not until he was at the entryway, and when he looked back, she was on her phone. Roark shook his head and tried not to think about that letter or anything Tamika Rayder had said.

The Dynasty Clubhouse was located down a winding path behind the manor and could accommodate up to twenty-four guests. There were six sleeping rooms, several lounge areas, a formal dining room, extensive gardens, a private pool and more space than Roark needed on this solo trip.

Even the room where Geoff had left Roark's bags was enormous. It was the size of the entire first floor of his flat in London. There was a grand four-post king-size bed on a platform to the far left, a work area with an antique-looking desk in the center and a cozy seating area facing a second set of windows. A fully stocked bar with leather stools, a walk-in closet and a luxurious bathroom.

Again, too much space, but for now, his home away from home. He removed his suit jacket and he walked across plush beige carpet leading into the sitting area. Two couches faced each other, a large square glass-top table between them. A fireplace with a flat-screen television mounted on the wall above was in one direction. The wall of windows on the other. Roark chose to sit on the couch facing the windows and let out the breath he hadn't realized he'd been holding.

Had he really come all the way out here just to see that letter?

Of course not. He'd come because he'd needed to get away from London for a while, to clear the fog that had settled over his mind in the past few weeks. After two days at the office and the reading of the will, he knew he wasn't ready to be back at work full-time, nor was he ready to deal with all that was on his shoulders as the head of his family. He had no choice about the latter, but where work was concerned, he'd notified his assistant that he'd be working remotely until further notice.

As for Ridge and Suri, in an effort to abide by his promise to keep them in the loop about everything, he'd sent a text last night, explaining he needed some time alone. Only Ridge had responded this morning, telling him to take all the time he needed. Suri was still angry with him about the autopsy. Roark didn't blame her. He'd been more than a little annoyed when Cade and Linc had kept information about his mother away from him. But he also didn't regret keeping the secret from his siblings. He'd planned to tell them everything eventually, he'd just wanted to get the full story first.

At any rate, the meeting with their criminal attorney, Ed Burrows and Detective Gibbons had taken place on Thursday, the day before yesterday. To Roark's dismay the police hadn't wanted a notarized affidavit. That was just as well because during the meeting, Roark, Ridge and Suri had each declined to answer anything other than the question of where they'd been during the timeframe in question. Gibbons hadn't been happy about their refusal to cooperate while he'd attempted to incriminate them, but Roark hadn't given a damn. They'd left the meeting, and Gibbons had been advised any further questions would go through their solicitor.

Still, the accusation weighed on Roark, that and the fact that he still had no clue as to who'd want to kill his mother.

And as if that weren't enough to be dealing with, there was Tamika Rayder.

On a huff, Roark lay his head against the back of the couch and scrubbed his hands over his face. He needed a drink. It was only a little after noon, but still, he desperately wanted a drink.

His ringing phone probably saved him from an early afternoon bender. "This is Roark," he answered after grabbing his jacket and retrieving the phone from the inside pocket.

Cade immediately began speaking. "Hey, just checking in with an update. I spoke to McGee about the fire late yesterday afternoon, and he didn't have anything new." Roark immediately sat up. "The fire chief doesn't want to go public with an arson declaration just yet. I suspect that's because it's also a murder investigation."

His temples throbbed, because this was exactly what he'd come to the manor to get away from.

A part of him had felt like he was abandoning his family during their time of need, but another part had acknowledged he was no good to anybody in the state he was currently in. He couldn't erase the picture of flames coming out of the windows of his familial home from his mind. The house's once-pristine white stone now had black stains surrounding those windows, stretching down toward the ground like vicious claws. So, no matter how far he got away from the house in Hyde Park, he still had to face the facts.

"Gibbons isn't gonna let McGee tell us much of anything anymore," Cade said.

"Because we're suspects—at least me, Ridge and Suri are." His free hand fisted before he could think to stop it.

"Your mother was worth five hundred million dollars at the time of her death. She was an equity shareholder in both Donovan Oilwell UK and Donovan International."

Roark hadn't needed Cade to tell him what he already knew. His mother had those holdings partly because of his father's will and also because Roark had insisted she be a part of any businesses he ran. At seventeen years old, he'd stood over his father's casket and vowed to always take care of his mother and siblings. Unfortunately, he'd failed Maxine when she'd needed him most.

"We have our own money." Not that he needed to explain their innocence this time.

Cade was a Donovan and while he hadn't gone into the family oil business but had instead decided he was better suited to be an FBI profiler, he still held stock in the family's American companies.

"I know that, and you know that. Now it's up to us to prove it to the MPD and figure out who did this."

Roark stood and walked to the window, holding the phone up to his ear in one hand, stuffing the other hand into the front pocket of his pants.

"I've got another member of my team working on this with me," Cade continued. "Since it's family and the FBI has no jurisdiction, I'm sort of operating under the radar for the time being. Anyway, Pierce splits his time between working with the Bureau and assisting Interpol on special cases, so he's got a bead on the international side and he was in Paris when the fire happened. He's got some vacation time so he's offered to stick around to give us a hand. First, he's gonna take a look at other shareholders and anyone who was maybe unhappy that you'd left the oilwell or that you and Dane started a new venture."

"Competitors, both on the Donovan side and on the side of Dane's other business, Imagine Energy," Roark added.

The clouds seemed thicker, heavier than they had just moments ago when he'd first entered the room, but still, the view from the east side of the manor was breathtaking. Gabled rooftops and cobblestone streets blended into the rolling hillsides just miles away.

"Right. I'm taking a different approach. I'm focusing on the arson." Cade spoke in the confident and succinct manner he always used when working.

"Because we know without a doubt that's what it was." Roark shook his head as the charred remains of the rooms on the second floor of the Hyde Park house flashed in his mind.

Cade continued. "We already know the type of accelerant used. The point of origin was at the nightstand on the left side of the bed."

"The side of the bed she slept on."

"McGee let that slip before he backtracked and clammed up with info. I'm gonna try and get into the Fire Brigade's computer system to see if I can pull his notes. But the coroner's report definitely states there was smoke in Aunt Max's lungs, meaning she was alive when the fire started."

"Alive but paralyzed so she couldn't scream or get the hell out of that bed before being burned to death." The words were like acid in his throat, and Roark closed his eyes to the incessant burn.

"Succinylcholine isn't an over-the-counter medication. It's only used by anesthesiologists in operating rooms. I'm going to start there and cross reference names of who made purchases in the last six months with the names of enemies on the list Pierce comes up with."

All the words replayed over and over in Roark's mind. Everything Cade was saying mixed with the coroner's report

Roark had read personally more than a dozen times. Suri's sobs the night she and Ridge had come to his flat after the reading of their mother's will and Roark had reluctantly let her read that same report

"Roark? You still there, man?"

"Yeah, I'm here. Sorry about that. Um, I'm gonna be here at the manor for a while. I can work from here and—" He couldn't say he felt closer to his mother here than he had at the Hyde Park house.

"I get it. Look, Aunt Birdie's staying in London for as long as it takes, or until Suri ships her back to Texas." Cade chuckled. "Linc's nearby for Ridge, and even though I'm back in the States, I'm just a phone call away."

"I know."

"We're gonna find out who did this and why, Roark. Believe that."

Roark did believe it. If there was one thing the Donovan family did, it was stick together. Now that they knew it was murder, none of them would stop until they found the person responsible and saw that justice was done. How justice would be meted out, well, that scenario could have a lot of variables.

After ending the call with Cade, Roark turned away from the window and its melancholy setting. He went back to the couch and dropped down heavily. There was just so much going on right now, so many unanswered questions.

He inhaled deeply and recalled a scent he knew was no longer near, but had remained embedded in his memory just the same.

Tamika Rayder.

She'd contacted him with questions of her own.

Roark could only sigh, because he didn't have answers for anyone at this point.

CHAPTER 5

*R*oark Donovan was fine as hell.

And rude as fuck.

But "fine" was definitely sticking in her memory more than the rudeness, and it shouldn't be. Tamika knew this and continued to reprimand herself as she drove from the Dynasty Manor back to the cottage.

He was tall, over six feet, she could tell even though he'd remained seated during their meeting because he'd stretched one leg out to the side of the table. That was after he'd read the letter, or rather, when he'd decided the letter meant nothing to him. She still chafed at that. But apparently not enough to forego thinking about how even that long outstretched leg had appeared muscular—from his thigh down, she'd detected muscles beneath the tailored pants. Not that she couldn't see from the waist-up view that he was in fantastic shape. His jacket had hung on broad shoulders, the collarless shirt he'd worn beneath had been molded to his chest. Her libido had kick-started into action the second she'd sat across from him.

And that was before she'd given any credit to his sculpted jaw and honey-brown complexion.

She tried to ease the car around a ridiculous round-a-bout in the center of the street and mistakenly swerved into another lane. Beeping horns yanked her out of her thoughts, and she cursed. Driving on the left side of the road was an adjustment and she'd probably end up crashing into something or, worse, somebody if she didn't get the hang of it soon.

"Roark Donovan's a jerk!" The words tumbled out as she struggled to right the direction of the car and to ignore the curses coming from drivers who'd rolled their windows down to yell at her—from the wrong side of the road as well.

He was a jerk because he'd been dismissive and curt and she should've demanded he listen to her, that he take her seriously. That was what she would've done with any other man. It was what she'd sworn she'd do in her life forevermore. Yet, she'd sat there and taken his flippant attitude. She slammed her hands on the steering wheel to keep from cursing again.

There was something to that letter—she was sure of it, because if not, her father wouldn't have kept it in his work file. He wouldn't have kept it at all. After going through all of his things because her mother hadn't been up to it, that was the only personal letter she'd found. It was the only letter from Maxine Donovan, and it'd been in a place where her father knew her mother would never find it. Why?

She didn't believe for one minute that her father had been having an affair, nor was she trying to get anything from Roark Donovan or his family. That was probably what the brooding millionaire thought. She'd considered that after she'd done her research on the Donovans. Rich people always thought everybody was after their money. Well, Tamika wasn't. Her mother was living comfortably off her father's pension and life insurance policies. She didn't need Tamika's financial help with anything, which maybe was a good thing, since Tamika was currently unemployed. Still, with no checks coming on the horizon, Tamika wasn't destitute and she'd never stoop to begging for anything, especially not from a stranger. She'd just thought the letter was strange and she'd wondered if Maxine's son would think the same thing. But he hadn't, because he was a very good-looking jerk.

She allowed herself to crack a smile as the visual of him sitting in that dining room acting so casually unbothered filled her mind once more.

Just as quickly as she smiled, Tamika's entire demeanor changed the moment she saw the first flashing light. Instinct had her pressing on the gas pedal harder until she almost slammed into one of the many police cars lined along the street in front of the cottage. An officer was waving in front of her car as she stopped and jumped out.

Of course, that officer continued his waving as he approached her. "Stand back, ma'am. Get into your vehicle and turn around."

"My mother's in there!" she yelled. "This is my mother's house!" The last word died in her throat as she inhaled a familiar scent and her heart sank.

Her mother's house was on fire and there was no doubt in Tamika's mind that she was still lying in her bed. Every inch of training Tamika had kicked in, pressing back the fear already bubbling in her throat.

"It's in the back," she said, pushing past the officer, who was either too frail or too inexperienced to stop her. "How many trucks were called?"

Without waiting for an answer, she ran down the path leading to the driveway and made her way around one fire truck. They'd need at least two more. She could already see heavy fire coming from one of the side windows. The sitting room beside the kitchen. Six firefighters were outside the house, several of them pulling two hose lines that attacked the fire from the outside.

"Somebody needs to go in!" she yelled. "There are people inside. Most likely two, but definitely one. Upstairs in the front bedroom, there's a woman—"

"Who the hell are you?"

Tamika turned when a burly man grabbed her arm and began pulling her away from the house. She met his gaze— beady and accusing dark brown eyes—and yanked her arm away from his. "I'm Fire Investigator Tamika Rayder, that's who I am, and I'm telling you now, you're gonna need to call in more trucks. And get someone inside to get them out!"

He shook his head and put his body in front of her as some form of barricade. "I'm Watch Manager Keyworth, and I don't know you. So, stand back!"

"I won't stand back." She pushed at him the same way she'd done the cop a few minutes ago, but this time that didn't work.

Keyworth was a lot sturdier than the cop. "Look, don't make me arrest you. Back off my scene!"

"This is my house!"

And he didn't care. All he was trained to care about was putting the fire out. He wasn't supposed to let her in, nor was he there to take orders from her, of all people. Tamika understood his position all too well, because she'd once been in his shoes. But now things were different.

"My mother's in there," Tamika said, this time her voice much smaller than it had been. "You've gotta get my mother out of there." Because she couldn't die. She just couldn't die…not like her father had.

Fear engulfed her in the next few minutes as she watched flames lick at the side of the stone walls. Thick black clouds of smoke filtered up into the air, and the scent, she coughed to keep from inhaling it. This was how it happened; it was the preamble to the reason her job existed. The fire that burned bright and full of energy but brought death and despair in its wake.

More sirens sounded, ones that were on the way combining with the ones already here. Lights continued to flash all around as firefighters dressed in turnouts, boots, gloves and helmets held on to the two lines, aiming water directly at the blaze. The fire wasn't dying. It was hungry and vicious and still climbing, ready to claim every life in that house.

Tamika's legs buckled; a sickly sound escaped her throat as she gasped. "Please," she whispered. "Please, save my mother."

Strong arms wrapped around her in that instant, holding her upright and pulling her back. "Let's get you someplace safe," the firefighter said. He was around her height, five feet nine, but his turnouts and boots made him appear larger than life. He wore a helmet and his face was covered with soot, as if he'd been in the house but was now out here with her.

"Why?" she asked, her voice raspy. "Why aren't you in there helping her?"

He continued pulling her back, stopping when they were at the back of an ambulance, its doors opened wide.

"I want you to take a seat," he said to her, and then, "Get her some oxygen!" That directive went to one of the paramedics.

When Tamika looked around, she realized there were

more people than when she'd first arrived. All of them in uniform, hustling around doing their job to contain the situation. This firefighter was trying to keep her calm. "I don't need oxygen," she said, shaking her head as he eased her down so she was sitting in the doorway of the ambulance.

"Ma'am, I need you to put this on your face and take deep breaths," a paramedic directed her.

"But—"

The firefighter shook his head, and the paramedic clamped the face mask over her nose and mouth. "We know there're people in there. We got somebody in there looking for them. There's nothing you can do but sit here and wait."

Because he wasn't lying, she didn't try to get up or swing on the paramedic who pressed the mask into her face with unnecessary force. Instead, she took slow and steady breaths, feeling her lungs silently thank her for the effort.

She hadn't noticed how much smoky air she'd inhaled while standing there watching her parents' house burn, hadn't understood the danger she'd put herself in. Because she didn't matter right now. She hadn't mattered for the last year. Nothing but finding out who'd set fire to her father's office had mattered. That was how she'd ended up losing her job, and that was why she was here in the UK tracking down the only leads she had.

"They're coming out!" she heard somebody yell and she immediately stood, pushing the face mask and the rude paramedic holding it out of her way as she ran toward the house. Two firefighters came from the side doors of the house, each carrying a body in their arms. As tears sprang to Tamika's eyes, more paramedics ran past her. Two of them were pushing stretchers, another two carrying large bags over their shoulders.

"This is the last time I'm gonna tell you to stay back,

lady!" The firefighter who'd been nice to her a few minutes ago was now pissed. Well, Tamika was okay with that—she was angry as hell too. Her parents' house was on fire and something, a deep dark something that'd been churning in the pit of her stomach for the last year, was telling her this wasn't a mistake. It was arson.

∼

"Dammit!" Someone else had been in the house.

He sat in his car across the normally quiet road from the country house and watched.

There was only supposed to be one person inside. He'd watched that housekeeper leave. When had she come back and why, dammit, why?

Gritting his teeth, he kept from cursing out loud, even though nobody would hear him if he did. In the forty-five minutes he'd been sitting here, nobody had glanced his way. The thought infuriated and empowered him. They had no clue he was here or that he'd been inside that house just an hour ago. His gloves still smelled like gasoline.

Lifting one to his face, he inhaled deeply, letting the scent seep into his soul. He'd had to move fast this time, because that housekeeper didn't take long when she went out to shop for food. He knew her schedule well. He also knew that someone else was now staying in the house.

Tamika.

His gaze narrowed on her now, standing on the sidewalk crying the same way her mother had when she'd watched him lift the can of gasoline and start to pour. He'd wanted to stand there and watch the fear fill her face, to pool into her eyes until they bulged out like a cartoon character. He'd wanted her to know she was going to die because of him. But he'd heard footsteps and he'd had to get out quick. Damn housekeeper! She deserved to die too for interfering.

Rage shot through his body in powerful thrusts just like the water bursting from those hoses. They were too late; the water wouldn't work. Sandra Rayder was going to die, just as she deserved.

The sight of Tamika climbing her big ass into the ambulance ripped him from the glorious thoughts, and his lips peeled back from his teeth. "No," he mumbled. "No. No. Fucking no!"

He slammed a fist into the dashboard as the doors of the ambulance were closed, but not before he got a glimpse of a woman on the stretcher inside. It was Sandra, no doubt and she must be alive. Otherwise, they wouldn't have let Tamika get back there with her.

The next sound that came from him was feral, ragged and animalistic, and more familiar to him than his own name. Sandra had to die. If she didn't, it would be his first mistake, and he didn't make mistakes. Not now. Not ever.

The ambulance whizzed by his car, and he switched on the ignition, planning to follow and to make sure this ended the way he wanted it to.

CHAPTER 6

*B*y six that evening, Roark was hungry and cranky. He wasn't sure if he should've upgraded that to "crankier," since he'd been in a foul mood for weeks now, but shrugged the thought away and continued to work on the memo he needed to send with his thoughts on last week's R&D meeting. His mind had been on other things during that meeting, but he'd managed to jot down notes. For the last few hours, he'd been sitting on the loveseat in his room, attempting to blend the notes into a cohesive summary.

The fact that he was still on the first page of the memo meant he wasn't doing too well. More often than not, Roark found himself looking away from his laptop, letting his gaze fall on one piece of furniture around the room and then another. His mother had selected every piece. Roark remembered being at the Hyde Park house with her one Saturday afternoon and commenting on all the design books and fabrics she'd spread out in the den. Maxine had loved working in the den at Hyde Park because it had a wall full of windows that faced the garden she'd tended to herself. She'd loved the scent and color of different flowers and had thus brought that love to the manor and the clubhouse, as was visible through the large vases of fresh flowers in every room Roark had been in so far. Just like the warm beige, yellow and cream hues in this room spoke of her calm spirit.

A rush of emotion soared through his body with those thoughts, and Roark closed his eyes to its intensity. With his fingers still resting on the keyboard, he took slow, steadying breaths, hoping the waves of grief wouldn't overtake him this time.

He could do this. He knew he could.

There'd never been anything he couldn't do, and that was mostly because his father had told him repeatedly when he was growing up that he was a Donovan and could do and be whatever he wanted.

"We were meant to be kings," Gabe Donovan would tell his sons as they'd sat with him in his home office or when he'd take them out for long walks. "The world will try to tell you differently. They'll try to break you down, brainwash you to believe you're no more than the slaves they created hundreds of years ago, but they're wrong. We were more before they stole us, and we'll be more long after they're dead and gone."

Roark believed every word his father had told him. As such, he'd studied and worked harder than anyone else in his classes, because he knew he was born to be more.

"You'll take this company to places I never dreamed of, Roark," Gabe had told him on his sixteenth birthday.

His father had come to his room early that morning, before Roark could get up and start his day with the celebratory breakfast his mother had orchestrated.

"You've got the passion for it deep in here," Gabe had

said as he'd reached out and touched a finger to Roark's chest. "I've been so proud, watching it blossom inside you."

Roark recalled sitting up in his bed, his father sitting on the edge beside him, looking as distinguished and debonair at seven o'clock in the morning as he did at one of their grand parties in the evening. "I won't disappoint you," he'd told his father, meaning those words with everything in his soul.

Gabe had shaken his head. "I know you won't, son. You'll make your mother and I proud. But most importantly, you'll make yourself proud."

Those last words hadn't mattered to Roark, not as much as the part about making them proud had. Opening his eyes slowly now, Roark acknowledged that was what had pushed him through his entire life, making his parents proud and living up to the Donovan name. No matter what was going on in his mind or his heart, he had to push through. He had to make them proud.

He typed for another forty-minutes, stopped and re-read the memo twice, and then moved to his work email so he could send the document to his assistant for final editing. The insane number of unread messages in his inbox startled him and with a grumble, he decided to go through them first, just in case there was something else he needed to address with his assistant or ask her to handle. He could put everything in one email.

Roark started with the latest emails received since Friday afternoon when he'd left the office. Not even twelve hours later, and he had one hundred forty-two new messages. He was making steady progress when half an hour later he stopped at a message from a familiar sender: Tamika Rayder.

I get this may have been a jolt for you, so I'm attaching the letter just in case you want to read it again. If you come up with some explanation, here's my contact info. If not, it was nice meeting you, Roark Donovan.

As he read the message silently, her voice echoed in his head. A little bit husky, and a lot sexy. Way too sexy for him to even contemplate while reading a message such as this. Who was this woman, and why was she so obsessed with this damn letter? Without a real answer in mind, Roark clicked on the attachment and re-read the lines he'd seen this morning. He had no idea who this man was, had never heard of him before and thus had no logical explanation for why his mother had sent this letter. Except for the most obvious— Maxine knew Lemuel Rayder.

Okay, so what? His mother had known a lot of people, and Roark wasn't so self-absorbed to believe he had to know each person she'd known. She'd been an adult, and he hadn't been in the business of keeping tabs on her.

That didn't stop him from clicking to another screen and typing in Lemuel Rayder's name. It was time to figure out who this guy was, even if just to give himself peace of mind.

Fire Chief, husband to Sandra and father of one— Tamika Rayder. Lemuel Rayder had been an upstanding citizen, born and raised in Arlington, Virginia. He'd attended community college for two years before entering the fire academy. After graduation he'd joined a station house, where he'd served for seventeen years before moving up the ranks to become first captain, then battalion chief and finally fire chief for the county. His wife was a social worker who'd retired two years before her husband's death in a five-alarm fire the day before their thirty-fifth wedding anniversary.

A fire.

The same way his mother had died.

Roark stopped reading and took a deep breath. He lifted his hands and scrubbed them over his face.

It was a coincidence, that was all. Roark didn't usually believe in coincidences.

But he was hungry. Closing the screen on Lemuel Rayder, he returned to his emails and closed out of the one from Tamika. He didn't delete it but instead moved it to a folder marked "miscellaneous." He'd think about why he'd made that decision later. After sending the memo and a few other assignments to his assistant, Roark closed down his computer and grabbed his jacket.

The walk from the clubhouse to the manor took only ten minutes, the cool evening air as refreshing as the dreary scenery filled with trees, rolling hills of grass, and dwindling daylight.

The lobby of the manor had less activity than when he'd arrived this morning, but there were two attendants behind the sleek black lacquer front desk. He'd changed out of his suit earlier and now wore jeans, boots, a black T-shirt and lightweight black jacket. His steps were muted as he moved across the gray-and-white marble floor and asked if there was a place he could have dinner.

"Absolutely, Mr. Donovan." Lily had come up behind him as he stood at the front desk. When he turned, it was to see her smiling, one arm extended in the other direction. "We have four five-star restaurants onsite with top-rated chefs. The Billiard Room is our premier steak house. We're aware that steak's one of your favorite meals. Correct?"

"Yes, that's correct," he replied as he followed her down three stairs into another area.

The floor here was a deep burgundy carpet, and in one corner there was a big glossy black piano, the man sitting behind it playing a jazzy tune. Wall sconces were lit along the dark-green painted walls as they approached double oak wood doors. Lily reached to open one, but Roark stepped around her and opened it instead.

"After you," he said and watched as the woman's smile

grew more nervous than cheerful. She'd glanced around as if she thought she'd get in trouble for allowing him to open the door, and Roark had to hide his irritation. "It's okay. I won't tell."

Lily walked into the restaurant, and Roark followed. She grabbed a menu and continued past the hostess stand. Roark smiled at the host dressed in all black who looked as if she had no clue what was going on. When he was seated at the table, Roark accepted the menu from Lily and immediately flipped to the wine list in the back.

"Would you like a Manhattan? We have Maker's Mark 46."

He shouldn't be surprised that she knew his favorite drink, since she obviously had a list of his likes and dislikes programmed in her mind. "Yes. Thanks. And I'll take the Delmonico, medium well, roasted potatoes and asparagus." The sides weren't on the menu, he knew, but it was what he liked, so he was certain Lily would make sure the chef accommodated him.

"Yes, sir. I'll bring your drink and let the chef know of your order."

He nodded in lieu of thanking Lily again and sat back with a relieved sigh when she was gone. Being born into one of the wealthiest African American families in the world, Roark was used to the finer things in life. Still, he'd never been comfortable with people waiting on him so attentively. When necessary, he tolerated it, but it wasn't a part of his life he cherished in any way.

His drink was perfect, the ambiance in the restaurant that of many traditional steakhouses he'd been in before. Only this one had a more authentic feel. He wasn't sure if it was the dim lighting or the luxurious décor, but the black tablecloth and sparkling crystal settings, the leather-backed chairs and the sterling silver stemware, all gave him an old, aristocratic feel, and he settled in to enjoy it.

"The place almost burned to the ground. It was an awful and amazing sight to see, especially here in Painswick."

"I agree, but Mrs. Marks is beside herself with worry. Reports say there were two women inside."

Roark had looked up from scrolling through his text messages when he heard the two men walking past his table speaking. They went farther back into the restaurant to take a seat at a table near the window, and he found himself wondering about the remainder of their conversation.

A fire? Here in Painswick?

His food arrived seconds later, and Roark pushed his phone aside and decided to forget about the overheard conversation. The steak smelled delicious, and his stomach growled in protest to the almost ten hours he'd gone without eating. After saying grace, he picked up his knife and fork and was about to cut into the meat when the words rolled in his mind once more: A fire in Painswick?

What were the odds?

Setting the knife and fork down, Roark picked up his phone and pulled up the internet. He typed in the words *fire Painswick UK* and waited.

Cottage in Golden Valley… Fire… Injured Tuppence Gregory and Sandra Rayder…

Roark grabbed his phone from the table and stuffed it into his pocket as he stood. He walked quickly out of the restaurant, intending to go to his car. But, of course, he bumped into Lily.

"Is there something wrong with your meal, Mr. Donovan? Something I can get for you?"

He was about to tell her no and keep walking, but then he

turned back to her. "Where's the nearest hospital to a place called Golden Valley?"

"Are you hurt, sir? I can get a doctor to come here to take a look at you?"

"No." He shook his head impatiently. "It's not me. Never mind, I'll just look on Google or something. I need to get my car."

"We can have it brought to the front door, Mr. Donovan. And I'll get the address to the hospital for you. Just follow me up front."

Lily was helpful, and more under foot than he liked, but again, Roark followed her. Minutes later he was running down the front steps of the manor and jumping into the driver's seat of his car. With the address to the hospital already programmed in his phone, he attached it to the dash mount and then drove. He didn't stop to think why it was so important that he get to that hospital; he just focused on getting there.

Tamika leaned over in the chair, her face buried in her hands, her mind repeating one thing—*don't cry*.

She couldn't cry, not here and not now. It wasn't going to help anything if she did, and besides, she didn't want to feel weak. The jury was still out on whether or not crying was really a weakness, but in her mind it was. And not just because Colin had said so, but because of how helpless she recalled feeling every time she'd ever allowed herself to cry over her circumstances.

No, she shook her head, took a deep breath and sat upright in the uncomfortable hospital waiting room chair. This was no time for tears. Running her fingers through her hair, she rotated her shoulders and declared she'd remain strong. No matter what those doctors said when they came to speak to her, she'd remain strong and she'd deal with whatever needed to be done. She really had no other choice.

There was no one but her. She had no siblings, and her father was gone. Tamika was as alone in life as she'd been in this large waiting room for the last five hours. Tuppence didn't have any family either, so that was another weight on her shoulders right now. What was she going to do if the woman didn't make it? While she'd been allowed to ride in the ambulance with her mother, Tamika had no idea what Tuppence's condition was. No doctors had come to speak to her yet, so all she could do was sit here and wait.

She stood and walked instead.

Folding her arms over her chest, she walked from one side of the waiting room to the other, back and forth. She looked over to the window periodically, seeing that the sky was now dark, lights from the street and other buildings prickling through the night. She continued to walk. Her feet were hurting, so she kicked her shoes under the chair she'd been sitting in and continued pacing.

No police had come to the hospital. That didn't make a lot of sense. Didn't they have questions? Wouldn't they want to know more about the two victims who'd been in the house? She definitely had questions, but they were buried somewhere beneath the heavy fog of fear for her mother's life.

What was she going to do if her mother died? How was she going to go on?

Shaking her head vehemently, Tamika kept walking, this time picking up her pace as if moving faster would get her somewhere. Anywhere but here.

"Ms. Rayder?"

She spun around at the deep voice, expecting to see a

doctor standing in the entryway. Her already pounding heart paused and then thudded as she looked into the searing russet-brown eyes of Roark Donovan. "What are you doing here?"

"I came as soon as I heard about the fire. Can you tell me what happened?" He took a couple of steps closer to her before stopping. She was still a few feet away from him and decided to stand still. He looked different from earlier. His jeans were dark, his shirt molded to his chest. But that wasn't the only difference —there was something about the way he was staring at her.

"I don't know anything," she replied when she remembered he'd asked her a question. Or had he asked two? "I don't understand why you're here."

"The reports said your mother was injured. Is she going to be alright?" He pushed his hands into the front pockets of his jeans, his legs were slightly parted, his brow furrowed.

"I don't know. The doctors haven't come out to speak to me yet."

He moved an arm, looked at his watch and frowned. "How long have you been waiting?"

"Hours," she replied.

"Too long." In seconds, he was gone, as quickly and dramatically has he'd appeared. Tamika didn't know what to say, but she blinked as if maybe she'd just imagined that entire weird exchange.

Why would Roark Donovan show up at the hospital?

After deciding she was probably losing her mind, Tamika resumed her pacing, this time moving closer to the window as she found the warm glow of the outside lights strangely soothing.

"Ms. Rayder, I have an update for you."

Again, she was spinning around to another strange voice.

This time it was a woman, a nurse, she presumed by the scrubs and stethoscope around her neck.

"Ms. Gregory is still in surgery. It's believed she fell trying to get Mrs. Rayder out of the house, and there was a laceration and internal bleeding that needed repair. Mrs. Rayder is being treated for first-degree burns and smoke inhalation. You'll be allowed to see her in another hour or so, as they're still trying to get her stabilized." The nurse stood next to Roark, speaking as if she were under some type of duress.

"Thank you. Can you please come and get me the moment I'm able to see my mother?"

"Yes, ma'am. I'll come get you personally." The nurse cleared her throat before glancing at Roark again. "And the moment the doctor is available, I'll send him down here to speak with you both."

Roark's stern facial expression remained unchanged. "Thanks."

At what seemed like his dismissal, the nurse hurried out of the room.

"Did you threaten her?" She didn't know why that was the first question to come to mind, but his shrug said he wasn't bothered.

"No. I just suggested she do her job." He was coming closer to her again, and Tamika wondered if she should take a seat or step out of his way, because he looked so determined, so intent. It was an odd sensation she was experiencing, as just watching him move kept her still and maybe a little bit aroused.

"I don't understand why you're here."

He stopped just about a foot away from where she stood. "Because I don't believe in coincidences."

And neither did she, which was why she'd sought him out in the first place. "My father. Your mother…"

"And now, your mother," Roark finished for her.

"I wasn't allowed in the house, so I couldn't tell if it was arson. But I know my father's was. I investigated that case until…" She paused and shook her head.

"You investigated? Are you a firefighter like your father was?"

So he did know who her father was. Or had he looked him up after he'd walked away from her this morning? "I used to be. Well, I mean, I was part of a station for about eighteen months before I figured out it wasn't really what I was meant to do. Then I took the courses to become an investigator."

"And you investigated your own father's murder?"

Hearing the question in someone else's voice sort of solidified the reason her boss had fired her. It was not only unethical for her to research her father's death, but it was against the insurance company's policy, because neither her father nor the city of Arlington were their clients. Which meant for the year since her father's death, she'd been abusing company time and resources to pursue a personal vendetta. That was the gist of it, but Tamika was convinced that sounded far worse than it really was. "I needed to find out what happened." It took every ounce of strength she had to keep her voice from cracking with that admission.

Roark simply stared at her. Not a hard or uncompromising stare, but a sort of communal look that acted like a force field between them, drawing her closer or him closer. They stood only an arm's length away from each other, in silence for much longer than she thought was normal.

He spoke first. "I'll wait with you."

When she didn't immediately reply, he moved away from her and sat in one of those uncomfortable chairs. After blinking a few times in an effort to decide whether or not she still thought she was dreaming, Tamika finally accepted this was really happening. Every heart wrenching thing that had happened since May third last year was devastatingly real, and there was nothing she could do about it. Not one damn thing.

She sat in the chair next to Roark, not because it was the closest to him, but because it was the closest to her, and she was exhausted.

Two hours later, the nurse returned and announced that Tamika could see her mother. "Five minutes," she instructed. "And the doctor will be waiting to talk to you when you come out."

Tamika stood still for a few seconds until Roark touched her arm lightly. She jolted at the touch and stared down at his hand.

"I can walk you to the door if it'll help."

This was the first time they'd spoken in the last two hours. It had seemed oddly comforting that they'd sat in silence for so long. She hadn't once felt the urgency to pace. "No. I'll be fine," she lied.

His arm fell to his side, and he took a step back. She was about to walk away when she remembered she'd taken her shoes off earlier. Finding them under another chair, she pushed her now-swollen feet back into the pumps and left the waiting room.

Minutes later, she was at her mother's bedside, staring down at a body that looked even more frail than it had when she'd left the cottage this morning.

There was a bandage going all the way up Sandra's right arm and one on her neck. An IV line was on the back of her left hand, a nasal tube in her nose giving oxygen, and stark-white sheets were pulled up to her chest. Other wires trailed down to hide beneath her hospital gown and were connected to the many machines that beeped and buzzed throughout the room. Shades were pulled down at the two windows on the wall farthest from the bed, and there was a chair a few feet behind her, which Tamika ignored.

Instead she stood directly beside the bed, her fingers lightly touching her mother's. "I'm gonna find out who did this," she whispered. "If it takes everything I have, I swear to you I'll find out why."

Her mother couldn't hear the words and neither could her father, but the part of Tamika that loved her parents above all else in this world felt content in knowing the declaration had been made.

Roark had made the decision to help her long before she'd left the waiting room. He'd spent the silent time they'd waited together running it over and over in his mind, trying to make some sense of it, but that was pointless. It didn't make sense.

He'd never met Tamika Rayder before today and had never heard of her parents before then. He had no idea how his mother had known this woman's father, or how any of this connected to his mother's death, but the two events were somehow intertwined. There wasn't a doubt in his mind that everything that had happened today was connected to what had happened to his mother a couple of weeks ago, and to Lemuel Rayder a year ago.

He could see her speaking to the doctor and knew he only

had a few minutes before she'd be back in the waiting room. With his phone still in hand from the call he'd made moments after she'd left the room, he hurried to make a second call. "I'm going to forward an email with a letter attached to you. I need you to tear it apart, find out any and everything you can about everyone mentioned."

"What's going on?" Cade asked.

"I don't know," Roark replied. "I really don't know. But it's something we need to figure out."

"Where are you? At the manor? Do you need Linc or Ridge to come out there with you?"

"No!" The answer was too vehement and probably too loud. Roark walked to the other end of the waiting room, boxing himself into a corner and turning his back to the entryway as he began to talk again. "For right now, just look into the email. Follow it wherever it takes you. I'll call you in the morning."

"Hey, man, you're scaring me. You okay? I can call somebody and have them there with you within the hour." And he could. Cade had more connections than anyone Roark knew. If Cade made a call to their other cousin Trent Donovan and his ex-mercenary friend Devlin Bonner, those connections would be tripled.

But Roark wasn't ready to wake those sleeping beasts. No, he'd prefer to keep this as lowkey as possible until they knew exactly what they were dealing with. "I'm fine. Just got an unexpected lead. One I don't think we should let the police know about just yet." Roark had no idea why he'd said that. He wasn't some type of private investigator. He was a businessman, but he was smart and he knew how to work a plan.

That was what he did for a living. He ran a company based on investigating and planning where to drill for oil next, and when they found the oil they were looking for, he developed a strategy for how to best market that commodity and negotiate deals with the highest bidders. Investigating and organizing were his thing, and he was convinced that whatever was going on here was part of someone else's plan.

"Roark."

He turned when he heard his name and stared at the woman who just might be a very integral part of that plan. "I'll check in with you tomorrow," he said to Cade and disconnected the call. "How's your mum?" Walking toward her seemed natural. He never questioned the need to be close to her.

Her eyes looked blurry, not like she'd been crying, but like she'd been trying her best not to. Roark knew that look well. "She's stable. Not awake. They said I should come back tomorrow."

"Is she going to be alright?"

"The burns can be treated. There were no internal injuries. Tuppence probably saved her life."

"Tuppence?"

"She's the caretaker at the cottage. She was there with my mother. The doctor's operated on her and she's critical right now, but they're optimistic she'll make a full recovery."

"Those sound like very good reports."

She nodded, but he couldn't tell if she agreed with what he'd said, or if she was just acknowledging that he'd spoken.

"Do you need to call anyone? Family?"

"My mother is my family," she said in a voice that sounded isolated and bereft. "Her and Tuppence. They're all I have." She'd been looking at something over his shoulder as she spoke, but then she shook her head as if bringing herself back to reality. "Ah, I need to find a hotel and then figure out if I can get into the cottage tomorrow. I'll have to see what can be salvaged and how bad the damage is. My mother owns the place and I'm sure there's insurance, so I need to find that paperwork and give the insurance company a call."

"I'll take you to the clubhouse. You can get some rest and make those calls first thing in the morning."

She looked at him as if she were seeing him for the first time. "The clubhouse?"

"Yes. That's where I'm staying at my family's B&B."

"I can't stay with you."

"Do you really want to stay alone in a hotel tonight?"

It took her less than a minute to reply, "No."

"Then, you're coming with me."

CHAPTER 7

This wasn't the way Tamika had envisioned things turning out. She hadn't imagined being at the Donovan manor again, and she certainly never thought she'd be in this private clubhouse with Roark Donovan, preparing to spend the night.

"I called Geoff, the concierge from the hospital, and told him you'd need clothes."

She walked closer to the bed while Roark talked.

"He's been here twenty years, which means he must be really good at his job. He said he'd have everything in this room ready for you. But if you need anything, just let me know."

She moved her fingers slowly over the three nightgowns laid out on the bed. The material was soft, silk no doubt. In bold colors—emerald green, fuchsia and royal blue. She spun around to face him again. "How'd you know I'd agree to come here?"

Because he was Roark Donovan, that was how. He didn't say that, but the confident way in which he was standing with his legs slightly spread, arms folded across his broad chest, and chin tilted, spoke volumes. Yeah, he wasn't the cockiest guy she'd ever met, but there was no doubt he knew all he'd had to do was ask. "I would've taken you anywhere you wanted to go."

"Oh." That was all she could come up with, and because his words contradicted what she'd thought about him and made her feel awkward, she clasped her hands behind her back and nodded. "Well, thanks. I'll be out of your hair first thing in the morning."

He let his arms fall to his sides. "We'll talk first thing in the morning."

"Is this what you do?"

"Excuse me?"

"Do you always just tell people what to do and they do it?"

A muscle twitched in his jaw as he stood there staring at her. Thinking. That was what he was doing, thinking and deciding what to say to her next. "I run a successful corporation. I'm good at leading." His voice was stern, but the look on his face was that of mild confusion.

"But you're not very good at being questioned. That's why you seemed so agitated at our meeting this morning. You like to have all the answers, but I caught you off guard." And now she was acting like being in this room, standing close to this bed, wasn't throwing her off just a little.

He took a step closer to her, and she willed herself to remain still. Not because she was afraid of him or of being alone in this room with him, but more so because she was uncertain what was going to happen next. "I don't like strangers approaching me with things I didn't know about my family. That has nothing to do with being a leader, but more to do with a man who protects what's his." His voice was deep with an edge of danger, or was that passion?

She couldn't tell; what she knew for certain was that she liked it. "I like finding the answers to questions. Which is why I became a fire investigator. I'm naturally curious, and I've been told I talk a lot."

He tilted his head, and she thought the corner of his mouth lifted as if he wanted to laugh at that comment.

"I didn't mean to offend you by asking about your mother. I just thought there was a connection," she continued when he hadn't responded.

"Get some sleep. We'll talk about it in the morning." He was about to turn and walk away, but he stopped and looked back at her. "We can talk about it in the morning, if you're up to it."

She smiled, not worried about what he may have thought by seeing her do so. "I like to talk over coffee."

There was no movement from either of them for the next few seconds. She suspected he was trying to figure her out, while she was reassessing what she already knew about him. He was an intriguing man. A sexy-as-hell, brooding and possibly unhappy, but damn intriguing man.

"Good night." He said those two words in a huff, and then he was gone.

She watched him walk through the sitting area and out the door he closed behind him with a quiet click. Then she continued to stand there for another five minutes while she digested everything that had happened.

Her messages had finally gotten through to Roark Donovan, and he'd agreed to a meeting. She'd come to this majestic-looking place and had sat across from a handsome man who hadn't wanted to hear a word she'd had to say. Then there was the fire, flames alive and hungry, licking along the stones of the cottage, ready to claim all she had left in the world. Tamika gasped, her knees giving out, and she dropped down onto the bed. Lifting her hands, she ran shaking fingers through her hair and then dropped her hands to her lap.

Her mother's feeble body with an oxygen mask that seemed as big as her face, lying on that stretcher, had her chest heaving, warm tears filling her eyes.

Then there was another flash of memory, and she could see the light-gray headstone at the cemetery in Arlington. "Daddy," she whispered the words as her voice cracked. "I almost lost her too."

Her head dropped, and she took deep breaths in an attempt to calm down. It wasn't working. A sob bubbled deep in her throat as she lay back on the bed and rolled onto her side. With her eyes closed tight, she dared any tears to fall, even as her body shook with more memories. She'd buried her father. Standing next to her mother, she'd moved her lips along with the pastor, reciting the scripture he was reading during the internment. With family and friends standing beside them, she'd held her mother's hand, promising to get to the bottom of what happened. Thirteen months later, and she still didn't know who'd killed him.

Or, now, who'd just tried to kill her mother.

Tamika rolled onto her back and took another deep breath, releasing it slowly. Opening her eyes, she stared up at the cathedral ceiling. With a start, she remembered she wasn't in the cottage but was at the luxury B&B formerly owned by Maxine Donovan. Easing herself up to a sitting position, her mind cleared a little more, and this time she sighed.

Seconds later, she eased off the bed and grabbed all three of the nightgowns before heading into the bathroom. "Damn," she said the moment she flicked on a light.

This place was like a movie star's home or those design photos on Pinterest. The bathroom was bigger than the bedroom, bathroom and kitchen of her apartment in Arlington. She took tentative steps over the glossy black marble floor. Double doors were to her right, and she assumed it was the linen closet.

She opened one of the doors, and bingo! After grabbing a towel, she moved further into the space. A double-sink marble vanity with dark gray cabinets beneath was on her left. Glass doors that opened to a shower big enough for six people was on the right. The wall of the shower—a stunning gray-and-white marble—matched the countertop of the vanity. The dainty crystal chandelier hanging from the center of the room matched the wall sconces between the mirrors above the vanity and another set over the freestanding tub.

"Who are these people, the black Rockefellers?" Shaking her head, she dropped the nightgowns and towel on the vanity top and went to open the shower doors. It took a moment to figure out the fancy handles, but once she did, she watched the waterfall-like spray shoot from the big square nozzle on the ceiling. Another few seconds were spent opening every drawer in search of a shower cap. There had to be one in here, because not everybody washed their hair each time they hopped into the shower, especially not Black women.

A fist pump came when she found the cap and then fitted it over her head before she removed her clothes. They smelled like smoke. Everything from her blouse to her trouser socks. The water was heavenly, just hot enough to leave a sting along her skin when it hit. She held her head back and for the next twenty minutes just let herself enjoy the glorious solitude.

The royal-blue nightgown felt like heaven sliding over her

skin. It fit. She turned in the mirror, staring at the cute crisscross straps in the back and noted the way the material hugged her F-cup breasts was even better than in her best eighty-dollar bra. "How did he know my size?"

The question was muttered while running her hands down her sides, over her full hips and thick thighs. Another turn and look over her shoulder had her shaking her head. The gown came to her ankles with slits up to her knee on each side. It was sexy and comfortable and not at all something she guessed would be just lying around in this fancy B&B. But clearly, she'd been wrong. It had taken them about twenty minutes to get here from the hospital—no way that concierge ran out to a mall and came back with these perfectly fitting garments in that short amount of time.

Anyway, it was late and she was bone-tired, so trying to figure out where these clothes came from wasn't high on her list of priorities. Instead, she returned to the bedroom and pulled back the comforter and sheets. She found her purse and retrieved her phone and charger, plugging them both in and setting them on the nightstand after checking for messages. There were none, and she was glad. Her mind couldn't deal with one more thing tonight.

She let out a soft sigh once her head hit the pillow and closed her eyes. Roark's face appeared, the warmth of his potent brown eyes lulling her to sleep.

A piercing scream yanked Roark out of his sleep. He bolted up in the bed, immediately kicking the sheets aside so he could get up. By the time he grabbed his sweatpants off the chair across from the bed, there was another scream, and he took off running. He yanked the door to his room open and headed down the hall. At the last door, he opened it and caught her just as she was about to step out.

She began talking the moment his hands gripped her shoulders. "I'm fine. I'm fine. Just a bad dream." Her hands went immediately to his biceps and two seconds later she started to pull away, but he held on.

"You screamed." A sound he didn't ever think he'd get out of his head.

"I was scared." She was blinking fast, like she couldn't believe he was there, or maybe she didn't think she was really awake. "That's what nightmares do. They…um, scare you."

"Where were you going?" he asked, because she was still afraid, even though he knew if he pointed that out, she'd deny it.

She shook her head. "Water. I always need…want water after the dream."

"There's a mini-fridge in your room." Her skin was cool beneath his touch, and soft.

"I didn't see it. But I'm fine, really. I'll just go downstairs, get something to drink from that big-ass kitchen and then go back to bed." She eased out of his grip, and because he'd been raised right, Roark let her go. But she only took a couple of steps before her legs wobbled, and then his hands were on her again. This time he wrapped his arms around her, holding her from the back.

"Are you sure you're alright?"

She nodded and lifted a hand to touch her forehead. "Just a little disoriented. A lot has happened today, and I was thrown off when I woke up and realized where I was."

"Let's go to my room. You can sit down, and I'll fix you something to drink."

"No, I'll be okay. This has happened before."

He didn't like the sound of that but didn't bother

pressing her with more questions. Instead he just guided them back down the hall toward his room. It occurred to him at the last minute to leave the door open because he'd rather not give her the wrong impression. "Here, have a seat." He stood next to her while she eased down onto the couch, and then he leaned over to switch on the lamp on the end table.

"Just water," she said in a tone as if she thought she had to reiterate that.

Roark tried not to be offended. She didn't know him except for whatever the internet had told her, and the first night she met him she ended up in this private residence with him. She had every right to make sure she was being perfectly clear about what she did and didn't want.

He went to the bar and grabbed a bottled water from the refrigerator beneath it. She hadn't been lying when she'd said a lot had happened today. Roark had been thinking that very thing as he'd lain in his bed trying to stay asleep instead of waking up every half hour like he'd been doing for the past couple of weeks.

He took a second bottled water for himself, even though he desperately wanted something stronger. Before walking back over to where she sat, Roark looked at her. She'd leaned forward, resting her elbows on her knees, her head held down. Whatever she'd been dreaming had really shaken her. He didn't know if he should ask what it was, or just focus on getting her to feel better. His experience with these types of scenarios wasn't plentiful.

When he walked toward her, he noticed the play of the light over her cinnamon-brown skin and felt the push of desire settle in his gut. Actually, it was more like a sucker punch, and he coughed to play off the sudden loss of breath. "Here you go," he said, because she was still holding her head down when he got close. "I didn't open it, but I can if you want."

"No. Thanks." She accepted the bottle.

While she twisted the top off, Roark stood awkwardly, wondering if he should sit next to her or move to the other couch. He was acutely aware of the scene and was determined not to give any false impressions.

"You can sit down. I'm not gonna start screaming again." She moved over on the couch to make room for him.

With the dilemma solved for him, Roark sat. He opened his water and took a long drink. When he was done, he cleared his throat. "You wanna talk about the dream?"

"No."

"Then let's talk about something else. Why don't you have a husband or a boyfriend?"

The question took her by surprise; he could tell by the quick way she turned her head so she could stare at him. As for him, he'd been thinking about the question for the past few hours. He'd been thinking about her a lot since he'd seen that news report.

"Well, that's certainly blunt."

"I don't really know any other way to be."

She shrugged. "I guess that works in your line of business."

He wanted to know everything she knew about him, but he wanted her to answer his question first. Roark was pretty sure there was no other man but he wanted to double-check, because the last thing he felt like tonight was having some guy banging on the front door looking for his woman.

"How do you know I don't have a husband or a boyfriend?" She took another drink of water.

Roark sat back on the couch, holding his water in one hand and letting his other hand rest on his thigh. "Because if you had a husband, you'd be wearing a ring, and even if you were the type of woman who took her ring off when her husband wasn't around, there'd probably be a tan line or indentation on your finger where the ring was supposed to be."

"What if I never wanted a wedding ring? Not all women like jewelry."

"But you do." He recalled how she'd been dressed when she'd come to meet him this morning. "You wore earrings and a necklace earlier today."

She shrugged again. "True. How about the boyfriend? What makes you so sure I'm single?"

"You're dedicated to your family, that tells me you're loyal. A loyal girlfriend wouldn't be spending the night with a man she just met twelve hours ago, especially without calling her boyfriend to let him know she was safe."

"What are you, a part-time private detective?"

He laughed. He couldn't help it. Her eyes widened, and she seemed shocked at the sound. That made him feel some kind of way. "I'm just very observant. And I'm curious to know why a woman like you doesn't have a man."

"Because every woman doesn't need a man."

He should've expected that response. It's exactly what Suri would've said if he'd made that comment to her. And it was Aunt Birdie's lifetime mantra. "You're absolutely right. But you're an attractive woman. That tells me your status is by choice." A statement which may have crossed another line, so he took a drink of water and wished like hell it was vodka.

"You're right as well. I am an attractive woman. I'm also pretty damn observant myself. I've never had a husband, and the last boyfriend I had, I dumped a year ago. You're single as well."

It was his turn to shrug. "You looked me up."

She nodded and sat back on the couch, mimicking his position. "I sure did. You were married to Katrina Neyone for three years before calling it quits four years ago. Now, you're a brooding bachelor. That wasn't on Google. I just came to that conclusion today."

Roark finished his water. "Now, we're both single, sitting on a couch in the middle of the night, drinking water like we're recovering alcoholics and avoiding discussing the one thing we have in common."

With those words, silence fell over them, and Roark immediately felt uncomfortable.

"I'm not going to try to seduce you," he said when he couldn't sit quietly any longer.

"And I'm not going to try to seduce you."

He turned to her. "That thought hadn't crossed my mind."

She stared back at him. "Really? It should have. Because just as you've noticed I'm attractive, I've noticed the same about you, and I'm not in the habit of denying myself any type of pleasure."

Did his dick just jump?

Roark swallowed, because his throat was instantly dry.

In that moment it dawned on him how good that nightgown looked on her. How had Geoff known her exact size? Because it fit her perfectly, right down to the way the silky material cupped her very ample breasts. His one hand clenched the water bottle, while the other pressed into his thigh. "I just wanted to assure you that nothing untoward was going to happen to you while you were here. There's something going on that we both need to get to the bottom of; mixing that with anything else would be a mistake." Some of those words sounded like bullshit, but he'd had to say them.

"We're adults. We can acknowledge there's attraction between us and decide whether or not to act on it. I had a bad dream, we're sitting in your bedroom...it makes sense that lines are a little blurred right now. But don't worry, I'm good. I'm not going to accuse you of anything and as I just stated, I'm not going to try anything." She stood. "Thanks for the water."

Roark stood too.

"I'm going to head back to my room now."

"Are you sure you're okay?" A part of him didn't want her to go, while a bigger part of him wanted her to get very far away.

She'd already started walking toward the door. It took every ounce of strength in him not to linger on the sight of her generous ass swaying in the blue satin. His dick had definitely jumped and begged for release at that sight, and his frown increased. "I'm going to be fine. As I told you, I've had nightmares before."

They were just about at the door, and Roark was still reciting the alphabet backward to keep from focusing on how good that nightgown really did look on her, when she glanced over her shoulder at him.

"You're a fixer."

"Huh? What?" It was his turn to blink in confusion, and he felt like a total idiot.

"You like to fix things for people. So right now, you're feeling out of sorts because you couldn't fix the nightmare for me. It's cool, really. I've forgotten it already, and now I'm ready to crash." When he didn't immediately respond, she turned and kept walking through the open door.

"I trust you know how to handle your nightmares, Tamika. But I'll be right here in my room if you need me."

He'd said her name. It rolled off his tongue and sounded in his ears.

"Thanks, Roark. Thank you for everything you've done for me tonight."

"You're welcome."

"Goodnight, again. For real this time." She chuckled, and he wanted to reach out and touch the cheekbone that rose with the action.

He wanted to slide his finger along the line of her jaw, to touch her full bottom lip. Fuck! He was hard and he wanted her in his bed. "Goodnight, Tamika. We'll talk in the morning."

Those words were for her and for him. He was going to talk to this woman about how his mother knew her father and how both of them dying in a fire couldn't be a coincidence.

He was *not* going to have sex with this woman.

CHAPTER 8

The next morning, Roark lay in the bed with a smile on his face and a hand on his dick. He lifted his hips slightly off the mattress, meeting the jerking motion he'd created to keep the tendrils of pleasure sifting through his body. That enticing blue nightgown had been pushed above her hips, and he'd eased between the softest thighs to sink deep inside her pussy. She'd welcomed him with open arms, lifting her legs to wrap around his waist. He pumped deep inside her, sinking in and pulling out, passion surging through him with every plunge.

An incessant beeping sound interrupted the dream, and for the second time he was jerked awake, eyes opening wide, heart hammering in his chest as he struggled to separate the dream from reality. The first sign he was no longer dreaming was the wetness on his fingers. With a frown and his free hand, he pushed the sheets back to see the crazy dream of being inside Tamika had almost led to a very real orgasm. Pre-cum still oozed from his tip as he grumbled and hurriedly yanked his hand from his dick.

The alarm on his cell phone he'd set before he was awakened earlier by Tamika's scream was still blaring, and he used his dry hand to stop the annoying sound. It was straight to the shower from there, where it took a good ten minutes of standing under a cool spray of water for his erection to subside. The embarrassment of being a forty-year-old man who'd almost had a complete wet dream would take a little longer to rinse away. By the time he was finished and had slipped on another pair of jeans and button-front shirt, Roark had managed to clear his mind of the odd sexual fantasy.

How long had it been since he'd thought of a woman in that way? Obviously too long, he told himself as he left the room and walked down the hallway. How many times had Ridge insisted sex was the key to survival for all men? And how many times had Roark frowned at his brother's obsession with the physical connection over a deeper emotional one? Not that emotion had worked out well for Roark, either. Katrina and their very real divorce papers was proof of that.

And why the hell was he thinking of any of this when there were definitely more pressing matters at hand? For example, the open door to the room where Tamika was supposed to be sleeping.

Roark stepped through that open door, moving further into the room. He didn't call out to her and kept his focus on the sitting area of the room, just in case she was still in the bed. Then what was he going to do? Walk over and wake her up with a kiss, or turn and leave, because what kind of creepy dude was he to be in her sleeping room early in the morning without her permission?

She wasn't in the bed. He hadn't been able to resist looking in that direction, and what he saw was a neatly made bed, that infamous blue nightgown tossed across it. Taking a deep breath, he pushed the memory of his dream from his mind. "I'm not having sex with that woman."

It had become a mantra rolling through his mind during his shower, and now he figured he'd say it out loud for stronger emphasis.

He went downstairs, wondering if Tamika had gotten up this early just to sneak out of the house before he awakened. But why would she have done that? It wasn't as if they'd actually had sex last night and she was somehow embarrassed and wanted to avoid the awkward morning-after confrontation. Shaking his head, he cursed the thought and his wretched mind for not being able to push sex with her completely out of focus.

When he was standing in the first-floor foyer, about to enter the parlor, laughter drifted from another direction. Unfamiliar with all the rooms in the clubhouse, Roark wasn't sure where the laughter was coming from, so he simply followed the sound.

"This doesn't fit too bad."

He heard Tamika's voice before seeing her and immediately stopped walking. It was coming from ahead, around a curving wall.

"Not entirely. But we can get your exact size delivered to the manor in less than an hour." That was Lily. He remembered her high-pitched voice from yesterday.

"I don't think it'll be necessary. I have suitcases of clothes back at the cottage that I hadn't even unpacked yet."

"But wasn't there a fire at your cottage yesterday? Mr. Donovan tore out of here in a flurry to get to the hospital to find you."

"He did?" Tamika asked, confusion clear in her tone.

Roark frowned as the member of his staff continued to run her mouth. "Yes, indeed. He was sitting in the restaurant one minute and running out demanding his car the next. I had no idea where he'd gone until I got to the front desk and Geoff was looking at a news broadcast on his tablet. Such a shame—I pass that cottage when I'm on my way to see my mum."

"Yes, it was...*is*...lovely. I'm going back there this morning to see how much damage was done. Hopefully, not much, and I can get my bags and head to a hotel."

"I don't think Mr. Donovan will let you go to a hotel. Besides, the manor is much better. And the clothes are no problem. Have you ever heard of CKDavis Designs?"

"No."

"Well, Camille Davis is actually Camille Davis Donovan. She's married to Mr. Donovan's cousin, Adam. They're Americans like you." Lily spoke in a matter-of-fact tone that held a hint of pride.

From where he stood in the hallway, Roark wondered if all the staff at the Manor were required to know everything about him and his family.

When Tamika remained silent, Lily continued. "We keep a good number of her pieces here. The lingerie I selected last night is part of that line. I believe another cousin's wife collaborated with Camille on those particular pieces. Her name is Tia, and she used to be a runway model."

"Wow, he's got one hell of a family."

"Oh, yes, the Donovans are a vast and talented brood. My family was so proud of me for getting a job here at the manor. And when we got word yesterday that Mr. Donovan was coming here for the first time, we were elated."

"Let me get this straight. Roark ran out of here to get to the hospital to see me last night. Then he called you and told you to find me some clothes?"

"Yes, well, he called Geoff, and Geoff called me. But that's how it happened."

"And you knew what size I wore?"

"I recalled seeing you with Mr. Donovan yesterday morning and took a guess. Geoff said you'd probably go right to bed after such a harrowing time, so I just grabbed nightwear and that jogging outfit you're wearing now. But I see that's a little big. I can order whatever you like from the catalog, and they'll have it delivered in a jiffy."

"Ah, I'd rather just get my own clothes from the cottage. And speaking of which, I'll get going now."

Roark moved from the spot he'd been rooted to. He turned around the curved wall and was immediately in the spacious gourmet kitchen. The strong smell of fresh-brewed coffee hit him immediately. He probably hadn't noticed it before, since he was so into their conversation. Eavesdropping like some kind of child. "We'll go to the cottage together. I've already arranged for some agents to meet us there." He talked as he walked in and went straight to the granite-top counter, where he spotted the coffee machine.

"Oh, good morning, Mr. Donovan." Lily hopped up from the chair where she'd been sitting next to Tamika. "I can get the coffee for you."

"It's not necessary, Lily. I'll get it. And thank you for everything you did last night."

"It was no problem, sir. I was just telling Ms. Rayder that the clothing comes from your cousin's collection and we can order anything she'd like to be delivered directly to the manor very quickly."

He nodded as he poured coffee into a mug, but didn't turn around to face either of them. "She should do that. Just in case." In case her mother's cottage had been damaged as much as his mother's house had been after the fire. Suri still wasn't able to return to their family home, but as soon as the Fire Brigade released it as a crime scene, Roark planned to have a construction crew in Hyde Park to begin renovations. He wanted it to be better than before.

"Very good, sir." Lily's gaze moved easily from Roark, back to Tamika. "If you give me your email address, I can send you the direct link. All you have to do is select what you want, and the order will immediately be sent to the warehouse in London and then shipped to us posthaste."

Lily was efficient and attentive, but Roark still wanted her to leave. He wanted to talk to Tamika alone. "She'll put in an order this morning, Lily. Now, if you don't mind I'd like to speak to Tamika for a moment." He did turn then so he could look at her and try to convey this wasn't an order of any sort. He'd never treated staff like they were beneath him and didn't plan to start now. Lily was already staring at him when he faced her. Roark waited a moment before offering her a smile. "Great coffee, by the way." He didn't bother asking how she knew he liked a strong French roast blend.

"You're welcome, sir. I know Geoff originally said you wouldn't need it, but the refrigerator and cupboards are packed with supplies. Dorianne's the head of kitchen staff at the manor; she'll be sending someone over within the hour to take care of your daily meals. For now, I just brought over some of the scones and muffins from the morning buffet, and the coffee, of course. You have my number should you need anything else, and Geoff plans to check in with you this morning also." She stood with her shoulders slightly back, her hands folded in front of her starched long black skirt and white blouse.

"Thank you, Lily. You've been wonderful since I arrived." It was a true statement, and he did appreciate the extra help of her finding clothes for Tamika.

"Very well, sir. I'll be on my way. Ms. Rayder, I've given you my card. As soon as I receive your email address—"

"Sent it while you were talking to Mr. Donovan," Tamika said with a nod. The smile she'd aimed at him was only slightly condescending, but when she looked directly at Lily, Roark noted it was sincere.

"Very well then. I'll take care of everything." With a slight nod, Lily left the kitchen.

And then they were alone.

Again.

Roark hadn't considered how he'd handle being alone with her after dreaming of her last night. He wasn't really good with morning-afters. "Good morning." That seemed like the most appropriate thing to say.

"Good morning to you. And thank you for having Lily get me clothes. Designer clothes at that. Do you always treat the women you bring home for the night this generously?" The sexy nightgown had been replaced with a black jogger jacket and he suspected pants to match. But since she was sitting and he was standing at the other end of the counter, he couldn't tell. There was some sort of animal print design on the shoulder of the jacket that seemed to work with what he suspected was Tamika's saucier personality.

"No. I'm not in the habit of buying women clothes, if that's what you're asking." Other than his mother, sister and ex-wife, Roark had never bought gifts of any type for any woman. Wining and dining, gift giving and spoiling women, all that was Ridge's area of expertise. Roark was about his company and his family. When a woman fell within those guidelines, he treated them differently. That had only happened once and it had ended badly.

He took another sip of coffee. "We're expected at the cottage at eight."

"Expected? By who? The police?"

Roark shook his head. "Not exactly."

She wasn't wearing any makeup this morning; however, her skin sill appeared silky smooth, thick, perfectly arched eyebrows lifted as she continued to stare at him. "What does that mean? I was wondering why no police showed up at the hospital to question me. Do you know something I don't?"

He suspected they both knew things the other didn't, and that was the reason for this conversation they were having now.

Roark moved to one of the stools near the end of the island closest to him. He pulled it out and took a seat. The island was at least nine feet long, so it seemed like she was a world away from him as she sat at the other end. "My mother was killed in a fire two weeks ago. We believe it was arson. The police suspect me, my brother, or my sister. Or possibly all three of us together."

There was a small white plate in front of her with an iced scone on it. He hadn't noticed that before, but now when she used her fingers to push it away, he did. "My father was killed in a fire thirteen months ago. I know it was arson. I walked the scene, saw the point of origin myself, so I'm positive someone set that fire with the intent to kill him." She spoke the words adamantly, but Roark caught the hint of emotion lacing each one.

"How do you know that for sure? That the fire was set to kill your father?"

"Because he was drugged. It must've been in his coffee, because that's all he'd had that morning after leaving home. His coffee that he brewed fresh in that awful little pot on the credenza in his office. Somebody put the drug in that, he drank and then—"

"He was paralyzed." Roark finished the sentence for her,

not totally sure he was right, but going with the feeling of dread he'd felt yesterday when he'd looked at his phone and seen the report of the fire at the cottage.

"Yes." She spoke the word on a whisper and nodded. "Succinylcholine."

Roark nodded this time, and they both sat staring at each other, letting the words they'd just spoken sink in. "Did you show your mother that letter?"

She laced her fingers, then let them slip apart. "No."

"Because you did think they were having an affair." During their first meeting she'd been sure to state there was no affair, but he suspected that's just what she'd wanted to believe. His mother had been a widower for twenty-three years. If she'd found someone to make her happy, Roark wasn't going to begrudge her that. But Tamika's father had been a married man.

She looked away from him, staring out the window across the room. The sun hadn't shown its face yet this morning, so the sky was still a muted gray hue. This part of the house faced the tennis courts and walkways leading to the manor's main building. "I never wanted to think of my father as a cheater." She turned back to him, her gaze pinning him with just a hint of sadness. "And that letter didn't really prove that he was. I couldn't ask him, and I didn't find anything else to support an affair. That was the first time I'd ever seen your mother's name or anything like that in my father's belongings."

"But you still didn't take it to your mother and ask her. She knew your father better than anyone. If you really didn't think it was an affair, why not ask her?"

Tamika pushed back from the island, the legs of the stool making a loud sound as they were dragged across the floor. She stepped down and grabbed her plate, walking it to the counter where she set it beside the sink. "After the funeral, my mother wasn't herself. She was quiet and withdrawn, and I didn't want to do anything to make that worse. I didn't want to make her have to think about losing him anymore."

She'd brushed her hair back from her face today so that it hung straight down her back, the dark color blending with the hue of her jacket. Yesterday she'd worn high heels with her outfit; today she had on black platform tennis shoes with the CKDavis emblem in gold on the back heel.

He remained silent while he waited for her to continue. She turned around slowly, planting her hands behind her on the counter as she leaned against it.

"My mother wasn't handling his death well. One weekend, two weeks after the funeral, she just packed up everything and came here to stay. She didn't even tell me before she left. I found out when I went to her house and saw the for-sale sign. When I called her, she said she wanted to be closer to him, and the cottage was the only place she could do that. I didn't fuss—I just went along with it."

"Because it was easier."

"No." She shook her head. "Because it was her life. I couldn't imagine how it felt to lose a husband."

"You lost a father."

"And I dealt with that. I've been investigating that fire since the day it happened, and I keep coming up with nothing. Except that letter."

"That letter could be nothing." Or it could mean everything. Roark was still trying to decide.

"You don't believe that," she said. "Because if you did, you wouldn't have run to the hospital last night. You wouldn't have stayed there with me to see what the outcome was, and you definitely wouldn't have brought me here. So why don't you tell me who we're meeting who aren't exactly police? And then tell me why you thought it made sense to call them."

There was a lot he could tell her, more pieces to the gigantic puzzle they'd both stumbled upon, but he wasn't sure the time was right. He glanced down at his watch before standing. "We should get going. We don't want to be late."

"Late? We're going to the scene of a crime, not showing up to the office."

There was something about her edgy sarcasm that rubbed him the wrong way, but that wasn't the part of Tamika Rayder that had Roark twisted in conflict this morning. The sexy allure of this gutsy and tenacious woman appealed to him in ways he'd never thought of before. She wasn't the type of woman he was normally attracted to and yet, she was just the type of woman he thought he might need at this moment in his life.

That last observation was oddly confusing, and that wasn't a feeling he wanted to keep. "I'm going out to the car. Be there in five minutes if you're coming along."

As he turned and walked out of the kitchen without waiting for her to say another word, his stomach twisted at the thought of him running from someone, or something. Roark never ran from a challenge or a fight—it wasn't in his nature. Yet, his legs couldn't carry him away fast enough from the woman who was awakening things in him he'd never known existed.

CHAPTER 9

Special Agent Pierce Rawlings looked like he should be on the front page of *GQ*. Dressed in a black suit, crisp charcoal-gray shirt, no tie and laced leather shoes shined to perfection, he stood in front of the cottage, appearing as out of place as Tamika had felt the first day she'd arrived.

"Nice to meet you," Pierce was saying as he pulled his sunglasses off and extended a hand to her.

Roark had introduced them and she'd been standing there ogling the very attractive, dark-chocolate-complexioned FBI agent with the ominous black eyes.

"Nice to meet you too," she managed to say and accepted his hand for a quick shake.

"We should get inside." Roark started toward the door, and Pierce immediately followed.

With the formalities over, Tamika stepped forward. "I have the key." It was a reminder to the men who were charging ahead of her without a means to get into the cottage. They both stepped to the side and let her pass them, and she hunted the key out of her jacket pocket. She hadn't brought her purse with her, had just stuffed her cell phone in one pocket, keys in the other.

"Fire Brigade's coming in at nine, so we've gotta make this quick." Pierce's voice wasn't as deep as Roark's and he didn't sound as if he were barking a command or suppressing his rage, the way Roark usually did.

"How do you know when they're coming?" she asked as she pushed the door open and stepped inside. The charred scent was still strong and filled her nostrils in seconds after entering through the hallway.

"I've got someone on the inside at the Brigade and the MPD. They said they think the fire started in the upstairs bedroom." Pierce was standing to her left, and he nodded ahead of them toward the front of the house.

Tamika took a breath. Pressing her lips together she pushed aside her personal feelings and stepped firmly into the role of investigator. "My mother's room. It's the largest one in the front. We can go up these back stairs."

When she glanced at Roark, saw his intense gaze steadily focused on her, she almost faltered. For whatever reason, there was an urge to sigh and admit that next to the day she'd entered her father's office after he'd died, this was the worst moment of her life. Instead, she turned away from him and led them both around a corner and down another hall to the second set of stairs in the cottage. These were used mostly by Tuppence to take clean linens and other supplies up and down without guests seeing her. "The fire stayed pretty focused on this front half of the house. It hadn't started to spread too far before the Fire Brigade arrived." She talked as she walked, looking at everything from the ceiling to the walls and the floors.

Focused now, letting the scents filter through her mind

without any emotional attachment was easier. Char patterns started on the floor and spread halfway up the wall in the hallway just before the first bathroom on this end of the floor. She remembered the wall was covered in a pale green wallpaper with tiny pink flowers. The parts of the paper that hadn't been scorched to a sooty black hue were bubbled and already starting to peel from the incessant heat. The char pattern stretched back toward the bedroom, and she followed it.

"From their preliminary findings, the Brigade noted the flames were most intense in this room here," Pierce noted.

Still staring at the blackened path, she tamped down on how hot it must have been in here during the fire and how frightened her mother and Tuppence were. "Started here, burned here the longest."

"And quickly spread down this hallway into the bathroom. First victim made her way up the other set of stairs, grabbed second victim and dragged her out into the hallway, but something happened, and second victim was injured. Firefighters found both down in the hallway, that way." Pierce pointed toward the stairs they'd came up.

"First victim is Tuppence Gregory. She's been working here for fifteen years," Tamika said as she stepped into the bedroom, her fingers shaking slightly. "Second victim is my mother, Sandra Paulette Rayder. She was in this bed."

Tamika stared down at the floor as she walked. Her pristine new designer tennis shoes crackling over the ash of carpet burned nearly to the floorboards. "Fire burns up in a V-shape pattern." Walking around the bed to the side closest to the window, she turned back and went to the other side, where there was a nightstand, about ten feet from the double-door of the closet. "See, this is a narrow V-shape, spreading out this way."

She pointed down to the floor and walked back out into the hallway, where she kneeled down and touched her fingers to the floorboard. Burned to a crisp. This fire had burned hot and fast. And her fingers were still shaking. Yanking them back, she stood and walked toward the bedroom again. Pierce and Roark were still standing in the room, Roark on the side of the bed closest to the window and Pierce looking in the closet.

"Smell that?" She inhaled deeply.

Pierce nodded, his nostrils flaring as he sucked in air and released it. "Yeah."

"Gasoline." Roark said the word with such finality, it seemed to reverberate throughout the room. "Did the doctor mention finding any drugs in your mother's system?" he asked her as they stared at each other across the bed.

"No. And I didn't think to ask. There was so much going through my mind last night, I never even thought of it." Shaking her head was the equivalent of Tamika mentally kicking herself for not thinking to ask that very important question. They'd found the succinylcholine when they'd performed her father's autopsy. For her mother, she'd need to request a tox screen, and then the doctor still might not do it based solely on her suspicions.

She looked down at the nightstand, which was barely burned, but the spot on the floor just three feet from it was scorched the worst of any other spot she'd seen so far. The char pattern pointed here. "He poured the gasoline right here. Not enough to be a puddle, but enough to get it going." She stepped closer to the bed, or what was left of it. The frame was still intact, the mattress, sheets and pillows burned to a crisp. "My mother always laid on this side of the bed. It was closest to the door. She took a fluid pill every day for high blood pressure, so frequent trips to the bathroom to pee throughout the night were common. He started this fire while she lay in this bed watching him."

"How do you know she wasn't asleep?" Pierce asked.

"It was too early. And I wasn't back yet. As long as I lived under my mother's roof, she could never get into bed and go to sleep until she knew I was home. It didn't bother her when I lived on my own, but if I was expected to sleep under the same roof as her, she wouldn't let her head hit the pillow until I was settled in my own bed, or at the very least in the house behind a locked front door." That habit of Sandra's had created some very tense teenage years for Tamika.

"There're lots of different ways to classify an arsonist," Pierce began.

"We're looking for a killer," Tamika corrected him.

She turned to see both men staring at her.

"You think whoever killed your father in that fire at his office a year ago came here to try and kill your mother last night?" Pierce's head was tilted, his gaze inquisitive. As if she'd taken too long to answer, Pierce switched his focus to Roark, who was still standing by the window. "In between her parents, he stopped off in London to kill your mother. Why?"

That was the billion-dollar question.

When neither of them spoke, Pierce continued. "Cade sent me the letter your mother wrote to her father."

Roark lifted a hand to run a finger over his clean-shaved chin. "And what'd you think?"

Pierce shrugged. "They were definitely familiar, and this didn't seem like the first correspondence they'd shared."

"So old friends?" Roark asked.

"Your mother was born here," Tamika added. "My father was born in Virginia."

This time Roark focused on her. "Do you have something against long-distance relationships?"

Tamika had something against this guy's voice, the way he stared at her—dammit, everything about him arousing her until she wanted to rip both their clothes off and mount him. She swallowed, trying to ease her now very dry throat before replying. "I already told you I don't think they were having an affair."

Pierce had moved from where he was standing, staring down at the bed and then over to the windows. "Cade sent me pictures of the scene from the Hyde Park house. Fire started in the bedroom there too. That says this is personal for him. He wants these women at their most vulnerable, undressed and in their bed for the night. It's also their most comfortable location."

She listened to his assessment but still had questions. "My father was at work, and why do you think it's a man doing this?"

Pierce nodded. "Right. It doesn't fit. And most arsonists are men. Socially isolated and lacking coping skills to deal with whatever it is that's really pissed him off." This last comment was said in a way that made it seem as if she should've known that as a fire investigator. Part of it she did know, but she'd wanted to know specifically what he was thinking in this case. When she'd been investigating her father's case, she'd presumed the arsonist was someone with a mental defect, perhaps a disgruntled employee that was now dealing with depression. She hadn't ruled out that being a man or a woman. He walked over to the window now and looked out. "Did your mother normally pull down the shades at night?"

"No." Tamika walked around the bed but stopped short of going closer to the window for fear of whatever Pierce was seeing as he stared out onto the street. "Why?"

"These shades are still up. She could see out the window directly across the street."

"What does that mean?" Roark asked. "She wasn't sitting at the window when the fire started?"

"No. But what if he was? What if he starts the fire and then sticks around to watch? Witnessing his handiwork and getting off from it." When nobody responded, Pierce turned away from the window. "I need to study those photos from Hyde Park again. And I'm gonna take a few pics before I leave here today, which we need to get ready to do before we're caught."

"Caught? This is my mother's house. I have a right to be here," she snapped.

"Not if you're gonna be considered a suspect," Pierce pointed out.

She paused, recalling Roark saying the police in London thought he and his siblings were suspects in their mother's murder.

"You wanted to get your clothes." Roark was standing right beside her now. Tamika wasn't sure when he'd moved, but his hand softly touching her elbow was as odd as it was comforting. "We can do that while he's taking pictures and then we'll leave. Do you want to go to the hospital to see how your mother's doing?" He was talking softly, in a gentler way than was normal for him, and damn her, she liked it.

"Yeah, sure. I was staying in the room down this way." Tamika walked out of the room, knowing Roark was close behind her.

She couldn't help but still look down at the burned floors and walls, but then she stopped when she saw blood. There was a narrow table against the wall; a brass mirror used to hang above it but was now broken and on the floor. "This must be where Tuppence fell with my mother. Wait, Pierce said the firefighters mentioned Tuppence must've been dragging my mom. I know my mom was very resistant about getting out of bed, but if the bedroom was on fire, she wouldn't have been stubborn enough to stay there. Unless—"

"She was drugged." Roark finished the sentence.

Or rather, he said what he thought she was going to say. Only, he had no idea that she was thinking her mother would've gotten up out of that bed when the fire started... unless she'd wanted to stay there and die. If Sandra died, she could be with her husband and they'd both be dead.

The breath whooshed out of Tamika in that moment, and she leaned back against the wall to keep from falling. Roark's arms were immediately around her, pulling her close to his chest. She didn't know what else to do, and what she was thinking was pretty heavy. It was also scary as hell to think her mother had loved her father so much that now she wanted to die to be with him. Tamika wrapped her arms around Roark and held on—for how long, she had no idea, but she had no intention of letting go until all the hurt and fear swirling around inside her like a hurricane was still.

"My mother loved maple-glazed pork loin. She cooked it every Christmas. And my Aunt Birdie demanded ham instead." Roark laughed at the memory, while at the same time wondering how they were going to make it through this Christmas coming.

"I'm ridin' with Aunt Birdie. Give me the Christmas ham all day and night." She forked another chunk of the haddock she was having for lunch into her mouth, and Roark tried not to stare.

"What else does your family do together?"

They'd been to the hospital to see her mother, but the doctor hadn't been available for them to speak to. Tuppence was still in critical condition, and to keep her calm, they weren't letting any visitors in her room.

They'd come back to the area, close to the cottage, because when Roark had sent him a text, Geoff had recommended this pub. Tamika hadn't seemed to mind being close to the cottage without actually returning there, but she hadn't wanted to talk about her family since this morning.

"Not as much as my mother would've liked. It was just us here in the UK—my parents when they were alive and my siblings. My father passed away when I was younger, and Aunt Birdie's in and out. If there's a cruise, she'd rather be on a boat, but when there's a big family gathering, she'll appear for that. Most of the Donovans are still in the US."

"You ever thought about moving there?"

Roark shook his head. This was his home. "Why didn't you move here with your mother?"

She chewed another bite of food and then lifted her glass of water to take a long drink. He enjoyed watching her eat. There was no real reason behind it; in fact, it seemed like such a normal event. The two of them sharing a meal because they'd both skipped breakfast and were now hungry. He shouldn't have thought anything odd about sitting across the table from her, yet watching her chew and smile as she enjoyed her food seemed sort of special. "For one, I didn't know she was moving here." She looked like that fact might still be a sore spot for her. "Then again, if she'd told me, I probably wouldn't have come. I have a life in Virginia. Or at least I did."

He wondered what that life had been like. "You don't anymore?"

"To tell the truth, I don't know. I lost my job," she said with a heavy sigh.

"Oh." He hadn't expected that. "What happened?"

"My boss said I was obsessed with my father's death. How can somebody be obsessed with their parent's death? I mean, that's huge, right? It takes a toll on you until you can't think of anything else."

Roark knew exactly what she was saying and could understand every word. As a son, he'd been rustling with the same things. As a CEO, he knew business had to come first. "Maybe you needed to take a break from your work anyway. It could be that the line of work you're in coupled with the circumstances of your father's death are just too much to deal with right now."

Her eyes widened at that suggestion. "I can multi-task."

"Didn't say you couldn't."

"You implied it," she shot back.

He forked his last piece of pork, stuck it in his mouth and chewed. When he was done, he picked up his napkin and wiped his mouth. "We don't have to be enemies or go back and forth each time we're alone."

She wiped her hands with her napkin. "I know. It's funny how we slip into that back and forth so easily, though. Almost like we've known each other a very long time and it's what our relationship thrives on."

"We have a relationship?" He hadn't meant to sound alarmed. Her words had seemed so deep, so meaningful. Up to this point he'd just been thinking of her as Tamika, the woman whose father knew his mother.

"Not in the traditional sense, but yeah, I think we do. I mean, I did crash at your place last night, and I'm probably gonna be staying there again tonight. So that makes us something." She wasn't wrong.

"Roommates," he said for lack of a better term.

"You just have to put a name on it, don't you? You're so strait-laced and organized. Everything has a meaning, a spot in your world, a purpose." She propped her elbows on the table and leaned her chin on a fist. The look on her face was so naturally pretty he almost forgot what they were talking about.

"Things should have a purpose. That's how life works."

"Life also works on spontaneity. Fate is unpredictable and yet can change the world as we know it."

Roark only stared at her. "I don't believe in fate."

She chuckled. "Of course you don't. Do you believe in lust at first sight?"

Busted. "I didn't used to. Attraction is a general effect. Sometimes it happens and sometimes it doesn't." Roark knew that was a thin explanation, but she'd caught him off guard, so that was all he had.

"Attraction can be mind-blowing. Or it can be deadly." The last word had been spoken so quietly he wasn't sure he'd heard her correctly. But that could've also been because he was more concerned with her previous words.

"Are you attracted to me, Tamika?"

"Well, there we go with the candid and sometimes abrupt questions."

"You started it this time. Does that make you uncomfortable?"

She took another drink of water and shook her head. "Not at all. And to answer your question, yes. I'm really attracted to you. When did you decide you were okay with being attracted to me?"

The question was so spot on he didn't even bother to refute it. "About two hours ago."

Her laughter came in a quick burst, the smile stretching

across her face and lighting up her eyes. "You're brutally honest, Roark."

"And you're a big surprise." He cleared his throat, because to his ears that sounded weird. "I mean, I wasn't expecting anything like this. When I came to Painswick, I just figured I'd get the meeting over with and then I'd spend some time walking in the gardens and sitting in the rooms my mother liked so much. I didn't think there'd be a woman like you."

"Well, I'm not going to ask if that's a good or bad thing, because you don't know yet. Neither of us will know until after we get the sex out of the way."

And she called him blunt. "We're going to have sex?" He felt like a teenage virgin asking that question, but the forty-year-old man wanted to make sure he wasn't getting mixed signals.

"Absolutely."

"When?" *Way to go, Roark.* That sounded pretty desperate.

She shrugged again. "Probably tonight. I've been on a hiatus from sex, but I'm thinking it's time to put a stop to that. How about you? When's the last time you've slept with someone?"

"Six months ago. Two dates and then sex. No calls from either side after that."

"Wow. Was that a pre-made agreement, or did you just not like the sex?"

He wasn't going to sit here and discuss his past sex life with this woman.

Last night and again this morning, he'd insisted he wasn't going to have sex with her, and now his dick was already pressing painfully against the zipper in his jeans. She wasn't helping matters by looking at him like she was ready to jump across the table and ride them both into an orgasmic haven. "It just didn't work out. Sometimes that happens."

"I agree," she said with a quick nod. "But I'm betting that won't happen this time."

"That's a bet I think you'd win." He signaled the server for their check.

The twenty-five-minute ride back to Dynasty Manor would have to suffice as Roark's contemplation time. Was he really going to have sex with this woman he'd just met yesterday? A woman whom he had nothing in common with and who might be part of a very dark time for his family?

All things considered; he probably could've made a better decision. Perhaps they should wait until after they got to the bottom of whatever was going on with their parents and these fires. Go on a few dates, spend some time together that didn't consist of reviewing scenes of a fire or sitting in a hospital waiting room? Decide how much they liked each other as people before they figured out if the sex was going to be good or not. All of those things should be considered, right?

His body vehemently disagreed.

As she sat just an arm's length away from him in the car, the heat that had been on a low simmer between them since yesterday morning was kicked up a notch. That was most definitely due to the conversation they'd had in the pub. The very candid conversation about wanting to sleep with each other. Roark had never moved this fast with a woman before, but it was something he knew his brother would be rooting for him to do at this very moment. Ridge was the go-all-out guy, the one who didn't give a damn about normal rules of dating or living his life for that matter. Roark was the conventional one, the one who'd dated a woman for an entire year before proposing and marrying her. He was also the one who'd been divorced after three and a half short years and who'd had nothing to show for that time but a divorce decree he kept in a file cabinet in his home office.

"Are you nervous?" She'd stretched a hand over the console between them, resting it on his thigh just as he turned a corner. He didn't jump like a nervous kid, but the touch did send a heated jolt straight to his dick, which had been hard since leaving the restaurant.

"I've had sex before, Tamika. Just as I'm sure you have."

"I did and I liked it. How about you? Do you like sex, Roark, or do you just do it because it's the thing to do at the time?"

This woman had some type of beam directly to his thoughts, and he wanted to know how she was pulling it off. "You really think I'm that rigid?"

Her response was to laugh, and Roark shook his head because despite what she was laughing at, he adored the sound. There were a few things he really liked about Tamika, things he'd noted more than once during their short acquaintance. She was tenacious, which initially he'd thought would be a problem, because he hadn't considered the reason she'd tracked him down had any merit. Loyalty, which was a huge thing for Roark, was obviously a big thing for her as well. No matter how many times he asked, or even when Pierce had hinted at it earlier today at the cottage, she held firm that her father hadn't been cheating on her mother. Some might see that as naïveté or flat-out denial, but Roark saw it as her dedication to the man she'd known and loved. Similar to the way he remained committed to his parents and their legacy. And then there was her laugh and her smile—

they both came quick and it genuinely and equally touched him in a way he'd never experienced before.

"I don't generally talk about sex as much as we're doing," he admitted. "It seems a little odd."

"I think it's best to talk about sex. State what you like and don't like so you'll be sure to get what you want."

"Have you ever not gotten what you wanted out of sex?"

Her instant silence was as big a tell as if she'd immediately poured out the detail of a horrific sexual escapade. When he looked over at her, it was to see that she was staring out the window. They were closer to the manor now, the car moving down the cobblestone roads just outside the property. While the hills and countryside were the backdrop, nestled in this area were what could be called quaint little stores and houses with thick wood doors and matching window boxes full of flowers. "I haven't always gotten what I want out of a lot of things. And eventually, I learned I needed to speak up for myself more."

"I can't imagine you ever not speaking up for yourself." But obviously there'd been a time, and his callous remark had probably just ensured she'd never tell him of that time.

He wisely remained silent for the duration of the ride, and she continued to stare out the window, lost deep in the thoughts of whatever had happened that had caused her to change. Roark hadn't considered how much he'd want to know more about this woman, but by the time they pulled up in front of the clubhouse, he'd decided she was definitely more intriguing than he'd first thought.

He stepped out of the car and wasn't the least bit surprised that she hadn't waited for him to come around and open the door for her. They were both walking up the front steps when the door opened and Geoff stepped out.

"They wanted to wait, sir, and I thought it best they not wait at the manor, as there are many eyes and ears there."

For a moment, Roark had no idea what the guy was talking about, but then he followed Geoff's gaze to the parking spaces at the side of the house and frowned. An official MPD vehicle was in the first spot.

Tamika obviously followed Geoff's gaze as well and sighed. "I was wondering when they'd show up. I mean, they weren't at the hospital last night, and they should've been."

But they shouldn't have been here. They shouldn't have known that she was staying with him, unless they'd been watching them.

Roark gave Geoff a nod. "You did the right thing. We'll speak with them. Call Ed Burrows and let him know they're here." He didn't bother to tell Geoff that Ed was his attorney, since the concierge knew everything there was to know about him already.

"Yes, sir. I put them in the parlor and gave them drinks—water, of course. They've been waiting for twenty minutes." Geoff spoke as he turned and went back into the house. Roark let Tamika go in ahead of him. "They're determined to talk then."

"Determined to accuse me is probably more like it." Her tone was somber and Roark didn't like it.

There were two of them, both sitting on a floral-print couch in a room that had far too much floral print for Roark's taste. They both wore stoic black suits, white shirts, slim ties and a look of skepticism and mild contempt the moment Roark and Tamika walked in.

"Mr. Donovan, we meet again." Donald Gibbons stood and met Roark's gaze.

"Forgive me if I skip the formalities and ask why you're here. I believe the last time we spoke, I directed you to my attorney with any further questions." Roark had no intention of making this easy for either of the policemen. He didn't like that they'd come here, nor did he like the way they were looking from him to Tamika as if they already had everything figured out.

"I'm Detective Horace Pennington from the Metropolitan Police Department. I was on the scene at yesterday's fire. I believe that was at the home owned by your mother, Ms. Rayder." The shorter of the two, Pennington was going bald in the center and had bushy eyebrows. Under Roark's severe gaze, the man smoothed down his tie and cleared his throat.

Roark directed Tamika to a spot on the loveseat across from where the detectives sat. Gibbons returned to his seat and Roark sat down beside Tamika. They might've looked like old friends having a visit. And cows might fly.

"I haven't had the pleasure of meeting you, Ms. Rayder. I'm Detective Donald Gibbons. I work for MPD as well, but I'm from the Major Investigation Unit. I'm sure Mr. Donovan has mentioned speaking to me before."

"He hasn't." Her tone was even, her gaze distrustful. "We're not in the habit of discussing policemen."

"Well, it's a shame to be having this conversation." Pennington interrupted. "But there are some questions I need to ask about yesterday's fire."

"Why are you here?" Roark asked Gibbons directly.

The man had the audacity to smile. "I want to hear the answers to those questions."

Pennington cleared his throat. "Ms. Rayder, you just arrived in Painswick, correct?"

"I came to visit my mother and I've been here for a week." She was calmer than Roark would've expected, but then, she was probably used to talking with police and other firefighters in her line of work.

Pennington pulled out a notepad and pen and began scribbling something. Gibbons kept his gaze on Roark, and Roark resisted the urge to punch the guy in the face. "Your mother and father own that house. It's normally a rental, but I see your mother made it her permanent residence about a year ago." Pennington looked up at her and waited for her response.

She nodded. "Yes, that's true."

"But this is the first time you've visited?" he pressed.

There was only a moment's hesitation on her part. "That is also true."

Gibbons sat forward, dropping his elbows onto his knees. "How do you two know each other?"

"We're sleeping together," Tamika snapped. "Isn't that what you're already thinking?"

That flash of spunk was another thing for Roark to admire about her.

Gibbons didn't even blink as he glared at Roark. "Your wife's in London. Did you know that? I had a nice chat with her before I was called to come here."

"My ex-wife is able to go where she pleases," Roark replied. He really didn't like this guy at all.

"But you come here to this big, fancy country house of yours and meet up with your new girlfriend just a couple of weeks after your mother is killed in a fire at her house. And bam, your girlfriend's mother is almost killed in a fire at her house as well. That's some coincidence." Gibbons was nodding, his keen eyes going from Roark to Tamika, then settling on Roark once more.

"I came here to relax after a very trying time." That was as much of an explanation as Roark planned to give.

"And I came to visit my mother," Tamika said.

"But there was a fire and your mother's now in the

hospital, is that correct?" Gibbons wasn't finished with his questions.

Tamika sat back and placed her hands in her lap. "That is correct."

Gibbons shrugged. "You two really don't see the coincidence here? I find that hard to believe, because you're so smart, aren't you, Roark? You just made a big move from one business to another, added your mother to that stock which, according to her will, all reverts back to you and your siblings. There's also a hefty life insurance policy to go along with the rest of her estate. That again falls to you as her personal representative."

"And you, Ms. Rayder," Pennington picked up as if the two had planned this little tag-team scenario. "Your mother also has a sizable life insurance policy, and the cottage is worth a decent amount. Nothing nearly as significant to gain as Mr. Donovan here, but considering you lost your job two weeks ago, and the lease on the apartment where you were staying—which was actually in the name of a Colin Hopkins—was up earlier this month, you're hurting for cash and a place to live right now. Not to mention you're experienced in this area. If anybody would know how to set a fire, it would be you."

"First, a ten-year-old could start a fire and end up burning down a house by mistake. It's not rocket science. Second, I'm not hurting for anything," Tamika replied. "And I have a BA in criminal justice, along with my certification as a fire investigator. I'd say I'm pretty employable, so definitely not desperate in any way."

"I'd say you're both lying," Gibbons announced. "After your break-up with Mr. Hopkins and his refusal to continue paying to keep a roof over your head, you were indeed desperate to find a place to live and someone else to take care of you. You somehow heard of Maxine Donovan's death and came here posthaste to shack up with Mr. Money Bags. He told you how to kill your mother for her insurance. Only, you messed up yesterday because you didn't anticipate that housekeeper coming home and saving your mother. Now, you've got to figure out what to do that won't make you look even guiltier."

The detective's reach to find motive had so many holes in it, Roark wanted to laugh at the effort. Unfortunately, rage at the man's audacity and overall dislike for both detectives at the moment had Roark standing instead. "That's preposterous, and you know it. And I'm done entertaining both of you. I want you out of my house. Now!"

Pennington had the good sense to look shocked as Roark raised his voice, while Gibbons continued giving Roark a smug sneer. Enough so that Roark took a step toward the couch, where the detectives had remained seated after his directive.

Pennington stood next, smoothing his tie again. "We just have a few more questions. Ms. Rayder, maybe you'd prefer to come down to the station house with me?"

"Perhaps you should contact her solicitor to request another meeting," Roark said to Pennington and prayed Tamika didn't say anything to contradict him.

She didn't. In fact, she came to stand beside him and echoed his declaration. "I won't be talking to you again without an attorney."

Now Gibbons stood, his flinty eyes narrowed on Roark. "I know who your solicitor is, Donovan. Just like I know I'm going to bring your ass down for this. Don't think for one minute that your money's going to get you out of a murder charge."

"Don't think for one minute that I'm going to be

intimidated by you. Now, Geoff will show you out." Roark wasn't intimidated, he was pissed the hell off.

As if on command, Geoff appeared in the doorway.

"Here's my card if you wish to contact me." Pennington pulled a card from his inside jacket pocket and extended it to Tamika.

She accepted it with a cordial nod. "I'll give it to my attorney."

CHAPTER 10

Six hours, a hot bath and a nap later, and Tamika was still irritated as hell.

How dare those detectives think she planned to kill her mother. Hadn't she sat at the hospital for hours after the fire last night, waiting with her heart in knots to see if her mother was going to survive? Hell, hadn't she tried to run into the burning cottage to get her mother the moment she'd arrived on the scene? How could any of those actions be construed as someone who'd intentionally set fire to the place with the intention of killing the one blood relative she had left on this earth?

Her fingers were still shaking with rage as she pushed her arms through the plum-colored dress and let the soft material slide over her body. This was a dress she owned, one of the few things that didn't smell like smoke, because even though most of her clothes had still been in her suitcase and duffel bag, in a room all the way down the hall from her mother's, the heavy clouds of smoke had still managed to permeate them. Clicking the link Lily had provided and shopping on the CKDavis Design website had provided a little calm to the stormy afternoon she'd had. And just as Lily had promised, the boxes of clothes Tamika had selected had been delivered within an hour of her clicking "place order." She suspected that had something to do with the fact that Roark was paying for the clothes and that she wasn't some random customer. While the thought of Roark buying her clothes had bothered her earlier this morning, after enduring the unfounded speculation that she and Roark had somehow conspired together to commit murder by the detectives, she'd decided to shop until her heart was content and hadn't felt one ounce of guilt when it was done.

After those detectives had left, Tamika had been a roller coaster of emotions. Roark had wanted to talk to her, but she hadn't been in the mood. They'd asked too many stupid questions, had made predictable assumptions and were dead wrong on all accounts. But no amount of pacing in this room, plopping down into the chair and switching on the TV she never actually watched, or gritting her teeth in anger, was going to stop the ball that'd already started running in their mind. Just like Roark and his siblings, Tamika was now a suspect in an arson case. How ironic was that?

She'd worked so hard to build a successful career and to maintain her father's respect in the field of fire prevention and investigation. It was something that had brought them even closer in her adult life. The last thing she'd ever do was disgrace him and his life's work the way the detectives had assumed she had. And it was her mother, for crying out loud! She'd never kill her mother for money! Who did they think she was, one of those unbalanced women on those true crime shows like *Snapped*? No, if that were the case, she would've directed her rage at Colin, which for a while she'd wanted to do. But even that jackass hadn't warranted her ruining her life to set him on fire.

Speaking of the gray-eyed devil, she snatched her phone from the nightstand where she'd had it on the charger and checked her text messages. Nothing. She sighed and gave silent thanks to the heavens.

If the detectives knew about Colin, there was a good chance they'd reach out to the cops in Arlington to find out more information. And the cops in Arlington might just go down to Colin's shop and have a little chat with him. Especially since a Black man who was also a former drug dealer turned barber shop owner and landlord to several properties in the city was just the type of guy the cops loved to question, for no other reason than because he fit some type of description. And if Colin got hauled down to the police station because of her, Tamika had no doubt his demented ass would waste no time giving her grief about it. In the two years they'd been together, Colin's favorite pastime had been giving her grief about one thing or another.

Huffing out her next breath, because she really couldn't believe the crazy turns her life had taken in the past few years, Tamika dropped her phone into the pocket of her dress—she loved comfortable dresses with pockets—and slid her feet into a pair of flat leather sandals.

She walked through the room that should've made her feel like a pampered princess, but instead reminded her of the precarious situation she was now in, and opened the door. The hallway was bright with the large chandeliers that stretched along its path. Thick Aubusson rugs lined the floors, and paintings of what was probably the scenic English countryside were on the walls. All things she found it hard to appreciate, considering how she'd ended up being here.

Taking the stairs, she tried to clear her thoughts. She

needed air and space from everything that was going on, if only for a few moments. Those thoughts carried her out the front door and down the smooth cement steps in front of the clubhouse. It had grown dark in the time she'd been shut in her room, and a cool breeze was blowing. She had no idea where to go or what to do at this point, so she simply turned to the left and began walking along a stone pathway.

Outside flood lights mounted along the house were a perfect mix of old and new, but she was grateful for them; otherwise, she'd have been drenched in darkness by the time she made it to the edge of the enormous house. There was grass straight ahead, small hills and big hills and more grass. To her right, the path continued to a raised area she thought might be the gardens Roark had spoken of earlier. Taking a chance, she moved to her right and smiled when she came upon an archway made of flowers and a black iron gate. Everything here seemed so ornate and elegant. She would've never pictured herself enjoying a place like this, but right at this moment, she felt giddy with excitement at seeing what was beyond the gate. Lifting the latch, she eased the gate open and entered a place she knew would be breathtaking during the day.

Since it was evening, there were twinkle lights strategically placed on the ground to illuminate the flowers or twisting vines along the wall of greenery. Feeling like she was entering a maze, Tamika continued to stroll, inhaling the fresh floral scents. She wasn't really big on flowers, had never received any from the guys she'd dated and hadn't seen them a lot in her home while she was growing up.

There was something pink just around the corner she'd turned, bursting from the green along the wall in a spray of color and scent. She stopped when she was close to the wall and leaned in to inhale deeply.

"I grew up smelling flowers every day and in every room of our house."

She startled at his voice, slapping a hand to her chest as she turned to see him standing just a few feet away.

"Sorry. I should've announced myself."

"You shouldn't be following me around in a garden at night," she snapped as she tried to regulate her breathing after being scared out of her mind.

"I guess you've got a point." Leave it to Roark to not give in totally.

Since the moment with these fragrant pink flowers was lost, she continued walking. "Have you been following me since I left the house?"

"No. Dorianne's dying to feed us, so I came up to your room to get you for dinner, but you weren't there. You don't have a car here and nobody had called one for you, so I assumed you were walking."

"This place is huge, Roark. How would you know I came here?" She felt like those detectives questioning everything now.

"When I came out, I saw you walking toward the gardens. I wasn't following you, just making sure you were alright."

And she was being a jerk. She pushed both her hands into her pockets and looked over at him. "Sorry. I'm in a bad mood."

"Understandable. I've been in a pretty crappy mood since they left, as well."

"I don't normally let people dictate my attitude, but I can't believe they think we're killers, or at the very least orchestrators of a murderous plot for money."

Roark chuckled. "The latter title sounds better."

She smiled, letting his lighter tone filter over her. "I have to figure out what's going on. I know this is connected to my father's death. I brought my files from the house, so I'm going to start looking at them as soon as I get back inside. The sooner I get to the bottom of this, the better for both of us."

He touched her hand at that moment, holding it until she stopped walking. "I think it'll be better for both of us the sooner I get this out of the way."

Tamika opened her mouth to question his cryptic words, and he swooped down, crashing his lips into hers, igniting the fire she'd known was on a low simmer between them.

If that sounded like a superhero entering the scene, that was precisely what it felt like. The moment his lips touched hers, the out-of-body experience began. His tongue eased inside her mouth with the intention of claiming and did an excellent job. She closed her eyes, melting into him, letting her tongue slide along his, tilting her head so she could take more of him. He'd dropped her hand at some point, his fingers now scraping along her scalp as he pushed through her hair, holding her face to his. He pulled back, just long enough so they could both take a quick breath before he plunged right back in. This time, her hands came up to quickly grasp his biceps and squeeze. Or rather, hold on, because her knees were now buckling. He felt so hard and strong beneath her touch. His hands moved to her shoulders, then down her back, where one continued until he was cupping her ass. She pressed into him, opening her mouth wider as he sucked her tongue. His dick was hard; she could feel it pressing into her belly, and her thighs quivered.

He was devouring her mouth, sucking first her tongue, then her lips, licking the top lip and then the bottom, teasing her tongue until she was reaching for him, licking and sucking along his lips in a silent duel for more. Her hands moved up from his biceps to his strong shoulders. He wore a long-sleeved shirt that fit every dip and bulge of his physique.

Both his hands were on her ass now, pressing her into his erection. When she gasped for air, he pulled on her dress, inching it up her legs.

"What... Are we... Out here?" She could barely think straight, so it made sense that her words were coming out in a jumble.

"Not out here. I just need to...to do this, right now." He didn't sound like his words were coming much easier, but they both forgot about that when he pushed her against the flowered wall and his hands ran along the bare skin of her ass, down to her thigh, then back up to her ass again.

His lips were on hers in seconds, this kiss hungrier, deeper than the other two had been. Frankly, she didn't give a damn how the kisses were described. All she knew was that she wanted every second of it to continue.

"Just need to...touch...you."

Well, shit, he'd been touching her. The scorch marks from his hands were all up and down her back and on her ass. What else could he possibly be thinking of touch...

The word died in her thoughts as his hand moved around to slip between her thighs. She adjusted, spreading them a little wider, but he knew where to go. He cupped her pussy first, his full hand grabbing her and holding until she thought she might come simply from the heat his touch was infusing.

"Damn!" He seemed to choke the word out before his fingers eased to the side, finding the band of her panties. Pushing the cloth aside, he pressed his fingers between her already wet folds.

Roark obviously knew what he wanted and how fast he wanted to get there, because there was no preamble to his fondling. He pushed past her pussy lips, grazed over her puckered clit and thrust his finger inside her within a three-second time span.

"I knew you'd be wet," he said and then made a low growling sound that had Tamika pumping into his hand. "Fuck! So wet!"

And she was. The way his finger moved so fast in and out of her sent pleasure rippling through her body, while the sound that action caused echoed around them. Was she really standing in the middle of a garden getting a magnificent hand job from this guy? Hell yes, and she was thoroughly enjoying every second of it. So much so, she lifted one leg and wrapped it around his waist. He groaned and dropped his head so he could kiss along her neck while his finger continued to move in and out of her.

"Had to touch you, feel you, right now." He was saying the words and moving his finger and tracing his tongue along her skin, all the things that were succeeding in driving her out of her mind with need.

Her hips moved to the rhythm of his finger. She wanted him to go deeper, harder. She wanted him to make her come, right here in the middle of this garden. "Never would've thought," she mumbled. "Feels so damn good."

"Yeah, it does," he said. "Yeah, it definitely does feel good."

Truth be told, it felt magnificent to her. Nine months, in comparison to Roark's six-month hiatus, had been way too long without sex, and even though this wasn't the thick-dick penetration she'd been thinking of earlier with him, it was still pretty close. Speaking of which, she pushed her hand between their bodies, easing down until she felt the print of his massive erection straining against his pants. If she pulled him out right now, she had no doubt he'd slip inside her and they'd be full-on fucking in the garden. Instead, she rubbed her hand over his length, gripping him through the pants and loving the sound of his breath quickening as she did.

"You want this dick, don't you?"

Man, if he wasn't asking the dumbest of questions.

"But not here," he followed up quickly. "Not. Yet."

Because he was too busy making her come with just his fingers. Yes, he continued to plunge deep inside her, pausing only to drag a finger back to her clit, where his quick circular motions had her breath catching between moans. Roark knew exactly what he was doing. She was pressing into his hand so hard, her thighs were already trembling, her orgasm just seconds away.

No, not seconds—it was there in full force when her body bowed in his grasp, her toes curled in her sandals, eyes closed tightly as bursts of color behind her lids signified the swirl of pleasure rippling through her body at this very moment.

She hadn't realized she'd gripped his dick until he moaned, "Fuck! You're trying to make me come too."

She wasn't, not at that moment, but damn, his dick felt good in her hand, almost as good as his fingers felt when he began massaging her pussy.

In the next moments after they'd both caught their breath, Roark eased his hand from between her legs. He lowered her leg to the ground and then stepped back to fix her dress. Tamika ran her fingers through her hair and cleared her throat, like that was going to shake the remnants of that terrific orgasm from her mind and body.

"I can meet you in your bedroom, or you can come to mine." His voice sounded deeper, but more controlled than ever.

"I'll come to you," she said, feeling a little shaky at how quickly she'd acquiesced.

None of this was like her, not the Tamika of the past. Colin would say it first, that her attitude toward sex had always seemed reserved or, worse, scripted. That could be because she'd always had to psyche herself up to have sex with him. This, with Roark, wasn't planned, it hadn't even been expected, and yet, here they were.

"I'll leave first. Don't be long."

In seconds she was standing there alone, still trying to wrap her mind around what had just happened and what was undoubtedly about to happen. To hell with that—she could think about all that other stuff later. Right now, she was going to get what she wanted, something she hadn't done in her past few years. Something she'd regretted allowing Colin to take from her.

Tamika wasn't going to be nervous. She was thirty-six years old and no stranger to sex. In some cases, she was no stranger to kinky and rough sex, but that was another subject. She stepped into her room and walked immediately to the bathroom. Once inside, she closed and locked that door and went to the sink, turning on the hot and then cold water. Then she just stood there, staring at her reflection in the mirror.

"Fine as wine." She whispered the words she'd been telling herself since she was sixteen. Why? Because if nobody else told her how good she looked, she'd always be there to tell herself. It had never been her inclination to depend on anybody for anything to be the woman she wanted to be, and yet, she'd once fallen into a trap that had threatened to steal her very soul.

But that wasn't what she was supposed to be thinking right now. With a shake of her head, she lowered her hands to the water, bent over and splashed water on her face. She repeated the action one more time for good measure before reaching for a hand towel. There was a pile of them folded neatly between both sinks now, as well as a smaller pile of washcloths. Once her face was dry, she grabbed a cloth and dropped it into the sink. Lifting her dress, she removed her panties, the ones that were now drenched in her very natural and extremely enjoyable reaction to Roark's touch.

After a quick wash-up, she turned off the water and stared at her reflection a few seconds more. She was going to have sex with Roark Donovan, a sexy millionaire who was accused of killing his mother. Well, that was something new to add to the list of the unexpected things that had happened in her life. And just as with the other things, she decided to stop questioning it now. *"Life happens fast. What's most important is that you stay in the driver's seat and keep moving."* That was what her father used to tell her.

Tonight, she was going to sit tight in the driver's seat and see exactly where this trip to Roark's bedroom would take her.

She didn't keep him waiting long—not because of his directive for her not to do so, but because she was ready.

His door was ajar, and she pushed it open further to step inside. The first thing she felt when she entered was the heat. Not the sexual heat that had engulfed them in the garden, but a real fire-blazing heat, and for just a second, she thought about the flames she'd seen stretching through the windows at the cottage last night. Giving herself a mental shake, Tamika closed and locked the door behind her.

When she didn't immediately see him, she walked over to the sitting area, where the fire was crackling in the fireplace. Moving closer, she stood there with her arms folded across her chest, staring at the blaze. She'd always been strangely drawn to fire, not in the "I wanna burn shit up" type of way, but in an inquisitive way that had pushed her to learn more about her father's career and eventually to carve out a notch in that world for herself. If she'd only known then what fire would really come to mean in her life.

She heard him come up behind her this time and instantly leaned back into his embrace as his hands went to her shoulders.

"If you're having second thoughts, it's okay. We can just sit and talk." How was it that this guy's voice could always wash over her and drape her in this cloak of comfort that was more than unexpected? In the life she'd sworn for herself, it was also undesired. And yet, it felt so good.

"If I had second thoughts, I wouldn't be here," she replied honestly, because honest was what she planned to be with any man in her life moving forward. It was something she'd told herself was a necessity and that she wasn't going to sideline ever again. "Are you having second thoughts?"

The first part of his answer was to lean forward and kiss her neck while his hands moved down her arms to wrap her in a warm hug. "Not at all."

Well then, she thought and turned in his embrace. When they were facing each other, she wrapped her arms around his neck and pulled him down for another kiss. The desire between them burned equally as bright as that fire and took barely nothing to be ignited. That was new too. There was no build-up with this guy, no slow burning of waiting and wanting. They'd both just known and as mature adults were acting on their wants. Score one for the grown and sexy folks.

His arms had gone around her waist, where he'd immediately grabbed her ass, squeezing her plump cheeks appreciatively. She pressed her body into his, enjoying the feel of his longing against her stomach once again. The memory of his rigid length in her hands a little while ago had a moan escaping as she thought of his hard dick being deep inside her very soon.

His mind was on the same track as he pushed her dress up once more. This time he didn't stop when it was at her waist but inched it up until they had to break the kiss and she could lift her arms so he could take it off completely. She wore only her bra and the golden glow from the fire behind her, and when Roark stepped back, dropping her dress onto the floor, his gaze plastered to her body, there was nothing but appreciation and maybe a pinch of awe in his eyes.

"You're amazing," he whispered.

As compliments went, that one was a winner, and Tamika pushed back every offensive and hurtful slur Colin had ever tossed at her in regard to her weight and body type. Folding her arms behind her back, she unsnapped her bra and let her heavy breasts fall free, because if he was going to admire her body, he might as well get it all in one gulp. And that was precisely what he did when she tossed the bra onto the floor to join her dress and his eyes rested on her breasts.

"Gorgeous," he mumbled and immediately touched a hand to each globe.

He kneaded and squeezed, taking her taut nipples between his fingers before moaning his appreciation. Her eyes closed momentarily to the warmth of this touch, and the tendrils of pleasure that soared through her breasts with his ministrations. When he lowered himself so his face was buried between her tits, she gasped and clapped her hands to the back of his head as if to hold him there forevermore. The sounds he made assured her he didn't mind being smothered by her plentiful breasts. In fact, if she wasn't thinking that he liked them, she knew for certain when he turned his face and opened his mouth wide to take a nipple inside.

This rich, fine man could suck titties for days, and she could definitely appreciate that. His mouth moved over her like he'd been starving for this feast she was offering. While he sucked one breast, his hand worked the other, squeezing and now pinching her nipple until a tiny spike of pain exploded and rained down more pleasure that trickled straight to her crotch. He moved to the next breast with no intention of slighting her in any way, sucking and squeezing until she was biting her lower lip in an attempt to keep from yelling out his name.

When he finally tore his mouth away and stood in front of her again, Tamika went straight for his shirt, pulling it from his pants and lifting it up over his head. His chest was bare before her now, and this time she sucked in a breath to keep from saying "dayuuuum" out loud. She'd known he was a nicely built guy, but glimpsing all that golden-brown skin stretched over nothing but muscle in the glow of the firelight made her mouth water. She ran her fingers over his thick biceps, loving the feel of physical strength there that matched the strength of his character she'd witnessed shining through earlier today, when he'd tossed those detectives out of his house.

He stood still as her palms flattened over the most defined pectoral muscles she'd ever admired close up. Why he hid all this under those dress shirts and ties, and even the fitting T-shirts she'd seen him in, was a mystery. Then again, he couldn't actually walk around with his bare chest out 24/7—women would be dropping their panties the second he walked into a room. Leaning in, she kissed one dark nipple then let her tongue run over it. His hands went to her head, holding her close in a way similar to what she'd done to him. Then his fingers were in her hair, scraping along her scalp as he'd done earlier. That, of all the things he'd done to her so far, was the most enticing. She'd never thought her scalp to be a pleasure point, but the slight tremble in her thighs with the first stroke of his fingers was a tell-tale sign. She switched to the next pectoral and he continued driving his fingers through her hair.

"Do you want the bed?" His voice was gruff with need that eased over her body like hot oil.

"Right now, I only want you."

Roark was apparently cool with that, because he lowered her to the floor, where she noticed the thick cream-colored blanket for the first time. It was positioned right in front of the fire. Obviously, Roark had suspected this would be their spot. When she was seated on the floor where he'd also placed a bunch of pillows she recognized from the couches in the center of the room, Roark stood beside her, easing the belt from the hoops on his jeans.

Okay, now she was getting a personal strip show. She was definitely down for that. He'd already removed his shoes and socks, another thing she hadn't noticed before, but his belt joined her pile of clothes on the floor and his fingers went to the snap of his jeans.

"Do you like what you see?" he asked as he dragged the zipper down slow enough to cause the beginnings of a cardiac event on her part.

She licked her lips. "I'm pretty sure I'm going to like it much more when you're finished."

He chuckled. "Damn, I enjoy your candor."

And she enjoyed his British accent. This clearly wasn't the first time she'd noticed it, but it was the first time she realized just how much she liked the sound of every word he said, because it sounded different than she'd ever heard those words spoken before.

The jeans came off and the gray boxers followed, and all that was left was his long, thick dick bobbing as if performing for her. She didn't lick her lips again, but she did swallow, hard, at the sight. With a stilted curse, he moved to their pile of clothes and found his wallet, which he hunted through to pull out a condom. For a moment she felt like an idiot for not thinking about protection in the time she'd been ogling him. Telling herself she would've thought about it before they went too far, she lowered herself down to the pillows as he came closer.

When he dropped the packet onto the rug beside them and began to spread her legs apart, he must've noticed her frown. "Not yet, darlin'. I need to taste you first." He looked like a predator, staring up at her while moving his body between her legs. As he pressed them open wider, his hands touched the skin of her ankles, up to her calves and then to the inner thighs.

"Is this, like, a taste test? Do you sample every part of me before you decide if you want to go further?"

His face had been buried in one thigh, his tongue stroking along her skin, his cheeks rubbing over her like he was feeling something special in the thickness there. "I already know how far I'm going to go with you, Tamika. The tasting is just the preamble to the main show."

She wanted to scream for him to take all of her right this very moment, but she refrained, clenching and releasing her fingers as anticipation mixed with arousal threatened to strangle her with the potent need.

With one hand, he spread her pussy lips until she was totally bared to him. If there were ever a time to be self-conscious, now was definitely it, because Roark certainly was looking at her as if he were surveying a new purchase. When he lifted his gaze to her, all she could see was fiery passion brimming in them. His lips were parted, and his breathing had picked up. He licked his lips this time, a motion that made her squirm beneath him when she imagined that tongue touching her very soon.

Soon wasn't fast enough, but when he finally lowered his head and did a quick lick of her clit, she almost jumped up off the floor it felt so damned good. Using his other arm, he grabbed her left thigh, lifting her leg and dropping it over his strong shoulder. Easing his other hand from where it still held her plump folds open, he pushed her right thigh back further and then he dove in, licking and sucking her as if she were a delectable meal that had been placed before him.

Tamika grabbed her breasts, kneading them in the same way he had, tweaking her nipples and then finally she lifted her hips to thrust against his hungry mouth. Pleasure plowed through her so forcefully she gasped and moaned louder than she intended.

"Let it out, darlin'. No need to be shy," he grumbled when he pulled away from her momentarily.

Shy was never something Tamika had claimed to be, but she could admit she was trying to hold back with Roark. A part of her didn't want him to see how very good everything he did made her feel. The thought of doing so made her feel too vulnerable, something she'd never wanted to feel again, but it was getting harder and harder to hold on to that restraint. It just felt too damn good.

He licked her hungrily, thrusting two fingers inside her now, pumping and sucking her simultaneously. She was so wet she felt her essence trickling down the crease of her ass. There was going to be one hell of a wet spot on this blanket when she got up, but Roark didn't act like he cared. To the contrary, he eased his fingers out of her, rubbing them along her slit, moaning and whispering how wet she was and how much it turned him on.

"Now," she whispered. Her eyes were closed at the time, her hands still cupping her breasts, legs spread in the position he'd put them in, and she was ready. Oh, sweet goodness, was she ready.

"Yeah, now is good," he replied and eased her leg down from his shoulder.

She opened her eyes to see him move away from her and reach for the condom packet. Normally, she liked the act of smoothing a condom down a man's rigid length, but her body was so taut with desire if she moved again before climaxing, she was certain something might break.

Roark must've sensed her desperation, because when he came between her legs this time, he lifted them both, pulling her closer to him as he rested her ankles on his shoulders. With his palms flat on the floor on either side of her, he positioned his dick, aimed and thrust deep into her in one quick push. He grunted and she screamed, and the preamble was over.

He rode her like he owned her, stuffing his thick dick so deep inside her Tamika knew he was touching essential organs. This wasn't lovemaking; it wasn't even sex—Roark Donovan was fucking her in a way she'd only dreamed of being fucked before, and she loved every second of it. Minutes later when he turned her over and put her on her knees, she backed her ass up against his dick and felt another sting of pleasure as he slapped both ass cheeks before pounding into her again. Her breasts bobbed with the motion, and his groans grew louder. Her screams had subsided a bit, but that was because they'd been exchanged with her repeating his name, as if verbally cementing the fact that he was owning her pussy at this moment.

"You come first," he grunted and pulled out of her quickly.

She was about to say something, but his hands were spreading her cheeks wide before she felt his lips on her pussy once more. He pumped his fingers into her and licked until she was trembling, her thighs quivering around his head, chest heaving as she struggled to breathe through the onslaught of pleasure.

"Yessssss," she moaned and felt that quick jolt of realization before her release seized her body.

"Yes, sweetness, that's what I want." When he finally pulled his face away from her, Tamika thought she was going to topple over, because every ounce of energy had been licked, sucked and drawn from her body. Instead, she realized Roark was switching their position once more. "I want you to make me come now."

He lay on his back and pulled her on top of him. Tamika shook her hair back from her face and prepared to take the driver's seat for the first time since she'd come into his room. She lowered herself onto his dick and marveled once again at how well he fit buried deep inside her. Then she began to ride, staring down at Roark as his hands reached up to grab her breasts, his face contorting with the sexiest sex face she'd ever seen.

"Bring it home, sweetness. Bring it all the way home." The last word lodged in his throat as she circled her hips, lifted off him until only the tip of his dick was still inside her and then slammed down onto him again. Her rapid pumps from that moment on led to him gripping her breasts tightly and, for the first time since they'd begun, him moaning her name in that deep, rich, accented voice. When his dick ceased pulsating inside her, Tamika eased herself down and was going to roll off him, but his arms went around her waist tightly and he pulled her closer for a sultry kiss that sealed the deal for her—Roark Donovan was the best sex she'd ever had, and no matter what happened from this point on in their lives, she'd never forget that.

PART II

**"Revenge triumphs over death; love slights it; honor
aspireth to it; grief flieth to it."**
—*Francis Bacon*

CHAPTER 11

She'd extended him the courtesy of going into the bathroom first, so now, Roark sat on the edge of his bed, waiting for her to come out. He'd pulled on a pair of basketball shorts and a T-shirt and allowed himself a few moments to think about what had just happened.

Pleasure still simmered in his blood; he could feel it easing along his veins, filling his body with an odd sort of satisfaction. It wasn't the act of sex itself—he was certain of that, because he'd had lots of presumably good sex in his life. No, this was different. Stronger, more intense, a desire embedding itself deeply inside him. More notable was the fact that it was unlike anything he'd ever felt after sex with any other woman, and he desperately wanted to know why. Roark didn't like not having all the answers. He'd been struggling with that daily in regard to his mother's death, and now, this. Lifting his hands, he scrubbed them over his face and took a deep breath.

The day had gone by and now it was almost ten at night. He wondered if she'd be hungry when she came out. They'd had a pretty big lunch, but then they'd also had a very trying afternoon and then...the sex. Dorianne would be gone for the night, but he'd instructed her to leave the food she'd prepared in the refrigerator and they'd reheat it when they were ready. She hadn't seemed happy about that, but she hadn't reprimanded him for skipping a meal, either. The look on the older woman's face said she'd wanted to do exactly that.

When it seemed like Tamika was taking a very long time in the bathroom, Roark stood. He walked to the other side of the bed and reached up to close the curtains at the window. He'd remembered to draw the ones in the sitting area closed before Tamika had arrived, which was a good thing, since they'd ended up together in that area instead of coming to the bed.

Katrina had never liked sex with the lights on, nor would she have ever agreed to sex on the floor. A smile ghosted his lips as he recalled pulling the blanket out of the closet and placing it on the floor in front of that fire. He hadn't known where that idea had come from, but something had told him Tamika would be totally down for the setting he'd provided. As memories of their sexual escapade floated through his mind, he realized in the end he hadn't appreciated the setting as much as the woman who'd made it complete.

Damn, she'd looked fucking phenomenal in the firelight, on her knees as he'd pounded into her and then as she'd ridden him. His body tightened with the thoughts, and he shook his head. "Phenomenal" didn't seem like an adequate enough word.

"Full disclosure."

Her words had him spinning around to see her standing in the doorway of the bathroom. She was wearing one of the heavy velvet robes that hung in the bathroom. It was black, with the Donovan insignia in gold on the right side. "Are you hungry? Do you want to go down and get something to eat first?" The questions came out in a jumble of words that made him feel ridiculous. He'd talked to women after having sex with them before, so acting like a nervous novice was way out of character for him.

She switched off the light in the bathroom and stepped further into the room, stopping before she could reach the end of the bed. With her hands buried in the pockets of the robe that was too big for her, she shook her head. "No. I want to get this out of the way." She cleared her throat and then began. "I lived with Colin Hopkins for two years."

Colin Hopkins was the name of the man Detective Pennington had brought up. He was the one whose apartment she'd been living in until recently. Roark had searched the guy online the moment he'd come to his room after the detectives had left this afternoon. So he knew a little something about the man she'd lived with, but now he'd wait to hear what she had to say.

"We met at a mutual friend's wedding. He seemed like a great guy and just my type, entrepreneur with just a touch of thug." She shrugged. "Some women don't shake the attraction to bad boys during their teen years."

Roark didn't speak. Her tone was different from when she was asking questions or simply talking about any of the things she liked to talk about. There was a hint of something in her tone, but he couldn't put his finger on it, not just yet.

"We went on a few dates, and you know how it is in the beginning, so romantic. Like, I'd be looking forward to each date all day long and when we were together, I didn't want the night to end. Then we took trips to Las Vegas and Miami. The first-year anniversary trip to Hawaii was the best."

Roark tried to ignore the immediate spike of jealousy at the smile on her face. She'd obviously enjoyed that trip.

"But the newness eventually wears off." These words were said in a snappish tone, and she stepped back to lean against the wall near one of the dressers. "No woman believes she's the type to stand for any kind of abuse."

His fingers fisted, and Roark resisted the urge to demand she immediately tell him what this idiot Colin had done to her.

She was shaking her head. "And believe me, I'm not. I was an only child, but I was a straight tomboy, fighting any and everyone who came at me wrong in my neighborhood. My mother used to get so mad when I came home with ripped shirts or scrapes on my legs and face because I'd been either wrestling or downright brawling with some kid who'd gotten in my face. And they got in my face a lot, because kids are cruel and they love to pick on the fat girl on the block. They just weren't prepared for this fat girl to fight back."

Now, his heart ached for her, for the bullying she must've endured in the name of childhood.

"And Colin was from the streets too, so he knew he had a straight ride-or-die chick on his side. I could get dressed in my suits and go to work at the insurance company and be as professional as I was trained to be, but if there was ever something to pop off while he and I were out, Colin knew I'd stand right there with him. In fact, that was one of the things he said he loved about me."

There was so much more to her though, so much more than Roark had seen in such a short amount of time.

"He didn't hit me, if that's what you're thinking. We would've been going 'round for 'round in that apartment if he had. But there are so many other ways to break a person down. It started with the quick jabs of 'you still hungry?' or 'you can't fit that.' I brushed those off, because I'd heard them before when I was younger and it wasn't that big of a deal. But then when he started complaining about our sex life because of my size, or the way I looked in pictures." She stopped and chuckled. "The funny thing was, I was actually a little heavier when I first met him, so I really couldn't understand where all this was coming from. My parents hated him, but I stayed with him. For whatever reason, he started coming at me about my job and about how I was trying too hard to impress my father, or to be like him—that's when he began to work my nerves. Nothing I did or said was right after the argument we had when I insinuated he was jealous of my father's college education and success. Colin didn't go to college, unless you count the college of the streets that earned him a ton of money, a bullet in his right leg and probation before judgment on a distribution charge."

Roark knew about the guy's criminal record and the barber shop he'd opened in Alexandria. The place that acted as a front for the drug enterprise he continued to run. "Why did you stay?"

It seemed like such a simple question, but Roark knew there was so much more to it than just walking away. He'd heard so many stories of women who'd been abused; when a woman on his staff had become a victim, he'd taken the time to actually read articles about the cycle of abuse. Eventually, his employee had decided to seek help, and Roark had made sure the company had provided her with all the resources she'd needed to get her life back.

"Maybe I thought it was easier." She shrugged. "I don't know. But I'll make a very long and distressing story short. I found out he was not only selling drugs again but was also investing in a strip club, where part of the job requirement for dancer was to sleep with him. He was trash—I'd known it for a while. That was the final straw, and I moved out. That was two weeks before my father was killed."

Just because his hands weren't fisted anymore didn't mean Roark wasn't still pissed the hell off. But he managed to ask the next question in as calm a voice as he could muster. "He just let you walk away?"

"Ha! Of course not. He took all the things I'd left in the apartment and brought them to my job, where he proceeded to burn them right there on the sidewalk."

Roark stepped toward her. "Your ex burned your belongings two weeks before your father died in a fire?"

She'd had a semi-smile on her face, but it quickly faltered. "He was the first person I checked out after I knew the fire at my dad's office was arson. He had a solid alibi for the time of the fire, and the person who started that fire had to be standing right there in the office with my father when he did it."

"What if he paid somebody to do it for him?" Roark asked and considered for a brief second that this was the strangest after-sex talk he'd ever had with a woman.

"Why? Killing me would've been easier. He could've walked into my office that day instead of dropping my things on the sidewalk then texting me to come downstairs so I'd see him burning it."

"But just as he stood and watched you grow upset at him burning your things on the sidewalk, he could watch you suffer at finding out your father was dead."

"Why wait a year to go after my mother?"

Roark shrugged. "She left. Maybe he didn't know where she went until now."

"But what about your mother? If Colin's hiring people to kill my parents to get back at me for leaving him, how does that explain her death?"

Roark didn't have an answer to that, a fact that was steadily wearing on him. "It's late. Let's eat and get some sleep. We can go over all this with fresh eyes in the morning." It was a suggestion made because he didn't know what was going on. When he'd read about her ex's criminal tendencies, he'd been annoyed but not suspicious. Now, he didn't know what to think.

She pulled her hand out of the pockets of the robe and pressed them to her face. After a deep breath, she let her arms fall down to her sides. "I'm not really hungry. Just tired." The words sounded so desolate as she turned to leave.

"Stay." He said it so quickly, his mind didn't have time to decipher whether or not it was a good idea. "I mean, I'm not an after-sex snuggler, but I want you to stay."

She turned around slowly until she was facing him again. With a tilt of her head, she smiled. "Did you really think you had to tell me you're not a snuggler, Roark?"

"Full disclosure," he replied with a tentative smile.

There were a few moments of silence that seemed to sit in the space between them like a boulder. He didn't know what else to say; he didn't want to push, and he didn't want to let her go to her room alone. Not tonight.

His heart thumped quickly when he saw her hands go to the belt of the robe. He watched her shrug out of it and then reach down to pull back the covers on the bed.

When she was in the bed, she patted the space beside her and said, "You coming?"

Roark had no idea what he was doing. Why now? Why this woman? More questions and more answers that eluded him. He climbed in beside her.

They lay in silence until they both fell asleep and sometime during the night, Roark turned over and reached for her. She was there, so it wasn't a dream, and he wrapped his arm around her waist, spooning his body against hers. Seconds later, his hand moved upward to cup her breast. She sighed in her sleep and snuggled back closer to him.

Roark held her tight and for the first time in weeks, slept deeply until the morning.

Her mother's hand was warm, her body was still, her eyes closed and Tamika's heart was heavy.

She sat in the chair beside the hospital bed the next morning, holding her mother's hand and letting her head rest on the rail the nurses had lifted along the side of the bed. Throughout her childhood, her mother had insisted they go to church every Sunday. Mostly, Tamika had just played with her dolls, lining them up on the dark wood pews. She'd dress them in their church clothes on Saturday night and stuff them into the backpack. It was the only time she played with what were considered "girl toys," and that was because Sunday was the only day her mother had insisted she wear a dress, tights and those shiny patent leather shoes—black in the winter and white starting on Easter and going through to Labor Day.

The memory made her smile, and Tamika wished she'd paid more attention in church all those years ago. If she had, maybe she'd know how to pray now. But even after she'd outgrown the dolls, she still hadn't gone to church to listen to the hymns or the sermon. By that time, she'd learned the church participated in a community basketball league and there were boys from the church wearing basketball shorts and tank tops instead of the ill-fitting dress pants and shirts she'd seen them in on Sunday mornings. However, seeing them in their basketball uniforms on

Saturdays during the games had changed her whole outlook on them when Sunday morning rolled around, so much so that she'd begun sitting in the back of the church with some of the other boy-crazy girls just to be closer to the boys.

She'd been such a child back then. That thought had her giving a little chuckle because what else was she supposed to be. Now, her mother needed her to be so much more. She'd spoken to the insurance agent on her way to the hospital this morning and had an appointment to meet the representative at the house the day after tomorrow, because that was when the Fire Brigade said the scene would be released.

The "scene" was her mother's home, and Tamika had no idea if Sandra would be able to return there. She had no idea if Sandra was ever going to wake up.

"Her vital signs are good. The burns will take a little more time to heal, but we're giving her plenty of pain medication to keep her comfortable. Skin grafts may be an option at some point, but that's nothing to worry about right now." That was what Dr. Duvall, the slim woman with coal-black hair that hung straight down her back, had told Tamika the moment she'd arrived at the hospital today.

"Is that why she's not waking up? Because of all the pain medication?" she'd asked.

"It could be. Sometimes after a traumatic experience such as your mother endured, patients will slip into a coma. It can be their body's way of dealing with all it's been through. But as I said, we're monitoring her carefully, and her brain activity is fine. She's just resting."

Tamika hadn't liked the word "coma" and had wanted to push it far out of her mind. Unfortunately, there was another word she'd needed to say at the moment. "There's a possibility she was drugged," she'd blurted out before the doctor could walk away. "I know you had to do blood tests while you were treating her, but did you run a tox screen?"

Dr. Duvall had shaken her head, her eyes immediately filling with concern. "She came in as a burn victim. We did run normal blood screenings, but there was no need to do a toxicology workup."

"There's a reason. What I mean is there might be a possibility she was drugged before the fire. Would it be too late to do it now?"

"It depends. I mean it's only been two days since the fire, but some drugs linger in the system longer. I could try to see if there's something notable."

Tamika had reached out to grab the doctor's hand at that point. It was totally unprofessional and definitely jarring for the other woman, but Tamika hadn't let her go. "Can you do that please? I really need to know if that's what happened to her."

The doctor's face had gone from concern to sympathy, and before she'd pulled her hand from Tamika's grasp, she'd given it a reassuring squeeze and said, "I'll let you know what I find."

"Thank you." Tamika had felt a wave of relief wash over her, only to replaced quickly by more concern. "What about Ms. Gregory? I still haven't been able to see her and I'm wondering why. How serious was her injury? How do you think she was injured so badly and my mother wasn't?"

The truth had been in the immediate hooded look of Dr. Duvall's eyes. "It's my guess that she fell into something while trying to escape the fire and it punctured her liver. There was a deep laceration we repaired during surgery. Unfortunately, she's developed an infection and we're trying to keep her stable while we wait for that to heal. Her body's not reacting to the antibiotics the way we'd hoped—that's another reason we've limited visitation, because we don't want her to incur any other infections while we're trying to fight this one. Does she have any other family we can contact?"

"No," Tamika had said around the tears that had clogged her throat. "I'm all they both have. Can I see her today?"

"We're trying a different antibiotic this morning, and since you've just mentioned the possibility of some sort of drugging, I'll do a toxicology screen on her too. I'll have the nurses come get you when you can see her."

Worry had mixed with a measure of relief that they were both still alive, and Tamika had thanked the doctor before entering her mother's room.

Who had done this to them? Who had started that fire and tried to kill both of them?

That question still loomed in her mind two hours later as her eyes remained closed like her mother's, and she tried to think back to her days in church, to the prayers the pastor would say. How did she ask for her mother's life to be spared when she'd never paid the least bit of attention when others had been praying? Would God even hear her if she did?

As she continued to wonder and chastise herself for things she knew she couldn't change, something happened. Her mother's fingers twitched.

Tamika's head shot up. "Mama?" She stared at her mother's closed eyes, at her naturally thick eyebrows and long lashes. Her high cheekbones and full lips and her black hair with the sprinkle of gray that had just begun to sprout at her roots. "Wake up, Mama. I'm here. I'm right here waiting for you to wake up."

Sandra's fingers moved again, and Tamika lifted her mother's hand to her cheek.

"Please, wake up, Mama. I need you to open your eyes and talk to me," she said and paused when her voice was cracking. "I need you to tell me everything's going to be alright."

The last was spoken on a whisper. A desperate plea to the woman who'd always made things better for her. But seconds ticked by as Tamika continued to hold tight to her mother's hand, staring down at her sleeping face, waiting and hoping.

"Please," she whispered as her eyes filled with the tears she hated so much. "Please, save my mother. Please."

The plea was spoken into the air, circling in the universe as Tamika closed her eyes and fought with everything she had to keep from crying. It wouldn't help, and she needed to be stronger than ever now. She needed to find out who'd done this and to make them pay.

CHAPTER 12

She'd been gone for a couple of hours. But she was coming back. Geoff had said he'd assigned a driver and a car to her because she'd wanted to go and visit her mother. All her things were still in her room, so she was coming back.

Why any of that mattered, Roark had no idea.

He hated the morning after sex, always had and always would.

He planned to hate this one even more, because Tamika had gotten up and left him sleeping in bed. He was used to being the one to leave first. Just as he'd been adamant he wasn't a snuggler. Yet, that had been what had finally wakened him this morning—the moment he'd rolled over to pull her into his arms once more and realized she wasn't there.

His laptop beeped with an incoming call, and Roark silently thanked the heavens for the interruption. Pressing the button to wake his screen, he accepted the call and felt a wave of relief when Ridge's face came into view.

"Hey, man. Just checking in to see how you're holding up." It was almost noon on a Monday, but Ridge wasn't in the office. Roark could tell because his brother's long locs were hanging free. Even though he'd worn his hair in this style for almost seven years now, Ridge never went into the office or to any business event or meeting with his hair out. It was either pulled back in some professional style or held with one of the many leather bindings Ridge had in his bathroom. His brother was very good at compartmentalizing his professional life from his personal, even as it related to his hair.

"I'm good. What about you? No work today?" Because just as Ridge was particular about his hair, Roark was particular about their family businesses.

"Had a Skype meeting at four with that group in India and their reps who're in the US. The time zones were all jacked up, but I made myself available anyway."

"Good move." Roark sat back and rested his elbows on the arm of the chair. "How 'bout Suri? Is she getting back to her normal life? I meant to check in with her and Aunt Birdie last night, but I got caught up in something."

Ridge threw back his head and laughed. "Man, those two are going at it every day and night. Those couple of days I spent with them were out of control. But you know Suri—she's cool. She can handle Aunt Birdie, and you know Aunt Birdie's a tough one, she can handle Suri. They're like a perfect match."

Roark couldn't help but smile at the happiness he clearly heard in his brother's voice. He knew it was just because Ridge was speaking about two people he loved dearly, and not a total depiction of how his brother was doing during his grieving process, but he enjoyed hearing it just the same.

"You better not let Suri hear you say they're a perfect match."

"Oh no, I have more sense than that," Ridge said. "What do you have going on out there? I thought you were heading to the country to get some time to yourself."

Roark wondered how much he should tell his brother. Keeping in mind the disagreement he'd had with his siblings before he'd left London, he wasn't really in the mood to keep secrets from them again, but he hated talking about the things he still didn't have an answer for. "Detective Gibbons paid me a visit yesterday." That was true and could also be considered cryptic. He knew Ridge would push for more details.

"What? Why? We gave him our alibis and told him to contact our solicitor for any further comments. What part of that doesn't he understand?" Ridge's smile was gone now.

"There was another fire here, and Gibbons thought it was a coincidence that I was here too."

"Wait, what? Man, that doesn't make sense. How did Gibbons even know you were there, and what was he doing out there in the country?" Ridge held up a hand before Roark could respond. "Are you telling me everything?" Again, Roark must not have been quick enough with his response, because Ridge continued. "If you're holding out on me again, Roark, I swear I'm coming out there, and you're not gonna like what happens when I arrive."

"Whoa." Roark spoke up quickly that time. "Don't get carried away with the threats, little bro. It's been a while since we've tussled, but make no mistake—"

"Oh my goodness, you're about to talk about that one time you pinned me down in less than five seconds. I was just recovering from a cold that winter and was still weak when you bullied me into a match. Then you refused a rematch."

Roark chuckled at the memory. "Champions don't have to entertain persons they've already beat."

Ridge laughed. "Yeah, whatever. But seriously, man, tell me what's really going on. We're in this together."

"There's this woman—" Roark paused when he saw Ridge shaking his head.

"Oh, no."

"Oh, no what?"

"Oh, no if you're starting off with 'there's this woman.'"

"Why do you say that?"

Ridge did something with his eyes that clearly relayed a "duh" expression. "Because you're not good with women."

Roark was about to reply to that comment with vehement disagreement, but then he thought there was a better use of his time. "Look, you wanted to know what's going on, so just listen."

Ridge sat back and smirked. "I'm listening."

There was no key Roark could hit that would take him through the screen so he could strangle his know-it-all brother. "This woman had been sending me text messages the week after Mum died. I ignored them, because I didn't know who she was. I met her out here Saturday morning when I arrived, and later that day, her mother's cottage was set on fire."

"Wait." Ridge leaned closer to the screen. "Some random woman wanted to meet with you, and you agreed to leave London to meet her. Then her mother's house catches on fire —is her mother dead? And Gibbons came to see you? Call me crazy, but I feel like you're still leaving something out."

Roark took a deep breath and released it with a huff. "Her mother's alive and in the hospital. Their housekeeper was also injured, and she's in the hospital too. A year ago, her father was killed in a fire. In her father's office, she found a letter written by Mum three days before her father died."

Ridge looked like Roark had felt the moment he'd heard about the fire at Sandra Rayder's cottage. "Whoa."

"Yeah, that about sums it up."

The raise of Ridge's brow said he was intrigued. "Does this woman have a name?"

"Tamika Rayder."

"Is she good-looking?"

Roark shook his head. "You're a jerk."

"Nah, I'm a man, and so are you, sometimes. So, is she good-looking or not?" Ridge wasn't about to let this go.

"She's fine."

"She's *fine* or she's fine as in she doesn't have a temperature or need medical attention?"

Roark chuckled. "Again, you're a jerk. Tamika came to me because she thought there might be a connection between her father's death and Mum's. Then her mother's cottage caught fire, and now Gibbons and another detective out here think there's a connection too. Actually, they think Tamika and I are conspiring to kill our parents for the insurance money."

"Wow." Ridge took a deep breath and released it the same way Roark had just done. "What are you going to do?"

"Cade and someone from his team named Pierce are looking into it."

"Well, there goes your calming retreat."

"Yeah. I thought I was going to have some quiet time here in the clubhouse alone, but now Tamika's staying here because she can't go back to the cottage and—"

"Whoa. Whoa. Whoa. This woman you can't tell me is good-looking or not is staying in the same house with you? Man, this is good! I mean, it's not good because people are being hurt and you're both suspects, but it is good, because if there's one thing that can help keep you calm, it's sex with a good-looking woman."

There was a knock at Roark's door, and he welcomed the interruption. "For the last time, you're a jerk," he told his brother with a chuckle. "And I gotta go. I'll call Suri later today and touch base with you about what's going on tomorrow."

Ridge was also laughing now. "Yeah, keep me posted. And seriously, man, if you need me to come out there, just say the word. Like I said before, we're in this together."

Roark nodded. "Yeah, I know, bro. I'll call you tomorrow." After disconnecting the call with his brother, Roark went to the door and opened it, his light mood taking a tumble when he met Geoff's gaze.

"Agent Rawlings is in the den, sir."

"Thanks, Geoff. I'll be right down. Have you—"

Geoff nodded. "After you asked the last time, I called Vaughn. He's the driver I assigned to Ms. Rayder this morning. He said Ms. Rayder was finished at the hospital but that she wanted him to drive past the cottage and then they'd be on their way back to the clubhouse. That was a short while ago, so I expect they'll arrive any minute now."

Roark felt a little embarrassed that Geoff had known what question he was about to ask. And that he was even asking the question, again. He shouldn't care where she was or how long it was taking her to get back here. She was an adult with her own life, and so was he. "Thanks, Geoff. I'll come down to see Agent Rawlings now."

Roark wanted to ask the man what he thought about Colin Hopkins being a suspect. Even though that wouldn't explain his mother's murder, Roark thought Colin was a good fit for wanting to kill Tamika's parents. From his track record and the way Tamika had described him, the guy sounded like the controlling type who would've been out of his mind with rage at the fact that she'd walked out on him. There was no doubt Tamika loved her parents above anyone and everything else, so it wasn't a jump to know that hurting them, killing them, would destroy her.

Roark found Pierce in the den, pacing, his black lace-up shoes moving over the plush forest green rug. "What's wrong?" he asked the moment he was close enough. The questions he'd just had in his head to ask were now lost with the look of concern etched on the guy's face.

Pierce looked up at Roark. "Where's Tamika?"

"She went to the hospital to see her mother. Tell me what's going on." Roark wasn't in the mood for waiting on an answer, especially not when the look on Pierce's face said he knew more than what he was saying.

"I'm calling Cade to loop him into this conversation, but we need Tamika here. Now." He didn't look at all bothered by the slight rise in Roark's voice with his previous comment. Probably because the guy was used to dealing with sociopaths and serial killers for a living. Standing here listening to Roark demand answers was most likely nothing to him.

"Hey. Are they all there?" Cade's voice sounded from Pierce's phone.

"Tamika's not here yet," Pierce told him.

"What the hell is going on, Cade? I want to know what you two know right now!"

That rise in temper may have done the trick, because Roark watched as Pierce's brows raised, and he could hear Cade exhaling deeply through the phone.

"It's about Aunt Max and Lemuel Rayder." Cade's voice sounded dour.

"What about them?" Roark asked.

"They were classmates." Tamika came into the room, supplying the answer to his question, and Roark turned to face her.

"My mother's awake and I asked her before I left," she said. She was wearing denim today, cuffed mid-calf, form-fitting over her soft thighs and glorious hips. Her jacket was a coral color, the shirt beneath white. She dropped her oversized Louis Vuitton bag onto the chair closest to her and turned her attention back to the conversation.

"She's right," Cade said from the phone. "They went to college together and, according to another classmate we tracked down after finding a picture of them during some rally back in the early Seventies, their group of seven was very close."

Tamika moved closer to where Pierce stood with the phone. "My mother just said Mrs. Donovan and my dad were good friends. All of them were friends."

"Did she know about the letter?" Roark asked, because he knew it was important for Tamika to keep believing her father wouldn't have had an affair.

"She knew, because your mother had sent her a letter too," Tamika answered.

"Now, we have this group of seven," Pierce interrupted. "Lemuel and Sandra Rayder, Gabriel and Maxine Donovan, Ronnella McCoy, Tony Graves and Kaymen Benedict."

"Okay, a group of friends from college—that's not out of the ordinary. How does this relate to the fires?" Roark needed Pierce and Cade to get to the point sooner rather than later.

"From everything we know about the fires so far, this guy is controlled. He's organized and intentional in everything he does." Cade cleared his throat before continuing. "Most arsonists set fires for the joy of the fire. They have an intimate relationship with it and with the method of their choice.

Once they set a fire, they stay and watch, because it not only gives them a sense of control, but for some it gives them sexual pleasure."

Tamika frowned. "Because things always needed to have the weird factor tossed in to be real."

"We think the arsonist might be going after people in this group," Pierce announced soberly.

"Revenge?" Roark couldn't believe that was what they were saying. People were actually dying—his mother had been burned to death in her bed—because of revenge? His hands fisted at his sides while he tried to come to terms with that thought.

"Revenge is a very strong motivator," Cade said. "And this guy's plenty motivated. He's traveling cross country to get the job done."

"My father died twenty-three years ago from a heart attack. He can't be included in this." Roark clenched and released his fingers.

Pierce shook his head. "No, your father wasn't, Roark, but he was part of the group. Your father was the first victim," he told Tamika.

"We believe something happened last year that reminded him of whatever went wrong in the group. The event would've been his stressor, and from that point on his plan to seek revenge by fire was hatched." Cade spoke matter-of-factly.

It was his work voice, Roark surmised. Cade and Pierce were talking like profilers, and he and Tamika had no choice but to listen to every word they were saying.

"I don't understand. You think somebody they went to school with forty plus years ago is now hunting them down and killing them. The guy would have to be in his mid-sixties by now," she said.

"Our profile puts him at sixty-five, the same age your parents were, and he's in relatively good shape. He'd have to be to carry the cannister of gasoline and whatever protective gear he's wearing," Pierce said.

Roark frowned. "Protective gear?"

"Yeah, because he wants to stay and watch them die," Cade said. "MPD has issued its official finding of homicide along with the Fire Brigade's report regarding your mom, Roark. Boot prints were found in the bedroom and the hallways leading down the stairs and out of the house. The prints showed remnants of gasoline and soot, meaning he stood there for a while watching and waiting for her to die. That's why he paralyzes them first, so they can see it's him who's killing them."

"Oh my——" Tamika slapped her hand over her mouth and turned away from Pierce.

Roark, even though he was feeling a little shaky after Cade's words himself, went to her, putting an arm around her shoulders. She leaned into him, and Roark nodded for Pierce to continue.

"We need to speak to your mother, Tamika. Find out what happened to their group and who could be the one doing this."

She shook her head but didn't turn back to face Pierce as he spoke. "You said it was a man, so you can scratch one name off the list from the group."

"We think it might either be someone who was part of the group or who knew the group while they were in school. But we're definitely looking at it being someone they all knew very well," Pierce said.

"Are you sure about this?" Roark asked. "There's another possibility. Her ex has motive to go after her parents."

Tamika tensed at his words, but Roark didn't move his

arm from around her shoulders, and so far she hadn't pushed him away. He'd take that as a good sign.

Pierce didn't look pleased at this new information. "Is that true?"

She turned around and moved out of Roark's hold at the same time. "Colin Hopkins. He burned some of my clothes and other stuff in front of my building after I broke up with him."

"Two weeks before her father was killed," Roark added. He didn't know if he wanted it to be Colin so Tamika could get some closure or so Cade would catch him and toss his ass in jail, where he'd be far away from Tamika.

"We did profile this as revenge attacks. The personal connection of the victims led us to that conclusion. It could still work for Colin," Pierce was saying.

"Except it doesn't fit for Aunt Max," Cade said.

Roark had known that was coming. He hadn't wanted to admit it out loud, but deep down inside, he'd known. "You're sure these fires are the same?" he asked Cade as if his cousin were standing in that room with them.

"The doctor is doing the tox screen on my mother and Tuppence today. She said she had no need to check for drugs before, because she thought they were both just burn victims, but she's going to call me with the results." Tamika didn't sound hopeful that they weren't going to come back with the same drug that had been in his mother's system.

"Ms. Gregory couldn't have been drugged if she was trying to get your mother out of the house." Roark tried not to ignore the obvious this time.

"She wasn't supposed to be there," Pierce said. "That and the fact that your mother is still alive is probably eating the unsub—that's what we call the suspect—alive. He'll be enraged now, and his timeline to kill the others on his revenge list will either move quickly or he'll circle back to your mother again."

"I don't know why this is happening," Tamika said. "Why kill my father and then come for my mother a year later? Or even come for Roark's mother a year later? What's he been doing all this time?"

"We're tracking the movements of each of the other three names in that group to figure that out," Cade said. "We just wanted to give you two an update and a warning."

Roark was already shaking his head. "We're not the targets. If this is revenge like you said, whatever happened was long before we were born."

"But you're here now and because the two of you knew something was off with these fires from the start, you're in his way," Pierce said.

"And being in the way of a killer is not a place you want to be, Roark. So I'm gonna tell you now to get some protection around the two of you and be careful." When Roark began to say something, Cade continued. "Don't argue with me on this, man. I know what I'm doing here, and I've seen these situations take horrible turns. I'm not trying to come back to London to bury you too. Now, either you're calling Trent to ask him about security, or I'm doing it."

Roark didn't like ultimatums and he particularly didn't like receiving them when he was in a room with people who weren't his family. His jaw clenched with anger but he waited a beat, measuring his words carefully. "I know how to take care of myself."

"And I do too," Tamika chimed in.

Now, Roark felt like an ass because he hadn't meant his words to reflect that he didn't give a damn about what happened to her.

Pierce looked as if he were growing impatient with both

of them. "We're still operating outside the lines here, Cade. If we're going to continue to track this guy and try to stop him, we're gonna have to pull in local law enforcement."

"My father was killed in America. Doesn't that make this guy an international murderer? So that would be over the heads of those two detectives who were here yesterday, correct? Because they were idiots." Tamika's voice sounded even steadier now, and if Roark was hearing correctly, it was tinged with a little bit of anger.

"I'll make some calls and let you know what our next steps are, Pierce," Cade said. "And you, Roark—"

"I already said I know what to do," he interrupted. "It'll be taken care of. Just do your part and find this bastard."

Seconds later, Cade was off the phone and Pierce was staring pointedly at Roark. "You need somebody here at the house and with you both personally when you go out. It might not be a bad idea to have someone at the hospital too. Pennington and Gibbons are probably already watching you two, but like she said, they're idiots."

"Got it," Roark told him with a curt nod.

"I'll be in touch as soon as we find something else. In the meantime, you should stop poking around the cottage." Pierce directed those words to Tamika. "We don't know who this guy is yet, so that means we don't have eyes on him. But he may very definitely have eyes on you."

"I'm not going to run and hide from some coward who uses fire to fix whatever petty argument that took place all those years ago," she snapped.

"You don't know that it was a petty argument—to him, it obviously means more. So much more he's ready to kill. You're an arson investigator, so you know about how deadly fires can be. You should also know how personal they are to the people who set them. How that personal connection can dement their mind until they believe whatever evil they've concocted in order to keep setting the fires. I'll tell you again, stay away from the cottage." Pierce added a very cold glare to his somber words.

Roark took a step until he was standing close to Tamika again. While he figured there was some truth to Pierce's words, he didn't like how harshly they'd been directed to her. "Don't worry, we're both going to be careful from this point on." He didn't touch her again, but he made sure Pierce got his message by giving the agent a very pointed stare.

Again, Pierce didn't seem ruffled or intimidated by Roark, but he did give up on dispensing anymore warnings. "I'll be in touch," he said before walking out of the room, leaving Roark and Tamika to stand alone in silence for a few minutes more.

"Let's go for a ride," Roark suggested after the quiet had grown to an irritating point.

Tamika made a huffing sound. "Didn't you just tell him we were both going to be careful? You think going out into the big bad world for a ride is smart?"

Roark turned to face her. "I think I'm a grown man, and I'll decide when and where I go. Right now, I need some air, and I'm guessing you do too. I'll get Vaughn to follow us. Is that okay with you?" He'd changed his directive to a question at the last minute and watched as she picked up on that change and offered him a half smile.

"That's fine with me," she said.

CHAPTER 13

"*D*o you believe what Cade and Pierce said?"

They were in the car, driving on a particularly curvy road that seemed to cut straight through the hills and valleys.

"I don't want to talk about that right now." And he didn't. Roark's mind was so full of fire and death that he could barely think of anything else.

Of course, it could be said that now wasn't the time to be thinking about other things, but Roark desperately needed to. The beginning of a headache was pressing against his temples, and his fingers were sore from clenching and unclenching them repeatedly. He tried rolling his neck, but that did nothing to relieve the mounting stress.

"Okay," she said, exaggerating the word as she looked out the window. "Why'd you come here, Roark? I know you didn't pack your bags, leave your office and set up house in the country just because I wanted to meet you."

If she were trying to change the subject, this question wasn't the way to do it, but Roark took a second before deciding how to answer her. "I came because I missed my mother." That was the simplistic truth. So why did it sound like it was a cop-out? "Getting the call from the security company that the fire alarm at the house was going off was something I'd never expected, and I was afraid from the moment I hung up the phone until the seconds when the firefighters told me I couldn't go inside that she wasn't alive."

He gripped the steering wheel, and Tamika reached a hand over the console to rest it on his knee. Roark glanced down at that hand for a moment and then returned his gaze to the road.

"Everything after that is such a blur, but it felt like razor-sharp pain at the time. I needed that pain to stop." Did that make him weak? Did it mean he wasn't the leader or the man his parents had always expected him to be? Roark had no idea, just as he didn't know why he was giving Tamika these answers.

"After my father died, all I could focus on was investigating that fire. I ignored my cases at work or I did the bare minimum on them just so it looked like I was at least touching them every day. But I couldn't think of anything except finding out what happened to him," she said.

"Different approaches to grieving," he replied. "That's what my Aunt Birdie told my sister when Suri asked why Aunt Birdie wasn't crying at the funeral home."

"Tuppence mentioned the grief process to me too. The night before the fire, she said I was in denial. But I don't think that's true. I can accept that my father is gone. I just can't accept how or why."

"Because a killer wanted him dead." Roark knew his words sounded cold and distant, and to ease them just a bit, he made a left turn, pulled the car off the road and switched off the engine. Behind them, Vaughn did the same.

Roark got out of the car and went around to the passenger side just as she stepped out. When he took her hand, he wondered if she'd pull away from him. Never before had Roark thought about a woman turning away from him the way he did with her. Perhaps that was because he didn't approach women nearly as much as his brother did, but whenever he had, the attention had been reciprocated. Up to this point, Tamika hadn't given him any indication that she wasn't receptive to his attention, yet that hesitation on his part was still there.

"Let's walk." He started toward the left, away from the parked cars.

They walked quietly, both of them enjoying the scene of lush green grass and the misty fog that hovered just inches above the ground, giving the area a haunted and intriguing appeal.

"I don't get this in the city," he said, breaking the silence. "The noise and business. Parties and endless meetings. That's my life there."

"Those are all the things that make you Roark Donovan. Did you know you were in the top three of the Millionaire Man Match?"

He frowned. "What in the world is that?"

"It's this matchmaking list composed of millionaires. I found it online when I researched you. There was this great picture of you in a black suit, white shirt and black tie, but your tie was loose, so it gave you a little bit of a bad-boy mogul look. I'll admit, when I first saw it, I imagined you with that shirt unbuttoned and showing your bare chest."

She made a growling sound when she finished, and Roark couldn't help but laugh.

"You should do that more often."

"What? Be entertained by a woman I just met?"

With her free hand, she pushed her hair back behind her ear. "No. Laugh. I mean, I guess I'm glad I'm entertaining you. Your laugh is so honest but it always seems like you're as shocked by it as whoever is around you. That tells me you don't laugh enough. Why is that?"

She was way too intuitive where he was concerned, but he didn't mind as much as he probably he should have. "I thought I laughed enough." Laughing actually hadn't crossed his mind at all. "I guess I'm mostly relaxed enough to laugh when I'm around my family. And I tend to be in the office more than at home with them, so that probably says a lot."

They were walking at an easy pace; the air was warm, but not humid. What Roark noticed most about where they were was the quiet. It was so peaceful here, and that was exactly what he'd been searching for.

"You have a huge family." She sounded almost amazed. "I saw so many names online and the businesses they're connected to. The Donovans don't half-ass in any industry, do they?"

"There are a lot of Donovans around the world, but not as many here in the UK. My mother hated that we weren't brought up in close proximity with the rest of our cousins."

"But you're still close to them, right? I mean, you and Cade sounded close on the phone earlier."

"I'm closer to Cade than the others from the US because Cade's been to the UK more. He comes when he's on special international cases. Like Pierce does, I guess. I've seen him more as an adult. My cousin Linc just moved here two years ago, so I've gotten closer to him and his family. He has two beautiful twin girls, and his wife Jade is pregnant again."

"Do you want children?"

Roark stopped walking. "Why would you ask me that? Do you want children?"

Her eyes widened and he presumed she was as shocked as he'd been by her question. She pulled her hand from his. This time she put both hands on her hips, an action that spread her jacket open wider and drew his attention to how tight the white material of her shirt was stretched over her breasts. "Relax, I'm not about to tell you I'm pregnant." There was a hint of laughter to her voice, but the look of irritation was clear on her face. "You're so uptight about everything. We used a condom last night, remember? I just noticed the way your voice became lighter when you mentioned Linc's kids. It sounded like someday you might want kids of your own. That's the only reason I asked."

He huffed and shook his head. "See, this is why I needed to come to the country. I can't even answer simple questions."

"You could if you weren't so worried about giving the wrong answer."

"I never give the wrong answer," he immediately replied.

"Then you're afraid of what the right answer is."

"I—" He was about to deny her comment but decided against it. Instead he started to walk again. "My mother wanted grandchildren. Katrina and I didn't stay together long enough to give her any."

She fell into step beside him. "My mom wants a house full of grandchildren. At least she did before my dad died. Every year for my birthday since I was twenty-five she gives me a pregnancy test as a way of nudging me toward that goal."

Roark chuckled. "Not too subtle, huh."

"Not at all. And if anybody ever buys my storage unit, they'll be in possession of a box full of pregnancy tests."

They both laughed.

"I'd like to have children one day." The admission had

Roark breathing a little easier, and he wondered why he just hadn't given that response before.

"Me too." Her reply came quickly, like there wasn't really anything for her to contemplate.

He stopped again, this time taking both her hands and holding them in his. "I like you, Tamika." Since he was being honest, he figured he should get that out of the way.

She looked up at him, giving the wide grin he was becoming accustomed to. "I like you, Roark." She shrugged and eased a hand away from his to brush hair out of her face when a cool breeze blew. "I think we showed how much we like each other last night."

And here it was, that awkwardness that came with the "morning after" that he always tried to avoid. Sure, it was nearing two in the afternoon, but this was actually the first chance they'd had alone. "I thought last night was really good." So good, he'd considered a repeat performance most of the morning.

She took a step closer to him, using her free hand to cup his cheek. "It was. But you know it was only sex. 'Relationships that start under intense circumstances, they never last'." When he only stared at her, she laughed. "That's what Sandra Bullock said to Keanu Reeves in *Speed*. You did watch *Speed*, didn't you, Roark?"

He shook his head but still managed to grin. "I don't have a lot of time to watch movies. But you're right, neither of us are in a position to start anything serious. You'll be returning to the States when this is all over, and I have my work in London."

"Right, that's what I said." She held tight to his hand and they started walking back toward the car. "We can get Dorianne to cook us something spectacular for dinner, and then we'll watch some movies. You came here to relax, and even though there's a psychopath arsonist on the loose, we're gonna take tonight to do just that."

Roark enjoyed the sound of optimism in her voice and the spark of energy in every step she took. He found himself chuckling again. "I take it you plan to pick the movies we're going to watch." It was more of a statement than a question, because Tamika definitely had a take-charge attitude.

In his life, Roark was used to leading, whether with his family or at work, so their personalities should've clashed, but they didn't. Instead, the more time he spent with her, the more drawn to her he felt.

"Absolutely! I have some great ones in mind, and I promise you'll love every one of them."

"Well, even if I don't enjoy the movies, I'm sure I'll enjoy the company."

They were at the car then and Roark reached to open the door for her, but she stopped him. She took both his arms and wrapped them around her waist, then she leaned into him while closing her arms around his neck. "I enjoy your company too, Roark. I enjoy it a lot."

With her palms pressed to the back of his head, she pulled him down until his lips touched hers. Roark held her tight and slipped his tongue between her lips. Her tongue met his, and the slowest, sweetest, melody began.

"Are you serious right now? You think John Wick was better than Robert McCall?"

She was sexiest when she was excited. It had only taken three movies, two bowls of Dorianne's chicken and dumplings, more dinner rolls than he cared to admit and two glasses of rum for him to figure that out. "Look, McCall was a smooth killer, I'll give him that, but Wick was brutal in his attacks. He went after everybody who betrayed him and even the people he'd originally worked for, all because of a dog." He'd actually enjoyed the movies she'd suggested they watch, including *Speed*, which had the romantic angle he'd expected from the quote she'd mentioned earlier.

She shook her head. "You're delusional. We're gonna have to watch the sequels to both so you can rethink your answer."

"Not tonight, I hope," he said. She'd already picked up the remote to the television in his room and was pressing the buttons to change it from the movie channel.

"Why? You ready to go to bed? It's only..." She paused and clicked on the TV's menu. "It's only twelve-thirty."

They'd been in his room watching movies since returning from their walk. After making the calls to arrange for a complete security detail for both of them, along with Tamika's mother and the housekeeper at the hospital, he'd changed his clothes. The button-front shirt he'd been wearing had been switched to a T-shirt, and he'd decided to forego shoes the moment he'd seen her walking barefoot. She'd actually taken her shoes off the moment they'd stepped back into the house. Then she'd gone to her room. When she returned to his room, her jacket was also off and her was pulled back into a ponytail. He'd sat on one end of the couch and she'd sat right beside him, one leg tucked under her butt. To anyone on the outside looking in, they probably appeared to be a normal couple having a movie night.

"I'm ready to go to bed, with you." It seemed so easy to tell her what he wanted. He didn't have to expect an interrogation or a counter to whatever he said. No, he wasn't going to compare her to Katrina—they were different women in every aspect. And yet, he was more drawn to Tamika than he ever recalled being to his ex-wife.

Standing from the couch, he extended his hands to hers. She turned the television off, dropped the remote and put her hands in his before standing.

"And I'm not just talking about sex," he continued. "I can't explain it, and that's something new for me to digest, but I know I liked sleeping with you last night."

"Roark Donovan, are you saying you liked *not* snuggling with me?" Her tone was teasing, but her eyes were telling him something else. Not quite arousal, but definitely a warmth that settled into her eyes as she stared up at him.

He'd been waiting for her to bring up that little inconsistency. "I've never snuggled with a woman before." It was an admission he wasn't sure he should've made, because her expression immediately turned serious.

"Not even your wife?"

Well, he was in it now, no backing down. "Not even her."

"How did she feel about that?"

As far as Roark knew, women didn't like to talk about a new lover's past relationship, but Tamika seemed genuinely interested. "To be honest, I don't really know. The subject never came up."

She tilted her head slightly like she was deciding whether or not to believe him. Then, dismissing it, she came up on the tips of her toes and dropped a soft kiss on his lips. "No wonder you never had children."

Easing her hands from his, she walked away, going toward the bathroom, but Roark couldn't let the conversation go so easily. He quickly turned off the lamp in the sitting area and followed her. "What's that supposed to mean?"

She was at the bathroom door when she turned to him. "It means if the two of you didn't communicate enough so you'd know whether or not she was bothered by you not holding her in the night, there was no way you were ready to have children."

He wasn't sure he subscribed to what she was saying. "We never even talked about children."

"That's my point exactly," she said with a nod. "Communication is key to any successful relationship. If you're not telling each other what you like and what you don't like, what you expect from the other person and why you're not getting what you need out of the union, what's the point in being together? You might as well just be friends with benefits."

"Did you and Colin communicate well?" He knew the moment the question was out that he maybe shouldn't have asked, but if they were going to discuss relationships, then hers had to be fair game as well.

Annoyance flashed in her eyes briefly, and she shrugged before replying, "No. And that's the lesson I learned from those two years with him. If I'd been honest with myself and admitted I wasn't getting any sort of emotional support or mutual respect from him, maybe the break-up would've come sooner. And if he'd have been honest about how he felt about my physical appearance, I could've told him to kick rocks long before the two-year anniversary. But we didn't, and so it ended, which again, proves my point regarding you and your ex."

She didn't wait for him to ask another question but instead continued into the bathroom, closing the door behind her. Moments later, Roark heard the start of the shower and he moved closer to the dresser, opening the top drawer and taking out a shirt he planned to give her to sleep in tonight, since she hadn't brought anything from her room when she'd come in earlier.

After placing the shirt on her side of the bed, Roark began removing his clothes. He left his boxers on while he waited for her to come out of the bathroom. He'd take a shower next and when he finished, he planned to snuggle tightly with Tamika tonight and to cherish this amazingly honest woman who was now waist-deep in a murder investigation with him.

In the middle of the night, Roark rolled away from Tamika. He removed the new boxers he'd donned after his shower and leaned over to the nightstand. Pulling open the top drawer, he grabbed a condom and covered his hard dick. When he was once again in the center of the bed again, he eased back into the same position he'd been in all night—on his side, his front pressed up to Tamika's back, one arm around her, hand cupping her breast.

She sighed and snuggled back against him as she'd done many times throughout the night, hence his rock-hard erection at three in the morning. But instead of falling back to sleep—which he was extremely grateful to be getting now —he pressed his dick to her ass and waited for a response. It came almost immediately when she wiggled against his dick. Roark moaned as the desire that had been on a slow simmer throughout the night fully blossomed. Her ass was so soft and so arousing, ready to welcome him should he dare to enter.

And oh, did he dare.

Burying his face in her neck, Roark trailed a line of scorching kisses to her shoulder. She lifted a hand to cover his on her breast.

"This," she whispered and backed her ass up on him again, "is one of the perks to snuggling."

This was a fucking awesome perk to snuggling in his

book. "It can get better," he replied and reluctantly slid his hand from her breast.

"Show me," she said in a breathy whisper when his hand continued down past her torso and belly.

She wiggled, knowing where he was going, and opened her thighs when his hand eased over her mound. His fingers slipped between her pussy lips easily, to brush over her already hardened clit.

"You're always so hot and ready for me." He groaned at the feel of the warm moisture on his fingers.

"That's because you're always making me hot with your brooding looks and sexy voice." She lifted her leg then, planting her foot on the mattress and giving him even more access to her slick, hot pussy. As the motion had her rolling back toward him, Roark eased his other arm around to grab her breast again. The weight of it in his hand always sent a bolt of arousal soaring through his body, and this time was no different. He kissed her shoulder again, running his teeth along her skin while his fingers dipped deep into her pussy.

"You like my voice, huh? What do you like to hear me say, my sweet? You want me to tell you how beautiful I think you are?"

She reached an arm back to cup the back of his head, her breaths coming faster as he continued to pump his fingers inside her.

"Or perhaps you'd like to hear how fuckin' hard you make my dick each time I think about being inside you?"

"Yes! Say that again."

With two fingers inside her, his thumb rubbed over her clit, and she arched back. "You can feel it, can't you?" He pressed his dick into her ass. "Feel how hard you make me. All I can think about is fucking you right now."

"Then do it. Do it right now!"

He didn't have to be told twice. Easing his fingers out of her, he let his hands slide down her thigh to the back of her knee. He lifted her leg up higher, shifting his hips so his dick slid down the crease of her ass. With a little more adjusting, he finally slipped into her and they both yelled out with pleasure.

When Roark began pumping, his whole body shook with desire. She held his dick so tight inside her while her essence dripped around him. He'd never felt anything as blissful before and didn't want it to stop.

"More," she groaned, throwing her ass back against his thrusts. "I need more, Roark. So much more!"

He was shifting them again, this time coming up on one knee and lifting her leg even higher. This position allowed for deeper penetration and for him to look down at her while he moved inside her.

"Mmmmm." She brought her hands up to cup her breasts that bounced with his strokes. "Yes, Roark! Yes!"

Tearing his gaze away from the sensual sight of her fingers squeezing her nipples, Roark stared down at his dick easing in and out of her pussy. It was erotic as hell and made him speed up his thrusts. Passion swirled like a torrential storm throughout his body, creating a funnel that eased down his spine.

She moaned his name again but this time arched her back while her thighs trembled. Roark groaned and gritted his teeth as her release covered him.

"I don't know what this is." The words tore from him in a ragged sound. "I don't know why now." He kept pumping, kept inching toward his own release as his muscles began to tighten.

"Just now," she whispered. "Just now."

Roark heard her words and focused on this, on being

buried inside her warmth and wetness, on easing in and out of her, stroking the embers of fire within them both. He focused on the intense pressure building at the base of his spine and the force of his pumps into her. He focused on her voice, on her. Until he exploded, and then nothing else mattered.

When he could finally catch his breath and had lowered her legs and eased out of her, Roark whispered her name. She pushed him onto his back and lay with one leg over his, her cheek pressed against his chest, her hand over his wildly thumping heart.

"What are we doing?" he asked because he just didn't know.

"What we can, for now."

"Right." He nodded, even though he knew she couldn't see him. "This is for now."

"Exactly," she whispered. "Just for now."

Roark lay there holding her, waiting for his heart rate to return to normal and telling himself repeatedly that just for now would be enough.

CHAPTER 14

London

He pulled on his boots and yanked the turnouts down over them. Standing, he adjusted the suspenders to keep the turnouts from falling down as he walked. The long-sleeved black shirt he wore covered him from his neck down to his wrists. He put on the jacket and buttoned it up before finding his gloves and slipping one on each hand.

There was no more preparation after that. It was time. But he still didn't move. Thoughts ran through his mind, memories that would never disappear. Pain and betrayal. Lies and deceit. Disappointment and heartbreak. All those things circled the memories, forming the endless black smoke he now yearned to see and to smell. That smoke meant something to him—it meant redemption.

Ronnella McCoy's house was in Hyde Park. Close to Maxine Donovan, and yet they hadn't kept in touch. Or at least not that he knew of, and he knew about all of them. He knew about their career success, their marriages, their children, everything. But most of all he knew their faults, the things they didn't show anyone in their new lives, the secrets they hid.

He drove to her house, parking directly across the street so he'd have a front row seat. It was well after midnight and he knew she'd be alone. Ronnella was always alone, a stark contrast to the vivacious former beauty queen she'd been in her teens and twenties. At one point she'd believed she had her pick of men and that when she was ready, whomever she'd selected would fall at her feet and worship her for the rest of her life. Forty-five years later, she'd never married, had no children and lived in this huge house alone.

He knew about being alone.

Stepping out of his car, he went to the trunk, opened it and removed the can of gasoline. The gun and syringe were in his jacket pocket. He grabbed the helmet and walked toward the house.

There was an alarm, but he already knew the code. Money really could buy anything, and what it couldn't, blackmail could. Ronnella's housekeeper was a flirty little brunette who talked a lot when she drank and fucked whoever was paying when she was drunk. He'd paid someone else to do the task for him, because the loud young woman wasn't his type.

With the code memorized, he walked around to the back door and jimmied the flimsy lock. Ronnella had paid for a sophisticated alarm system but had a cheap lock on the doors, and he couldn't muster up enough sympathy to feel sorry for her stupidity. As soon as he was inside, he closed the door quietly behind him and hurried to the control panel to punch in the numbers that would kill the alarm.

She should've heard the chirping sound of someone

entering the house. He'd heard it and hadn't been at all disturbed. He wanted her to know he was here.

With purposely slow steps, he moved through the house, going by the description the flirty housekeeper had given. He made a wrong turn and ended up in an exercise room instead of her bedroom, but he corrected that and three minutes after he'd entered her house, he was standing at her bedroom door.

He had twenty-seven minutes with her before it'd be time to leave. And time for her to die.

With a gloved hand, he touched the knob and let the fresh memory of that night so long ago seep into the forefront of his mind. For a few seconds he stood there with those thoughts, closing his eyes so he could clearly see every movement, hear every word, watch every flame again.

Pushing the door open, he stepped inside and stopped abruptly.

A naked man was on top of her, his ass cheeks clenching as he pumped into her. Ronnella lay beneath him, giving herself to him the way she gave herself to every man who suited her, every man who showed her the attention she craved. Another memory slammed into his mind, the one where he used to be the man Ronnella had wanted.

Fresh rage layered his purpose in the same instant she looked up and saw him. The two had been so engrossed in their sex, her moaning, the other man's grunting, that they hadn't heard him enter the house or the bedroom. Proving again how self-centered and foolish they were.

Ronnella screamed, and the other man turned.

"What the hell?" the man yelled.

A jolt of recognition hit him at once. The other man was Tony, his old friend and roommate. Tony was fucking his girl, again.

Tony grabbed the sheets to pull around him and pushed Ronnella behind him. "What do you want? How'd you get in here?"

Ridiculous questions. Why wasn't Tony jumping out of the bed and looking for something to defend himself with, to defend Ronnella with? Because he was a selfish coward and even though he wasn't in the plan for tonight, he was meant to die as well.

"You know what I want," he said, walking closer to the bed. He set the can of gasoline down and felt a spurt of satisfaction as they both huddled together on that bed, fear evident on their faces.

That was what he wanted, their fear. He wanted to watch it contort their faces and fill their souls as they acknowledged the inevitable.

He pulled the gun out of his pocket, aimed it at Tony's chest. "I want you to die," he said, his voice raspy.

"Wait! Wait! If it's money, I've got it. I can get you whatever you want. You want a jet to get out of here, cash, a car? I can get all those things at the drop of a dime, and nobody has to know. Nobody has to get hurt," Tony insisted.

The idiot didn't even know who he was. Tony came from money. Just like Gabe had. That made them both assholes at times, because they used that privilege whenever it suited them. He and Lem, they didn't have money, but the four of them had bonded anyway. They'd forged a friendship in college, four Black men who were going to run the world. But that had never happened.

"You still trying to buy your way outta shit," he spat the words, hatred filling every crevice of his damned soul. "I never gave a damn about your money."

Ronnella gasped, and he knew that was the moment she recognized him. "No," she whispered. "It's impossible."

He took a second to look at her, to really see her this time. She was still pretty, her skin a soft sand complexion and those same expression-filled hazel eyes. Her hair was shorter now with no gray at all. Ronnella would've never allowed it to turn gray. Out of the corner of his eye he caught a movement and shifted his attention, firing the gun when he saw Tony extending his arm to the nightstand where the phone was.

Tony yelled as the bullet ripped through his shoulder, and Ronnella screamed again.

"Kaymen, no!"

His twisted mouth moved into a position he recalled as being a smile, and he chuckled. "You remember me." Of all of them, a part of him had hoped she would.

The others hadn't, not until he'd told them and then they'd begged and lied just as they always had.

He wasn't going to wait for that now.

With Tony cupping his shoulder and screaming in agony, his blood dripping onto the light-colored sheets, Ronnella continued to stare and shake her head. "Kaymen."

He hurried around to the side of the bed where she was then, still pointing the gun at Tony as he dug his free hand into his pocket and pulled out the syringe. "Lay back!" he instructed her.

Tears were rolling down her face now, and her hands were shaking. "Kaymen, please."

"Shut up and lay back, or I'll shoot you in your lying face right now!" For the first time, he trembled.

He'd wanted to save her for last, but he hadn't been able to track down Tony—now he knew why. They were together, and that was just as well. A two-for-one would give him extra pleasure.

She lay back slowly, her entire body shuddering as she

sobbed now. She was afraid and probably just starting to feel the icy pricks of regret. Well, good for her—she should have regrets. All of them should.

When she was down, he moved faster than he normally did, jabbing the syringe between her toes and listening as she screamed again. That noise would stop in just a few seconds, and then he'd only have to deal with Tony. Because he'd presumed Ronnella would be alone, he'd brought one syringe, but that was fine, his gun was working just fine to keep Tony still.

"You lay back too!" He directed his former roommate and walked around to stand in front of the bed. "Since you two were always fucking around behind my back, it makes sense that you both get to lay there and die together."

"Dammit, Kaymen! Hold the hell up, man! What're you doing?"

Kaymen leaned down and removed the top from the can of gasoline. "Shut up!" His head was throbbing now; the headaches he'd lived with for forty-five years was more intense than he'd ever felt it before. Anger boiled inside him and his hands trembled momentarily. "Shut up and lay there! Lay there and die!"

"Kaymen!"

He ignored Tony's next call and started pouring the gasoline right there. From the second it splashed onto the carpeted floor and the scent wafted up to his nose, Kaymen went into a zone—the place where there was nothing existed but the heat, the scent of burning flesh, the sound of ferocious flames licking along the skin and tearing it away until there was only bone. The sound of screams, his this time, echoing in his mind.

He walked faster, pouring gasoline all the way around the bed. When he was on the side where Tony was holding his shoulder, the stupid motherfucker tried to lunge at him. Kaymen landed one hard punch to Tony's jaw and when he fell back on the bed, Kaymen poured gas directly on his ex-friend's screaming body.

When the can was empty, he searched his jacket pockets for the lighter he always carried, but it wasn't there. He cursed as he searched again.

A whispery sound came from Ronnella and he jerked his head in her direction. She was staring directly at him. Her eyes so glassy now they looked fake, her lips trying to move. He paused for a moment and then walked closer to her. With a flame-resistant gloved hand that had been splashed with the gasoline, he touched her cheek and then her hair. Tony continued to howl from across the bed, and Kaymen leaned down closer to Ronnella.

"I'm...sorry...Kaymen," she whispered, her breath hitching as the drug relaxed every muscle in her body. "I'm so sorry."

He tried to kiss her forehead the way he used to do whenever she felt sad, but it didn't feel right. It felt dirty and sordid and he yanked away from her, yelling, "It's too late to be sorry."

With purposeful movements, he yanked his jacket open and reached down into the pocket of the jeans he wore beneath the turnouts. The bright light of victory soared through him as he felt the lighter in that moment.

A match would've been preferable to some, or anything with a flame that he could've dropped onto the gasoline-drenched floor and ran as the flames exploded, but Kaymen had an up-close and personal relationship with fire. It obeyed him. So when he kneeled down and flicked the lighter's switch, that flame hit the gasoline, and a blinding spark of yellow-orange erupted. He stepped back then, as easily as if he'd been moving from one room to the next, but he didn't leave. He only moved back enough so he could watch the flames without any of them getting on him.

Ronnella opened her mouth to scream again, but the sound was stilted by the drug steadily seeping into her system. Tony yelled and intended to jump off the bed, but as soon as his legs went over the side, they were met by the rising flames that had traveled along the gasoline path. In seconds, the bed was surrounded and two of the people he'd thought would be his friends for life were about to take their last breath.

Painswick
  One Week Later

"This isn't the cottage," Sandra said as she stepped into the front foyer of the clubhouse. "It's too fancy."

"Yes, this place is fancy," Tuppence answered from behind them.

Tamika rolled her eyes but vowed to remain silent as she and Roark ushered the women inside.

The cottage needed renovating as well as cleaning work as a result of the fire, and after a spirited debate with Roark about who was going to pay for everything—she'd won—the contractors were scheduled to start work next Monday morning. She'd let him buy her clothes and she was staying at this gorgeous—or as her mother had just said, "fancy"—B&B free of charge. No way was she going to let him take on the price of the renovations to her parents' home. Even if the insurance company hadn't indicated they'd pay the claim,

Tamika had a comfortable savings account she would've drawn from without hesitation.

"It's just temporary," Tamika reminded the two prickly women. "As soon as the repairs to the cottage are complete, you can move back in."

Geoff had sent them to the hospital in a limousine this afternoon so her mother and Tuppence would have comfortable space during the twenty-minute ride back. Two black SUVs with armed guards rode with them. Tamika was glad to hear her mother talking so much, but a little worn by all the negativity and speculation in Sandra's tone.

"Looks like royalty lives here," Tuppence was saying as they moved into the parlor.

It was the closest room right off the foyer to the left, and she'd wanted them to sit down for a few minutes to catch their breath before going up the stairs to the rooms Dorianne had prepared for them.

"Not royalty," Roark said as he helped Tuppence onto one of the floral couches. "My family owns the place but we rent it out, similar to the way you used to rent out your cottage, Mrs. Rayder."

"Your family." Her mother sat back on the end of the couch Tamika had taken her to, and Sandra stared across the room at Roark.

Tamika had noticed her looking at Roark this way in the hospital when he'd entered her room and Tamika had introduced him. Both she and Roark had wondered how her mother would react to hearing his name. Tamika had already told him and Pierce that her mother admitted to knowing Maxine Donovan had been sending her father letters, but her mother hadn't mentioned anything about that conversation since that day over a week ago. And truthfully, Tamika had been afraid to push for more information, because her mother looked so fragile with bandages still covering the scars on her arms and neck.

"You've got a big family, don't you?" Sandra asked Roark.

He stood next to the couch where Tuppence was sitting and nodded. "Yes, ma'am, I do."

"Then you're blessed," she said. "Never forget how blessed you are to have a lot of people who love and care about you."

"No, ma'am, I won't." Roark glanced at Tamika then, but she looked away from him because she didn't want to see his subtle push for her to find out what her mother knew about their group of friends and any grudge one of them might be holding against the others.

While Tamika wanted to find out who was doing this, she wasn't willing to risk her mother's sanity for it, and something deep inside told her it was only going to take one more thing before Sandra went to the point of no return with her depression.

"Bet y'all have had some big parties here," Tuppence said. She was short, so her feet didn't touch the floor, and she looked around the room, eyes wide as she took everything in.

Each time Tamika stared at the woman, her heart warmed. Not only because Tuppence had helped save her mother's life, but that she was still here with them also. The infection that had begun after her surgery had cleared up quickly, which was why she'd been released along with her mother. There'd been no drugs in Tuppence's system, but traces of succinylcholine had been detected in her mother's.

"Actually, we've never spent time here as a family," Roark said and then frowned. "I don't really know why not, but this is the first time any members of my family have been here."

"Shame—this is a great room. A big 'ole Christmas tree would look wonderful in that corner near the window. And all the presents spread out. The fireplace would be lit, and somebody could start singing Christmas carols." There was a light in Tuppence's eyes when she spoke. "You remember we talked about our favorite Christmas stories, Sandra. We sat in front of that little tree, the only size I could carry by myself, and just talked for hours."

Sandra rolled her eyes. "You talked, Tuppence. I listened." Because five months ago she hadn't been in the mood to talk. Tamika hated that she hadn't been here sooner, to help her mother get through her grief.

"Well, Dorianne has promised to cook a big dinner, so we'll all sit together in the main dining room and it'll be just like having a family dinner." Roark's announcement shocked Tamika a little, because in the time she'd been here with him, he hadn't talked about this place with the adoration she saw in his eyes and heard in his tone now.

"Ah, that's right. If you'd like, we can help you both upstairs to your rooms, where you can get some rest until its dinnertime." Now that they were here, she wanted them to get as much rest as they could. Their healing was her number one priority at the moment.

"Is there a television in my room?" Sandra asked.

"Yes, Mama, there is. And it has all the premium channels, including one that runs classic Black movies, so you can settle down and watch some of your favorites."

"I'd rather have a window than a television," Tuppence began easing herself to the edge of the chair, attempting to get up on her own.

Roark was immediately at her side, wrapping an arm around her and taking her hand to ease her off the couch slowly. Sandra continued to stare at him. "There's a huge window in your room, Ms. Gregory, and I'll move the chair closer to it so you can sit and look outside."

"I don't know how many times I need to tell you to call me Tuppence, but yes, I'd like to sit in front of the window for a while. Seems like I've been laying down forever."

As Roark moved past them with Tuppence, and Sandra lifted shaking fingers to cover her mouth.

"Are you alright, Mama?"

For a few seconds, Sandra didn't answer. When Tamika kneeled down beside her and placed a hand on Sandra's knee, her mother finally shook her head. "I'm fine." Sandra cleared her throat. "Just need to take a nap."

"Are you sure?" Tamika asked. "Does Roark remind you of someone?" His father maybe? The man she'd gone to school with and whose wife had been killed almost a month ago.

Sandra's gaze shot to her daughter's quickly, her eyes opened wider than they'd been before. She'd dropped her hand from her mouth and now just blinked at Tamika as if she were confused. "I need a nap," Sandra repeated, and this time, Tamika helped her upstairs so she could take one.

It took twenty minutes to get her mother out of her clothes and into the more comfortable cotton lounge pants and matching top she preferred—the items were new since, all of her mother's things had been destroyed in the fire. Like the renovations, Tamika had paid for her mother's and Tuppence's replacement items. Her savings was taking a big hit, but she didn't care. When her mother was settled, she went in to check on Tuppence, who loved the window seat Roark had created for her.

Now, Tamika was walking down the stairs again, in search of Roark. He hadn't been in his room when she'd checked, so she'd assumed he was either in the kitchen trying to coax Dorianne to let him taste whatever she was cooking, or in the study on the computer continuing to search the names of each member of the group Pierce had given them last week.

She'd just come to the bottom of the stairs when the front door opened and in walked a man she'd never seen before with Pierce right behind him. The guards out front already knew to let Pierce in, so she presumed this other guy was safe as well.

"Hey, Tamika, where's Roark?" Pierce asked after he'd closed the door behind them.

The other guy with the startling sexy gray eyes—or were they green?—continued walking until he was just a few steps away from her.

"I was just coming to find him." She answered Pierce but continued to stare at the guy who was also staring at her. "Hello," she said when the staring was getting out of hand.

He extended his hand to her and cracked a brilliant smile. "Hi, I'm Cade, Roark's cousin."

Were all the guys associated with Roark hot as hell? If so, she was gonna have to call up some of her girlfriends in Arlington and introduce them to these fine-ass men. Of course, that would have to be after this investigation was over.

"Hey, man. What're you doing back here so soon?" Roark came in, walking directly to where she and Cade still stood shaking hands.

"Had to come make sure my big cousin was safe." Cade stared at her a few seconds longer before casually gazing at Roark.

"Yeah, okay, let her hand go." Roark touched Tamika's wrist, removing her hand from Cade's since it didn't seem like Cade was going to do what he'd just asked him.

"We don't have time for this." Pierce's tone was stern and tinged with urgency.

Cade immediately sobered. "Yeah, he's right. We've got some news for you."

Roark nodded and linked his fingers with Tamika's. "Okay, let's go in here and sit down."

Roark directed them to the parlor, where just a short while ago they'd been sitting with her mother and Tuppence. She didn't release Roark's hand until he guided her to the couch and waited for her to sit down. He remained standing, just as Pierce and Cade did. Tamika didn't know how to feel about all that testosterone surrounding her.

"There was another fire," Pierce said without preamble. "A week ago in London, about six miles from where your mother lived."

Roark folded his arms across his chest. "And someone died in this fire?"

Cade held up two fingers. "Two people. Ronnella McCoy and Tony Graves."

Now Tamika stood. "That means the arsonist has to be—"

"Kaymen Benedict," Sandra said, and everyone turned to see her standing beneath the archway. "Max said he was going to come. In her letter to me, she said she knew he was alive and he was going to come for us." Sandra lifted a shaking hand to her chest and swayed.

Roark was immediately by her side, holding her up. "Come and sit down, Mrs. Rayder."

"No. No. I don't want to sit. I want my Lem back." Her mother looked exhausted, and Tamika walked over to her.

"I know, Mama. I want him back too, but that's not possible. Now, we're trying to stop anyone else from being hurt."

"I couldn't sleep 'cause it's time y'all know." Sandra

sighed. "He wants us all dead. That's what Max said. He told her he wanted us all dead, for real."

Tamika shook her head as her mother said those two words again. She couldn't figure out what they meant and by the way her mother was shaking, she was afraid to ask her for any information Sandra wasn't willing to provide.

"Do you know where he is?" Cade asked in a calm and compassionate tone.

Sandra finally let Roark and Tamika lead her to the couch. "No," she said, shaking her head. "I haven't seen him since he stood over my bed and told me it was my turn to die."

PART III

"Only love and death change all things."
—*Khalil Gibran*

CHAPTER 15

*R*oark watched Sandra as she talked. Her frail fingers were clasped and resting in her lap. The white gauze bandages going midway up her arms and around her neck were a stark contrast to the dark cranberry-colored robe she wore. Earlier today he'd watched as Tamika had brushed her mother's hair back and styled it in two neat braids. Sandra's eyes, which were almost identical to Tamika's in shape and color, searched the room until she found the fireplace and let them rest there, even though no fire was lit.

"Tony was the oldest." She began talking after everyone in the room had been quiet for a few minutes, giving her the time and space to decide if she wanted to say more. "He'd turned twenty-one that Wednesday, but we all had lots of studying to do for mid-terms the next week. We couldn't risk going out on a school night."

Roark noticed Pierce had taken out a notepad and pen and was scribbling something as Sandra spoke. Tamika sat on the arm of the couch where her mother was seated. She'd had one arm wrapped around Sandra's shoulders when her mother had first sat down, but once Sandra was settled, she'd pulled that arm away. Cade stood closest to the fireplace, his gaze intent but compassionate as he watched Sandra carefully. Roark inhaled a deep breath and prepared to hear about a time in his parents' life that he'd never thought he needed to know.

"Friday night, we were all ready to party." Sandra chuckled, but the sound died in her throat as she blinked and shook her head slowly. "We were still so young, no matter how the years kept piling on our lives. We had so much growing to do."

She crossed one ankle over the other and took a slow breath. "Lem and I had been going together for three years by then. We'd met at freshman orientation and had been inseparable from that moment. Lem was studying business because his father wanted him to get a desk job, maybe as a supervisor or something at the Social Security Administration where he worked. Maxie, that's what we called your mother." She looked at Roark then and blinked a few times as if waiting for him to say something.

He smiled. "I've never heard that nickname for her."

"You look like her a little. Right around your eyes and when you smile." She was nodding now. "I can definitely see Maxie in you when you smile. That's because she was such a happy spirit. She loved to dance and sing, and she could write so well. We all thought she was going to go on to become a great novelist. But then we all knew she and Gabe were gonna get married too. They were so in love you could feel it vibrating between them whenever they were in the room. I didn't know Gabe had died so young. Not until Maxie mentioned it in that first letter she sent to me."

"When was that, Mrs. Rayder?" Cade asked the question, but his tone was anything but profiler-like. He was speaking in a smooth, calm tone Roark figured must work on witnesses they were trying to get to remember painful things.

"About two years ago," Sandra replied. "I remember because it was just before me and Lem's thirty-ninth wedding anniversary. They'd been at our wedding, Gabe and Maxie, and so she sent us an anniversary card, but it came addressed only to me. Inside the card was a letter. That's when she told me all about Gabe's death and her children and how she'd led the best life. By the time that letter was finished, I knew something was wrong. But I just thought maybe Maxie was sick or something."

"Did you ever write her back, Mama?" Tamika asked.

Sandra nodded. "I did. We exchanged a letter every month from that time up until the month Lem passed."

"Was she writing to your husband that long, as well?" This was Pierce asking, and Sandra jerked her head around to see he'd taken a seat in the chair near the window.

"I don't think so. At least, Lem didn't tell me about getting any letters from her until early last year. He said she'd sent it to his job instead of to the house. I guess she could've been doing that all along, but Lem would've told me." The way Sandra inhaled deeply, her shoulders sagging a bit more when she exhaled, answered the question Roark was sure everyone in the room was thinking.

Would Lem have kept it a secret if Max had been writing to him longer? Sandra said she didn't know for sure, but Roark suspected she knew it was a possibility.

"Lem came home one day and just said he didn't die." She began shaking her head again and this time started to rock her legs as well. "He kept saying he didn't die for about ten or fifteen minutes. My husband dealt with so much death on the job I just thought he was talking about somebody who'd been caught in a fire. But he wasn't."

Tamika returned her hand to her mother's shoulder.

Sandra cleared her throat and continued. "That night long ago we all went out for Tony's birthday, we piled into his Lincoln Mark VII. That's when cars were big and fancy lookin'. We were heading over to the next town to this club where they served liquor to minors. Tony didn't think he should've been the only one getting drunk that night. Anyway, it didn't matter that they were serving any age, 'cause me and Max didn't drink anyway. Ronnie did. That girl loved to drink, and she could dance too. But she danced like those women in the clubs, not like Max did. Ronnie could do things with her hips that even me and Max couldn't understand. And she was beautiful, all that long, pretty hair hanging down her back and those light-colored eyes. Kinda like yours." Sandra nodded toward Cade. "Men loved Ronnie, and she loved them right back. But most times though, she loved Kaymen."

Everyone in the room perked up at the mention of his name.

"Those two had that explosive-type love. Like one minute they'd be kissin' on each other like they were about to have sex right there in front of you, and the next minute they'd be arguing so hard and loud you'd take cover because you weren't sure when punches or furniture might start to fly."

"Kaymen Benedict was violent." Pierce was probably just speaking out loud as he wrote, but Sandra immediately looked at him.

"Kaymen was a good guy. He wasn't an angry man. He was smart and had good sense. He was going to college to make something out of himself. But he and Ronnie, they just weren't meant to be.

"Everybody got drunk except me and Max, but we didn't have our license. So Gabe drove, because he wasn't as drunk as the others. It was late, and we'd just decided to pitch in and get a motel room. We had to use the money we had on us and not any of Gabe or Tony's family money. Their parents would have a fit if they knew we were that far away from school and going to motels at that. But then it started raining, and the car was going so fast until it just seemed like we were flying." Sandra pressed a hand to her chest.

"Do you want to stop? Do you need something to drink? I can get it for you," Tamika said.

"Yes ma'am, if you need a break, we can definitely take one," Cade said.

"No. I need to get this out." Sandra lifted her chin and took a slow breath. "The car ran off the road, and we went down into a ditch. Thank the good Lord we all managed to get out after the immediate shock. We made it up that little incline and to the road and just started walking as fast as we could. If anybody found us out there, we'd have been in a world of trouble. Underage drinking for some those of us that weren't twenty-one, drunk driving for Gabe and the crash. Gabe told Tony to just report the car stolen when we got back to school. We were gonna walk the short distance to the motel and get that room and then in the morning call a couple of cabs to take us back to school.

"Rain was just pouring. When it rained like that while the sun was out, my momma used to say it meant the devil was beatin' his wife." Sandra was back to clasping her fingers again. "It was pitch black the night of the accident, but I think the devil was born in that fire."

"What happened when you got to the motel?" Pierce asked.

"That's when we noticed Kaymen wasn't with us," she said slowly. "We all thought he was there. I mean, we just kept walking through all that rain, and it was so dark and cold. Nobody was talking much after Gabe told us what we were gonna do, so we just walked. But when we realized he wasn't there; we didn't go back."

The room was silent again.

"Tony said if Kaymen didn't get out with us, he must've been dead. So we didn't go back. None of us slept that night, either. And in the morning, we saw on the TV in the motel room that a car had exploded in a ditch and was burned to a crisp by the time the police got there." Tears ran slowly down her face.

"Kaymen was dead for real. That's what we all thought, and we knew we couldn't tell anybody, or we'd all be in trouble. There was nothing more to talk about, we just left that motel. Ronnie cried for weeks, and me and Max had to finally get her to snap out of it before she got us caught. We couldn't get in trouble. Me, Lem, Ronnie and Max, we didn't have the type of money Gabe and Tony had. Their rich families would've gotten them good lawyers, and they probably would've never gone to jail. But us, I know my daddy didn't have no money and he would've been so pissed at me that if he did have money, he wouldn't have given it to me. He'd have said I need to take whatever repercussions came from what I did."

"Oh, Mama." Tamika wrapped her arm around her mother's shoulders again.

"No, don't feel sorry for me. We should've told somebody about the accident that night. That way they could've gone back to look for Kaymen. We never should've left him there to die."

"But he didn't die," Pierce said. "Because if Kaymen died, then he couldn't have been the one who set that fire in London last week, or—"

"Oh, it's him." Sandra insisted. "I looked right in his face that night at my cottage. There's not much left of his face, burns all over, but I knew his eyes and his voice. It was a little raspy, but he still sounded like Kaymen to me. Besides that, he said he was gonna make sure I died for real, just like he did with Max…and Lem."

Roark sucked in a breath. He let his arms fall to his side and gritted his teeth. For weeks he'd wanted nothing more than to know who'd killed his mother, and now he knew. And he knew why.

"Mrs. Rayder, did Maxine tell you how she knew Kaymen was still alive?" Pierce continued his questioning when everyone else remained silent.

Cade was a professional, but he was also hearing the motive and intent of the man who'd killed his aunt. He may not have been as rocked by Sandra's statements as Roark, but he was definitely feeling something, because it showed in the grim look on his face.

Sandra lifted her hands to wipe the tears from her face, and Tamika stood to get her some tissue. "I didn't believe her. I wrote back and told her there was no way he was alive, that he'd burned to death in that car. Right where we left him." When Sandra stopped speaking this time, she closed her mouth so tightly her lips thinned and she rocked her body back and forth in the chair.

"We left him there, and that was wrong. He was our friend, and we should've helped him," she whispered after a few moments. "We should've called somebody to help him because he was our friend. We did that to him, to his face and his hands—we did all that. We left him there and that fire burned him, it burned straight to his heart, and now he's after all of us. He'll kill us all! He's gonna come back for me and finish the job, and then I can be with my Lem. I can be with my love and I guess my friends again. We'll all be together." Sandra's words had begun to slur, tears falling faster, and the way she continued to rock in that chair had Roark standing and moving closer to her. But Tamika was already there and she turned to everyone, saying, "That's enough. I'm taking her back to bed."

Roark agreed Sandra needed to rest now. She needed to let everything she'd just remembered settle back into the recesses of her mind, for her sanity's sake. "I'll help you," he said and went to the other side of the chair to help lift Sandra up.

Tamika didn't say anything at first but by the time they made it to the stairs, she stopped to look up at him. "I can handle it from here."

"I want to help. We can get her settled, and then I'm sure Pierce and Cade will have more to talk to us about."

Tamika shook her head. "No," she said quietly. "I can't do it right now. I need to make sure she's alright. That's all."

Roark had never before seen the look of fear and distress in her eyes. He'd never heard her voice in such a shaky tone, but he did recognize the grief that rested heavily on her shoulders even as she tried to support her mother. He could see it in the way her hand was tightly gripping her mother, pulling Sandra close to her body. Protecting her and trying desperately to hold on and keep her mother here with her. If Roark could've held on to his mother before Kaymen had come for her, he would've. There was no doubt he'd have never left Maxine's side, held her hand, made her smile, any and everything he could've done to keep her here with him; he would've done in a heartbeat.

For that reason, Roark took a step back and dropped his arms to his sides. "Whatever you or she needs, Tamika, I'm right here. All you have to do is say the word, and it's done."

She tilted her head as if she were trying to decipher what he said or how to respond. Both of which were unlike her. Tamika always knew what she wanted to say in any given situation. "Right now, she just needs to rest," she replied finally and then took the first step with her mother.

Roark didn't leave immediately. He stood watching and when Tamika turned back to look at him, he was ready to jump to do whatever she requested.

"Thank you, Roark," she said. "Thank you for everything."

That hadn't been what he was expecting and as he walked back into the parlor, Roark was still examining the tightness that had gripped his chest at the finality he'd heard in her tone.

"Is she gonna be okay?" Cade asked.

The sound of his cousin's voice immediately snapped Roark out of his thoughts about Tamika. He could admit to himself that he was grateful for that fact. "Yeah, she probably just needs to rest. Traveling from the hospital and then, well, all this, has been a lot." Much more than even he'd anticipated. He pushed his hands into his pant pockets.

Cade nodded. "Yeah, I can imagine." He was standing now too, and so was Pierce.

"I had a tech guy who's retired from the MPD doing background checks on all the friends in that group. Just sent him a text that I need those reports ASAP," Pierce said.

"Good," Cade told him. "Now that we know who it is, we need to track him, grab his ass and this'll be over."

Roark wasn't so sure about that. "What happens in the meantime? You heard what she said—he's coming back for her."

"We knew that already," Pierce said, and Roark looked at him, unable to hide is irritation.

"You knew she was a sitting duck?"

"It made sense, considering the profile," Cade interjected. "His endgame will be to kill himself after he's taken all the people he blames for betraying him. That's why I told you to get the added security."

"And I did."

Pierce nodded. "Well, now we have enough to go to the local police with. They'll do more to keep Sandra safe."

It wasn't just Sandra Roark was worried about at the moment.

"Look," Cade continued. "She's the last one of the group. He's gotta come back to her—his psychosis won't let her live. And when he comes, we'll be ready for him."

"And she's bait?" The words were bitter in his throat.

"He's already on our radar the minute we see him we're grabbing him. He'll never get near her," Pierce said in a tone Roark figured normally ended all argument from a victim's family.

But Roark wasn't a normal family member. "I'm not going to just sit here and wait for that bastard to show up. Reacting isn't my thing. I'm more inclined to be prepared, to strike before I get struck."

"I know," Cade said, stepping closer to Roark. "But in this case, I need you to stand down and let us do our jobs. We'll get him, Roark. I promise you we'll get him for you and Aunt Max. We'll get him for all the lives he's taken."

Roark stared at his cousin, feeling the sincerity of his commitment and believing with his whole being that Cade would do whatever it took to bring Kaymen Benedict down. But it wasn't enough. Not for Roark. "Fine. Keep me posted," he said tightly.

Cade nodded, but he didn't step away from Roark, nor did he stop staring at him.

"I'm gonna head to the MPD now and give them all the information we have so far. The more eyes we have looking out for this motherfucker, the better." Pierce moved toward Roark. "Keep the security here tight, and we'll handle the rest."

It was Roark's turn to nod at Pierce before the guy left the room.

"Don't do it," Cade said the moment they were alone. "Whatever you're thinking about doing, just don't. Let us take care this, Roark. This is what we do."

"Well, it's not what I do. I don't wait for somebody to strike me or mine."

"I know—"

"Yeah, you do know, because you're the same way. Don't stand here and tell me to allow somebody else to do the work."

"I'm standing here telling you that this sadistic bastard killed my aunt! He drugged her and made her watch as he burned her to death, all because he's got an ax to grind. I'm not taking that shit lightly either, Roark. But I'm the one who's trained to handle this, not you."

"I'm her son!"

"Yes, you are! And your responsibility is to your brother and sister right now. Think about them before you go running off ready to hunt this idiot down yourself. Think about that woman up there who's trying to be strong for her mother but couldn't help looking to you for comfort. Think about everything you've got here in this house with you right now before you go putting yourself in the path of a killer."

Roark didn't reply—not that Cade had stuck around for anything else he was gonna say, anyway. It didn't matter. Roark knew what he needed to do. The second he was alone, he pulled his phone out of his pocket and made a call. "Yeah,

Devlin, I'm going to need that extra package we talked about last week. Can you get it here tonight?" After a brief pause, Roark continued. "Good. Thanks."

Roark disconnected the call and gripped the phone tightly in his hand. He wasn't promising Cade anything, and his cousin knew it. Devlin Bonner was a former Navy SEAL turned mercenary turned private investigator and husband to Roark's cousin, Bailey. Together, those two made a deadly combination, but Roark hadn't wanted Bailey involved in this. He hadn't wanted his former Navy SEAL cousin, Trent, involved either, which was why he'd gone straight to Devlin for the security detail. And Devlin hadn't let him down. With contacts all over the world, he'd been able to dispatch a team of elite soldiers dressed in black suits and ties to the clubhouse within three hours after Roark's first call last week. Now, he was going to send Roark more assistance, because everything had changed. He'd never considered himself a violent man, but then again, he hadn't been raised to cower or run from anyone. And if Kaymen Benedict was on a killing spree, Roark was gonna be there to stop him, once and for all.

CHAPTER 16

Hyde Park
London

"I'd kill for the chance to come up to your place."

"It doesn't have to be that drastic," Suri said before laughter bubbled up from inside her.

Durant had her pressed against the front door of the building. One arm was around her back, the other was beneath her thigh, holding her leg as she wrapped it around his waist. "It's your fault. You shouldn't be so freakin' sexy," he whispered before thrusting his tongue inside her ear.

That was probably the least sexy thing he could've done at that point. Suri hated a tongue in her ear. "I think you're more hung up on the freakin' part. You want another taste of what you had before and lost when you couldn't keep up."

He'd moved from her ear to dragging his tongue along the hills of her cleavage. Now that she could get with, since as she recalled, Durant could suck the hell out of her titties, enough to make her come and want to beg him for more. But Suri never begged.

His hand moved back until it was running over her ass cheek, gripping it tightly. She pressed into him then, remembering how good he was with her ass as well.

"We can have it all again, Suri. Just say the word." He looked up at her and waited until she opened her eyes to look at him. "Just say the damn word."

She knew it was as simple as that; she'd known it even before Durant had called her last week and asked for this date. It'd been months since they'd seen each other, since he'd walked out after she'd confessed her attraction to men and women. "No," she whispered and thought seriously about retracting that one simple word.

Durant was great in bed, there was absolutely no doubt about that. He was a computer geek who could—and most likely did—hack into any and every computer worldwide. Working as a private contractor and being in high demand meant he had his own money, so he wasn't after the Donovan funds. One of the main things her brothers had warned her about was guys coming at her just for her money. As if she'd be naïve enough to fall for a scam like that. But that wasn't the case with Durant. He owned a mansion and a luxury yacht where he preferred to sleep. And he'd offered to give her the world, his heart included.

She'd turned him down then, and she was turning him down now.

"Stop," she said when he'd continued to kiss her breasts.

He did exactly as she said, pulling his mouth away from her and letting her leg down slowly before taking a step back. "What do you want from me?" he asked, his tone as tortured as the confused look on his face.

She cleared her throat. "Nothing. And everything."

He dragged a hand over his bald head. "You can't have it all, Suri. Me. Them."

Suri knew the "them" he was referring to; she knew and she hated that he couldn't even bring himself to say it. "Would you rather I lie to you and to myself?"

"I'd rather you not think you can be with me and have a woman on the side too."

She frowned. "That's not what I think."

"It's what you said," he argued.

"No, Durant, that's what you heard. And you heard that because your big ol' ego was bruised. How dare I lay in your bed and let you do all those delicious things to me, come in your mouth, all over your dick, yell out your name, and then tell you I like girls too. How fuckin' awful of me to be honest with you!"

"I don't know how that works, Suri. I didn't know what you wanted me to say then, and damn if I know how I'm supposed to offer myself to you now." He was frustrated, and once upon a time so was she.

But Suri was over that now. She was secure in her wants, accepting the fact that some would think that made her different. What she hadn't quite figured out yet was how her happy ever after would look as a result. "To be honest again, I don't know, either." She reached into her purse and pulled out her key. "And maybe it's best if we just don't see each other while I try to figure it out."

He cursed. "You said that the last time, and I left you alone. If you still weren't sure, why'd you agree to this date?"

"Because I wanted to see you again." She'd wanted to see if she could hate him the way she'd tried to do in the months she hadn't seen him. That answer was no. She didn't hate Durant, and therein lay her biggest problem. "But I understand what you're trying to say. I won't agree to another date from you, Durant."

"Suri—"

"No," she said and held up a hand to keep him from stepping close to her when that was exactly what he'd tried to do. "It's not fair. This is who I am, and I can't ask you to accept that. I won't ask you to accept me."

He opened his mouth to say something and then clapped it shut before shaking his head.

"Goodbye, Durant." She closed her fingers so tight around her keys, one pressed painfully into her skin.

"Bye, Suri." He said those words and turned to walk down the steps. Suri watched him get into his car and drive off, all while telling herself she'd done the right thing. Again.

She couldn't help who she was, not even to make the guy she thought she might be in love with happy.

With that thought in mind, she took a deep breath and was about to turn around and unlock the door when she saw him.

He was standing between two parked cars across the street. Had he been there the whole time? She didn't know. Durant had come around from the driver's side to get her out of the car as soon as he'd parked. And when she'd stepped out, they'd stood at the car with her back against the hood while he'd kissed her hungrily. She'd never looked around.

The guy was staring right at her now. She couldn't see his face, because he wore a long black coat with a hood pulled down low. And he wasn't moving.

She turned immediately and almost dropped her key as she fought to get it into the lock. Once it was in, she pushed the door, hurriedly stepping inside and then slamming it shut behind her. The front door to the building where she'd been temporarily staying was paned glass at the top, so she could look out again to see the guy hadn't moved. Now fear eased its sharp claws over her skin, and Suri ran to the stairs, taking them two at a time until she was on the third floor, where her flat was located.

She fumbled with the keys again, cursing her shaking fingers until she got it to work. Rushing into the flat, she slammed the door behind her and ran through the living room. "Aunt Birdie! Aunt Birdie!"

Suri ran from the living room to the kitchen to the powder room, screaming for her aunt, because she had to be here, and she had to be alright. The woman drove her insane, but she couldn't be hurt, she couldn't be…

"Aunt Birdie!" she yelled louder this time and ran down the hallway toward the three bedrooms. Aunt Birdie was staying in the biggest one all the way to the back.

Suri slammed into the door, her hand slipping on the knob as tears clogged her throat. "Aunt Birdie!"

When the door finally opened, she burst inside and was about to scream when to her left, another door opened.

"Chile, if you don't stop making all that noise at this time of night… Folk are tryin' to sleep. Or if they ate that last bowl of buttered beans before going to bed, like I did, they were probably stuck in the bathroom too." Aunt Birdie closed the bathroom door behind her and walked toward the bed.

Suri leaned over, pressing her hands to her knees as she tried to catch her breath and calm the adrenaline pumping through her. "I just needed to make sure you were here and alright," she said between breaths.

"Well, where else would I be? Unlike you, I don't hang out 'til all hours in the morning with some no-good man."

Suri shook her head as she came to a full stand again and looked over to her aunt. She was wearing a long pastel-colored nightgown, as she did every night. Her head was wrapped with a silk scarf, and the eye mask she always slept in was hanging by the elastic string around her neck. Her ensemble was made complete by those ridiculous slippers with feathers or something fluffy on top. "He's not a no-good man, and it's called a date."

Aunt Birdie pursed her lips. "Hmph. Well, last week you were on a date with a no-good woman. You need to make up your mind."

Suri could only shake her head; she was in no mood to argue with her aunt tonight. It was enough that the mean-as-a-rattlesnake-woman was alive and well. "Alright, I'm sorry I disturbed you. Good night, Aunt Birdie."

She didn't wait for her aunt to respond but left her room and moved through the house until she was once again in the living room. She hadn't turned on any lights when she'd come in because Aunt Birdie was a staunch believer in conserving electricity, so empty rooms had to be pitch-dark at all times. Thankful for that tonight, Suri crept toward the window. Pressing her side against the wall, she eased an arm around slowly, pushing the curtain until there was the barest space for her to peek through.

Her heart thumped and then stopped. He was still there, and his head was tilted back as if he were looking up at her.

"Fuck this," she snapped and released the curtain.

Going back into her room this time, she yanked the shoebox from beneath her bed and pulled out the gun she kept there. A quick check of the bullets, and she released the safety before heading out again. She had to close the front door quietly, because she didn't want Aunt Birdie coming out to see where she was. Running down the steps with gun in hand, Suri had no idea what she was going to do beyond telling the bastard to get lost, but as she arrived on the first floor and made her way to the front door, a loud boom and then a bright burst of light sent her flying back.

~

At a little after midnight, Tamika sat on the edge of Roark's bed and sighed. "I told myself to stay in the room with my mother all night."

Her initial plan had been to slip into bed with him and lose herself in the warmth of his embrace, because for a guy who was still relatively new to the snuggling thing, he was pretty damn good at it. But Roark was awake. He'd been sitting up in the bed, his laptop open, notepad, pen and a blue spiral-bound book with a burst of white flowers on the cover next to him.

"How's she doing?"

"That's just it," Tamika said and turned sideways, lifting one leg onto the bed so she could look at Roark. "While she was in the hospital, Dr. Duvall had a psychiatrist come down and speak to her, so she's now on an antidepressant, along with her pain medications, which I'm not totally sure is a good cocktail of meds. But besides that, she's been on the antidepressants for about five days now, so when she began talking I figured that was the reason why. I had no idea she needed to talk because she'd been holding in so much."

Roark closed his laptop and leaned over to set it on the nightstand. "I wish my mother had talked."

Tamika had wondered how he felt about everything her mother had said earlier this evening. If it was hard for her to hear that her parents knew the man who wanted them dead, and had pissed that man off by leaving him in a burning car, then it had to be even harder for Roark to hear his mother had known for at least two years that this man was alive.

"How did they live with this for so long?" she asked. "And how did your mother finally find out Kaymen was alive?"

Roark shook his head. "I don't know. That's what I've been sitting here trying to find out. I hadn't gotten around to closing out her email accounts and lucky for me, my mother was extremely organized. She kept all her passwords written down in her planner. I've been going through each email, trying to find some mention of Kaymen."

She kicked off her slippers and pulled both her legs up on the bed, scooting back so she could lean against the headboard the same as him. "I don't know what I'm going to do if something happens to her. If he gets—" She stopped talking when she felt his hand covering hers.

"It's not going to happen."

For endless moments, she continued to stare down at his hand over hers. This was exactly why she'd tried to force herself not to come in here. "So much is happening." She hadn't realized she'd said that out loud until he squeezed her hand.

"That it is."

"Which means we should try to focus on one thing at a time, right? Prioritize. Sex was good. It was fun in the midst of all this…um, darkness. But now we have to concentrate on protecting the people we love and keeping our focus on them. Tell me that's what you're thinking too. Tell me I'm not the only one deciding to stop whatever physical was going on between us while we get to the bottom of all this killing. Dammit, open your mouth and tell me, Roark."

She dragged her gaze away from their hands and looked up to see that he'd been staring intently at her. Tamika knew she'd just babbled all the things that had been running through her mind in the last five hours. She also knew she was being a rambling idiot. What happened to that woman who was so in control of herself, her thoughts and her body? The one who'd said yesterday that they could just have sex until it was time to move on?

With waves of embarrassment swarming through her, she sighed. "I'm sorry."

"Don't be," he said. Then he moved, using his other hand to pick up the pad, book and pen and toss them all onto the floor so he could slide closer to her on the bed. When he was still again, he lifted her hand to his lips, dropping a soft kiss on each of her fingers. "What I'm going to tell you is that Cade and Pierce are going to find this sonofabitch and they're either going to kill him where he stands or they're going to haul his demented ass to jail. That's what I know without a doubt in my mind."

Her heart was still fluttering from the sweet kisses he'd just dropped on her fingers; now she was looking into his eyes and feeling the potency of his words.

"The next thing I'm going to tell you is I'm here for you in whatever way you need me to be tonight. No judgment and no regrets."

And no promises. She didn't say that, but the words immediately popped into her mind. But what the hell? There were no promises to be made. If not for Kaymen Benedict and his crusade for revenge, she and Roark would've never met. She may have come to Painswick to visit with her mother but there would've been no reason for her to promise a steak dinner to her friend in the IT department at the insurance company where she used to work to find Roark's personal phone number and then insist they meet. They didn't run in the same circles—her family worked good jobs, had pension plans and social security to look forward to in retirement, while his owned luxury B&Bs and ordered designer clothes like she ordered groceries.

"I—"

Whatever she was gonna say was cut short by an insistent knock on the door. She and Roark both jumped as if they'd been caught doing something they shouldn't have. With a frown, Roark rolled off the bed first, and Tamika followed him. She hadn't been prepared for what they saw when they opened the door.

A woman wearing a pink-and-gold silk scarf wrapped around her head and a pale-pink quilted robe. Another woman wearing a great black cocktail dress and red boots laced up to her knee. But the outfit wasn't what stuck out most about this woman, it was the flecks of what Tamika was certain were blood along her face, neck and upper chest.

"Suri? What the hell happened? What are you two doing here?" Roark fired off questions while Tamika stood beside him waiting for the answers.

"Apparently not as much as you're doing up in here," the older woman wearing the pink and gold said. "Now, get out here and show me to my room. That woman downstairs was all flustered and could barely tell me her name, said she was going to call somebody named Geoff. But I need to lay down and get some sleep. I don't have the time nor the inclination to wait for somebody else to come and talk to me."

"No problem, Aunt Birdie. I'll get you settled," Roark stated briskly.

Tamika touched his arm. "I'll do it, Roark. Just let me get my shoes and I'll get Dorianne, and we can have the rooms on the first floor set up for them."

"Who are you, and why are you coordinating rooms at his B&B? Roark, are you sleeping with the staff? Lord have mercy, this family has gone straight to hell in a handbasket."

"She's not the staff," Roark insisted, but the woman's

words had already taken Tamika back to the thoughts she'd been having before the knock on the door.

"I'm Tamika Rayder," she said and extended her hand to Suri first, because she knew this one would be receptive.

Suri extended her arm slowly, and Tamika immediately looked down to see that the back of her hand had specks of blood on it too. Roark must've seen it as well, because he moved quickly, stepping in front of Tamika and wrapping an arm around Suri so she leaned into him immediately.

"We need to get you medical attention," he said and scooped his younger sister up into his arms.

That left Tamika with Aunt Birdie.

"I can take your bag, ma'am." The bag was actually a signature Louis Vuitton makeup case Tamika was certain cost over three thousand dollars. It made the eight-hundred-dollar bag Tamika had that had been a splurge purchase when she'd received her tax refund last year look like a cheap imitation.

"You wanna take my bag, but you're not the staff." If it were possible, Aunt Birdie held the handle to her case even tighter and fell into step behind Roark.

Tamika ran back into the room for her slippers and came out again when Roark and his family were halfway down the stairs.

A guard was positioned inside the clubhouse, while two were out front. She'd heard Roark talking to someone named Devlin earlier today and they'd agreed that having two additional guards at the manor would also be helpful.

"They said they were family," Jackson the guard, said the moment he saw Roark. "I checked it out before I let them in and I wanted to call you first, but she insisted on going straight to your room."

"He sure did," Aunt Birdie snapped. "Holding us out there like we were common criminals. It's absurd."

Tamika was quickly surmising that Aunt Birdie was the complainer in the Donovan family.

"It's okay, Jack," Roark said before giving the guy a conciliatory nod as if he already knew what Aunt Birdie had put him through while he'd checked out who they were. "Can you call the paramedics?"

"Already done, sir. They should be here at any minute."

"Thanks." Roark carried his sister into the parlor, and Aunt Birdie followed.

Dorianne came up to Tamika's side as she walked in behind them. "I didn't know what to do or say to her," the woman confided in Tamika.

Tamika could only nod, because she wasn't real sure what to do or say to Aunt Birdie, either. "It's fine, Dorianne. They're going to need rooms. I can help you get them ready." Tamika almost frowned when she realized her words did sound as if she worked here.

"No. No. I can take care of it now that I know what's what. Just give me about fifteen minutes. There's hot coffee in the kitchen. I did manage to get that started when I figured it was about to be an interesting night." Dorianne was wearing a robe as well, hers a navy blue and white checker-print, her black scarf tied in a knot on her forehead.

"Thank you, Dorianne," Tamika said before turning her attention back to Roark and his family.

"What the hell happened?" Roark asked as he sat on the couch beside Suri.

"She got blown up, that's what happened," Aunt Birdie snapped. "We were both almost killed."

Aunt Birdie dropped down into the chair Tamika's mother had previously sat in and put her case on the floor beside her. When she sat back in the chair, Tamika could see how tired the older woman really was. Tired and afraid. Her eyes closed as she released a heavy sigh. She didn't fold her hands together and let them fall into her lap the way Tamika thought she would; instead she clamped her hands on the arms of the chair as if that action was somehow steadying her.

"There was an explosion," Suri said, her tone much calmer than Aunt Birdie's had been. "I came home from a date, and there was someone standing across the street. A guy I believe, dressed in all black and wearing a hood over his head. I went inside to make sure Aunt Birdie was okay. She was, but when I looked out the window, the guy was still there. That's when I grabbed my gun—"

"Whoa, wait a minute. You have a gun?" Roark was clearly surprised by that revelation.

Suri gave him a look as if that were old news. Tamika found the exchange endearing, even though the circumstances were dire. "Yes, I have a gun, Roark. I'm a thirty-year-old woman who knows how to protect herself."

Roark looked as if he wanted to say something else, but thankfully thought better of it and just waited for her to continue.

"I grabbed my gun and ran back downstairs. I was just going to point it at him and tell him to get lost. I never planned on shooting anybody, even though I'm a damn good shot." The last was said with an edge of pride. "But before I could even get to the door, it literally blew up in my face."

"He planted a bomb at your house." Tamika spoke slowly, letting the words and the weight of that comment settle in.

Roark jerked his head in her direction. "She's not his target. He doesn't even know her."

Tamika swallowed, trying to wrap her mind around all the things that were happening, and dread settled in the pit of her stomach. "But you don't believe in coincidences. Don't you remember telling me that?"

"Will somebody tell me what's going on?" Suri asked.

"How'd you get here, Suri? Didn't the police come? Who in the hell let you walk away from an explosion without calling for an ambulance and sending you both straight to the hospital?"

"Police and ambulances arrived. Firefighters too. They say it was a car bomb, in one of the cars across the street. Right where I saw the man standing." She gave a shaky sigh. "The blast wasn't close enough to the house to cause more than broken windows to the front. Or the bomb wasn't big enough. I forget which one they said."

"They?" Roark pressed. "The cops or the firefighters?"

"Detective Gibbons. The one we spoke to at the solicitor's office that day. He was there and he said that if this were meant to kill us, it would've. He had so many questions. He wanted to know where you were and whose name the flat was in, and when was the last time I saw you. Aunt Birdie yelled at him to get a warrant and arrest us if he thought we were guilty of a crime. I told him to contact Mr. Burrows, and then we packed up some stuff, got in the car and came straight here. I didn't know what else to do."

Roark pulled his sister gingerly to him for a hug then. "You did the right thing," he whispered.

"Paramedics are here." Jack came in with two men on his heels, both wearing medical jackets and carrying duffel bags.

Tamika watched for a few seconds as Roark stayed close to his sister while the medics began examining her. Then she turned her attention back to Aunt Birdie, who'd been uncharacteristically quiet in the past few moments. Not that she knew the woman all that well to know it wasn't usual for her to be quiet, but since their impromptu meeting, the woman had much to say, so to be silent now was a little alarming.

Moving closer to the chair where the older woman still sat, Tamika took a chance and put her hand on top of hers before clearing her throat. "Miss...um, Bird...uh, ma'am? Are you alright? Is there something I can get you, or do you need to be seen by the paramedics as well?"

The woman cracked an eye open slowly, peering at Tamika as if she suspected she might be trying to steal something from her. "I take my coffee with lots of cream and sugar. And while you're getting it, tell that woman to hurry with my room. I need to lay down."

There was no sarcasm or edginess to her words, just simple statements spoken in a tone that said she'd been through a lot. For the second time today, or night, Tamika felt a pang of sorrow for the suffering people around her were going through. She'd known Aunt Birdie for about fifteen minutes, and yet that didn't stop her from hurting for the woman who'd probably never experienced anything like this before.

Well, that made two of them, because as she left the parlor and headed to the kitchen, Tamika thought about the chaotic turn things had taken in her life. She didn't know how it was all going to end and that frightened her, so much that she stood in the doorway of the kitchen and once again considered praying. Realizing the right words still wouldn't come to her, she repeated what she'd said before, "Please. Please." She hoped they'd be enough.

CHAPTER 17

*I*n the week since Roark had been at the clubhouse, there'd never been as much activity as there was right now.

It was a little after ten in the morning, and breakfast was being served in the main dining room. This announcement from Dorianne had brought everyone downstairs to sit at the massive glossed oak table with its matching high-backed chairs. In the center of the table was an enormous fresh flower arrangement, and table settings had been arranged for each of the guests in the house.

"Like I said yesterday, fancy," Sandra said when she made her way to the table and was about to take a seat in one of the chairs closest to the door.

Tuppence was right behind Sandra and immediately touched her arm. "It's a beautiful day, Sandra; let's sit closer to the window. And maybe later we can take a walk in the gardens. Roark told me all about them while he was helping me yesterday. He said his mother had a beautiful garden in London, but this one was bigger and better."

Roark watched the two women walk and talk. There was a friendship there, not just an employee/employer relationship. He'd often seen that with the way his mother had always dealt with the staff at their home in Hyde Park and the way his father had taught him to work alongside his staff at the oilwell. This line of thought steered him back to Aunt Birdie's comment about him sleeping with the staff last night. Tamika hadn't seemed too bothered by it, but it hadn't sat right with Roark, and he wondered belatedly if he should've said something more to set his aunt straight.

There'd been so much going on last night that he hadn't really had time to think everything through. Even now, after they all had finally been able to go to bed and get some rest, Roark still didn't know what to expect next. This big "family" breakfast, for one, wasn't anything he'd ever thought would be taking place. Not here, not with these particular people and especially not now.

"Good morning," Suri said when she entered the room. "I was told to come down for breakfast."

His sister looked a lot better this morning. Sure, she still had the marks from the glass that had shattered into her face, but as the paramedics had cleared her last night, she was going to be just fine. She'd pulled her hair back into a neat ponytail that made her look younger and wore white high-waisted pants with an orange top. As usual with Suri's very coordinated style, there were orange bangle bracelets on one arm and orange hoop earrings in her ears.

"I was too," Roark said when she came to stand beside him.

"This place is really nice. It's a shame we haven't been out here before now."

"Yeah, it's a shame about a lot of things," he replied and then decided he didn't want that to be the mood this morning. "Mum loved it here. She spent a lot of time decorating and redecorating. And she's trained the staff to keep things exactly the way she wanted them."

"Impeccable," Suri said. "She had impeccable style and grace, and I've seen that here in the clubhouse at least. After breakfast I'll go explore the rest of the grounds and the manor. I have a feeling I'll be visiting much more frequently."

"Maybe we should all make it a habit to visit more frequently, as a family." The last was said as he watched Tamika and Aunt Birdie enter the room and take seats at the table.

When Tuppence signaled her, Tamika went to sit between her and Sandra. That meant she wouldn't be sitting near Roark.

"Let's sit," he told Suri and escorted his sister to seats across the table from Tamika and her family.

Aunt Birdie went directly to the seat at the head of the table and sat down with the regal air she always carried. "Now this is more like it," she said as she took the white linen napkin from the table, snapped it open and set it in her lap.

Moments after everyone was seated, Dorianne came in to announce, "The buffet is open."

Roark thought Aunt Birdie was going to explode at that announcement. During the repast after his mother's funeral, Aunt Birdie had made it clear how much she despised a buffet. "I'll fix your plate," he told his aunt.

His aunt who was in the process of rolling her eyes with much drama before she spared him a glance. "Thank you. Don't skimp on the bacon. I'm not one of those ones with a sudden affliction to swine. And scones, I love vanilla scones."

"Yes, ma'am," Roark said and stood from his seat again. Just as he'd finished fixing Aunt Birdie's plate and got her a cup of coffee, Roark noticed Cade entering the dining room.

He immediately started walking toward his cousin, and that was when he noticed Pierce coming in behind him. And Ridge. "Oh, well, the gang is really and truly all here," he quipped.

Ridge didn't hide his annoyance. "Cade called me this morning, but I'm wondering why neither my brother nor sister thought about picking up their phone last night."

At the sound of his ire, Suri forked a chunk of French toast dripping with maple syrup into her mouth.

"I'll make the introductions, and then we can go into the parlor to talk," Roark stated.

Cade had already walked past him. "And after we talk, I'm having breakfast." He stopped at the head of the table and bent to kiss his aunt. "Aunt Birdie, my love. It's good to see you as always."

Aunt Birdie lifted a hand to cup Cade's cheek. "Always the fresh one. Good morning, Cadence."

Aunt Birdie liked to call everyone by their given names, even though she'd always gone by her nickname. It was something nobody in the family was allowed to question.

"We should talk. Now," Pierce said. "Introductions can come later."

Roark was used to being the serious and unyielding one in his family, but in this past week, Pierce had taken over that spot.

"Yeah, now," Ridge said without going to speak to Aunt Birdie or anyone else at the table.

Roark followed them but paused to glance back at Tamika before leaving. She was about to stand and come join them, but he shook his head. "Stay. I'll fill you in later."

He was certain she didn't like that, but her mother leaned over to whisper something to her, and she looked away from him. Roark left the dining room and walked toward the parlor.

Cade was last to come into the room, chewing on a piece of bacon while holding a sausage in his hand.

"How can you eat at a time like this?" Ridge asked.

"Easy." Cade took a bite of the sausage. "Like this."

Ridge shook his head, and Pierce moved to stand in what Roark was thinking might be the guy's favorite spot in this room—near the window. "How the hell could you not call me and tell me that our sister and aunt were nearly blown the hell up?" As Ridge was normally the more laid-back brother, this burst of temper was different, but not surprising. His brother was right, again.

"I should've called, but to be fair, I was dealing with a lot here. Aunt Birdie and Suri showing up in the middle of the night looking like they'd been in a battle, learning that our mother was hunted and killed by her former classmate, having to secure this place like we're in a war to keep everyone safe. I had a bit on my plate at that time, Ridge."

"That's not an excuse," Ridge replied. "We agreed to no more secrets."

"And I wasn't keeping any. I told you everything that was going on, up until last night. It's ten in the damn morning, man. Cut me some slack." Roark may have been asking for slack, but really, he wasn't giving Ridge much choice. He wasn't going to defend himself against not telling him about the explosion again; the explanation he just gave would have to suffice.

"I think we have more serious things at stake," Pierce stated evenly.

"Yeah," Cade said, brushing his hands together because he didn't have a napkin. "Here's the thing. Our profile described Kaymen as an organized serial arsonist suffering from a psychotic break. Now, while we're clear on the car accident/fire forty-five years ago. And the fact that his friends left him for dead in a burning car. That's the central incident. But we still haven't closed in on what the most recent stressor was that took him from just being angry at his friends to wanting to see each of them dead."

"Okay, give me a second to catch up. The last status email I got from Roark was yesterday morning, and all it stated was that the fire investigator's mother admitted she knew Mum and that you two had figured out there was a group of friends from college that connected Mum to the victims of the most recent fire. Now, we know who the killer is and we're just sitting around here talking about it instead of going out to arrest his sorry ass." Ridge was still angry.

"There was another fire in London last week, and it killed two more members of the group of friends. That's how we know who the killer is." Pierce was obviously irritated that he'd had to go over that part again.

"His name is Kaymen Benedict," Roark said. "Does that ring any bells for you? Have you ever heard Mum talk about him?"

Ridge frowned. "No. I've never heard that name before."

"Okay, you're all caught up," Pierce snapped. "Last night's explosion is out of character for the killer we profiled."

"What? He left a bomb with the hopes of killing my sister and my aunt. How is that out of character?" Roark asked.

Cade shook his head. "He doesn't do bombs. He starts fires, and that's probably because a part of him died in a fire. That explains why he wants his former friends to watch as he burns them alive, because they left him while he essentially did the same thing."

Roark sighed. "I get that, but—"

"Changing his methods isn't part of the profile," Pierce said.

"Unless he's devolving," Cade added.

Ridge frowned. "He's what?"

"Unraveling, rapidly losing all grip on reality because the scenario he set up to avenge his grievance is starting to go wrong. Sandra didn't die in the fire he set at the cottage." Cade's expression was serious as he continued. "Then when he went to kill Ronnella McCoy, he stumbled across his other friend, Tony Graves."

"How do you know he didn't already know Graves was there with her?" Roark was listening to his cousin and to Pierce, trying to follow their line of thought.

"Because after I left the MPD yesterday, I drove to Hyde Park and questioned some of Ronnella McCoy's friends. They said she wasn't dating anyone and she wasn't even supposed to be in town on the night of the fire. She'd been booked on a cruise but had cancelled for some reason. I checked out the cruise logs, and she was booked on a three-week Mediterranean cruise. My friend at the MPD had already performed a data dump on Ronnella and Tony's phones. They'd been in contact on and off for the past three months, but almost every day in the past two weeks. Tony called her an hour before she was supposed to leave for the airport the morning of the cruise."

"So she cancelled a cruise for a date and ended up dead." Ridge rubbed a hand over his jaw. "What the hell is going on?"

"We're thinking that maybe if your mother warned Lemuel and Sandra Rayder about Kaymen being alive, she would've also warned Ronnella and Tony. Now, they may not have believed her, just as the Rayders didn't take it very seriously. But, there's no way Ronnella wouldn't have heard about your mother's death; even if, by chance she and your mother had no other contact with each other, they lived close to each other, and news of the fire was in the local papers," Pierce added.

"You think they were talking about the fires, wondering if it were Kaymen?" Roark asked.

Cade shrugged. "We'll never know, but whatever was said on that last call made Ronnella cancel her trip and put both of them literally in the line of fire less than twelve hours later."

"Now wait, you're saying this guy is angry with his friends why?" Ridge asked. "I mean, who gets angry enough to go around killing people he hasn't seen in however many years?"

Cade and Pierce looked to Roark and Roark sighed.

"Mum, Dad and their friends, they got drunk one night and there was an accident. They all got out of the car and ran away from the scene because they were underage. Kaymen Benedict didn't get out."

"What? You're saying our parents, the ones who wouldn't tolerate us even lying about not eating broccoli, left someone to die and never said anything." Ridge was speaking the very thoughts Roark had yesterday after the conversation with Sandra.

"They were young and they all thought he was with them," he said but then stopped because there wasn't any more he could provide by way of an excuse. It was an awful thing to happen, but nothing they did or said at this moment was going to change it.

"Our current issue is figuring out Kaymen's next move. His endgame," Pierce said.

"He'll want Sandra dead. She's the last one, the only mistake he made. He'll come for her," Cade told them. "Now, whether he plans it to be a murder/suicide or he thinks he's gonna walk away and somehow feel better about himself, I don't much give a damn. My priority is to keep Sandra alive."

"If his plan is to walk away, won't he just kill again? Shouldn't the plan be to kill this bastard?" Ridge asked.

"He's only killing those who wronged him. For all intent and purposes, the killing should stop once Sandra's gone." Pierce didn't sound convincing at all.

"And what if it doesn't?" Roark asked the question he knew everyone was thinking.

"We're going to focus on the first step for now, Kaymen's endgame," Cade said. "Stopping him before he can put his plan in motion."

"How are you going to do that? Do you even know where this guy is?" Ridge asked.

"Once we knew it was Kaymen, we dug up everything we could find about him. It wasn't much, especially not after the accident. His parents even had a funeral for him. Everybody thought he was dead. We know somebody had to help him out of that ditch. He would've been injured, badly burned, so there's no possibility he just walked away on his own. Besides, if he had, he would've immediately gone in search of his friends." Pierce shook his head. "We didn't find any medical records, and there's nothing on Kaymen after that time. No credit cards, no jobs, no home, no action on his social security number at all. He's basically been dead for forty-five years."

"So why did he come back now?" Ridge asked.

"That's a good question," Cade said. "But more importantly for us, how did Aunt Max know he was coming back long before he walked into her house and burned her alive? And why, if she knew he was eventually going to come for her, didn't she do something to try to stop him, or at the very least protect herself?"

"Cadence, the food is getting cold," Aunt Birdie shouted from where she stood in the doorway, and the four men turned to look at her.

"Uh, yes, ma'am. I'm coming now," Cade said. "We're on top of this. All you need to do is keep your security detail. Pierce and I will work out the rest."

Pierce nodded. "Right. I'm circling back to the MPD now to speak with the Chief Detective about last night's developments. I'll touch base with you later today, Cade. Since you've got to go eat your breakfast." The sarcasm was thick in Pierce's tone and if he weren't such a serious, strait-laced agent, Roark might have chuckled at him.

Cade only grinned. "No shame in my game," he quipped and turned to walk toward Aunt Birdie.

Pierce had left the room first but before Cade and Aunt Birdie could leave, Geoff appeared.

"Sir," Geoff said, looking directly at Roark. "Dorianne informed me earlier this morning that we had more guests. Is there anything else I can get for you or them?"

"No, Geoff, thank you. We're okay for now," Roark said.

"You work here too?" Aunt Birdie asked Geoff. She was staring at him strangely, and Roark moved to stand closer just in case she went off on a tangent and he needed to get her out of the room quickly.

"I do," Geoff said. He turned to Aunt Birdie and bowed in front of her. "I'm Geoffrey Ewing, Concierge of Donovan Manor, and I'm at your service."

Aunt Birdie continued to stare at him. "I knew a man named Ewing before," she said quietly and then just as abruptly she waved Geoff out of her way and continued walking back toward the dining room.

Cade followed her, leaving Roark, Ridge and now Geoff to stare after them.

"Love her to pieces, but I swear she's a strange one," Ridge said when Aunt Birdie was clearly out of earshot.

Roark didn't reply but he was surprised to hear Geoff say, "We all have one in the family, I guess."

Geoff walked away, and Ridge looked at Roark. The brothers both shrugged and chuckled before going back to the dining room to join the others.

"Hey, you." Roark breathed a sigh of relief at the sight of her. When she lifted her head and smiled, he inhaled even deeper at the quick onslaught of desire that punched him in the gut the moment he realized she was sitting in the hot tub.

"Hey. Long time no see," she replied.

It'd been a long time, all day and a good portion of the night, which was why he'd gone around asking everyone currently staying in the clubhouse if they'd seen her. He'd finally lucked out when Dorianne said she'd suggested Tamika come here for a little peace and quiet.

"I see you found a place to hide out for a while." He continued walking toward her.

The clubhouse had an indoor and outdoor pool, just like the manor. This part of the house was located on the far west end. She hadn't switched on all the lights, so it was dark when he'd looked through the glass doors, but something had told him to enter anyway, and Roark was more than glad he had.

"Aunt Birdie and Tuppence have a war of words going anytime they're in a room together. My mother's crying a lot, and Suri looks at me like she knows something I don't." She shrugged. "It just got a little overwhelming."

"I can imagine." He was closer now, the steam from the

bubbling water reaching up to make the skin on his arms feel warm.

After dinner, he'd gone for a run around the property. It served a double purpose, one because he'd been off his workout regimen since coming here and two, he'd wanted to see the security he and Devlin had put in place. He wanted to make sure they were being protected from all ends. Ridge had opted not to stay at the clubhouse even though, after learning what was going on, Aunt Birdie had thought it best they all stay in one place. Ridge thought that would make them all sitting ducks, and he'd walked out amid Aunt Birdie's ramblings.

She leaned back against the lip of the hot tub. "I heard you went for a run."

He nodded. "Yeah, I did. Relaxed me a bit, I guess. Then I had a shower before coming to look for you."

"Oh, well, then I guess inviting you to get into more water wouldn't make sense."

The bubbles in the water created a frosted layer so he couldn't tell if the burgundy halter top she wore was a one-piece or two-piece bathing suit. It didn't really matter, because the thought of her only wearing a bathing suit beneath that water had already begun to arouse him.

"Water's one of the best things for a body," he replied.

She chuckled. "I think that refers to drinking water, not sitting in it until your skin wrinkles like a prune."

"Whichever. I'm game." If he grabbed his shirt and pulled it up and over his head too quickly, so be it. He wasn't about to deny that sitting in a hot tub with Tamika was a much better way to spend the remainder of the evening than going back to his room and continuing to look through his mother's emails.

"Good, because this water feels divine." She let her head

fall back and made a groaning sound that caused his dick to throb.

Roark went into the water, wearing only his boxers. He took it slowly even though his body was already rigid with arousal, because the water was hot as hell. Refusing to back out for fear of appearing weak in Tamika's eyes, he kept going, praying the heat didn't scorch the skin off his legs.

"I used to treat myself to spa days once a month." Her voice was soothing, and Roark decided to focus on that instead of the water temperature; besides, once he'd lowered himself all the way in, it felt a little better.

"I used to hit the gym at least three times a week," he added when he was able to sit back and almost relax.

"It shows," she said, but her head was still back, eyes still closed.

There was so much more he wanted to ask her, more he wanted to know about her, but right now she obviously wanted to push everything out of her mind that didn't make her feel good. He could relate to that—he just wished he were as good at it as she appeared to be. "I believe there's a gym at the manor, along with two more pools and a full-service spa. You should check it out tomorrow." The B&B was meant as a luxury getaway, even if they hadn't been able to enjoy it in that way.

"We're not on vacation," she said as if she were reading his mind. "If we were, I'd be asking for a refund."

Roark chuckled. "Yeah, I'd be with you on that request. There's definitely a lot going on, but you know what? We can take this break. The house is secure, the manor is secure and Pierce and Cade have gotten the MPD involved now, so everybody's looking for him. We can take this moment right here for ourselves."

"That's what I've been telling myself for the past half hour."

She hadn't moved, and he could no longer resist. Roark reached out and ran a finger along the line of her jaw. "I'd like to see you in action on a real vacation. I bet you're the type to do all the excursions offered, especially the daredevil ones."

That comment got her to not only open her eyes, but to raise her head and let her arms fall into the water. "If I'm the daredevil, then what are you? Let me guess, you're the 'lay on the beach with your cool-ass shades on' type of vacationer. You get the bartender to keep refilling your drink, and you've got a book you never really plan to read sitting on the towel beside you. That's how you spend your day until it's time to go in and take a meal. And in the evenings, you go for a swim, because the sun has gone down and its less crowded in the water."

"That's precisely what I'd do if I ever got around to taking a vacation," he admitted.

He wasn't surprised when she pursed her lips and shook her head. "It's a shame I've got you all figured out."

Yes, that was a shame, because he still didn't have her figured out yet. "But, if you were there, on that beach, I'd probably be persuaded to do anything you wanted."

She perked up. "Jet-skiing? Or no, ziplining. I was in Vegas last summer with one of my co-workers for her bachelorette party, and we were supposed to go ziplining, but one of the other girls got food poisoning, so we all hung around the suite that evening to make sure she didn't vomit everywhere while we were out."

"That was...um, very noble of you." He tried not to frown at the visual that had popped into his head.

She shrugged. "It was no big deal. We ordered tons of

room service and got drunk as hell. Had almost as much fun as if we'd gone out. It definitely made for a good memory. But I'd still like to go ziplining."

"Uh, well, you should definitely go ziplining then."

"But you wouldn't do it, would you?"

Roark paused to consider it, then shook his head. "I can be a very good cheerleader from the ground."

She exploded with laughter and smacked a hand on his shoulder. "You're so predictable." It wasn't said in a sarcastic or nasty way, she'd just said it, much like she would've said the grass was green or this water was hot. Still, it pricked something deep inside Roark.

He'd let his hand fall from her face as they were talking, but now he wanted to touch her again. This time he dipped his hand under water to find hers before lifting it up and bringing it over to his face. Just a few months ago, he'd worn a thick beard. The morning after his mother's death, he'd shaved it off.

Tamika instantly took over, rubbing her fingers along the line of his jaw and not jerking away at his obvious five o'clock shadow.

"I think about your touch a lot, Tamika."

She tilted her head. "Do you?" Her hair was piled on top of her head in a messy bun. Several tendrils had fallen to frame her face and as a result of the steamy air surrounding them were wet and sticking to her skin. She wore no makeup, and her skin appeared fresh and clear. Her lips were plump and kissable.

He nodded. "More than you could ever imagine. I mean, like, probably on the brink of being porn."

She smiled again, and the sight slammed into his gut like a hammer. He did enjoy her smile.

"But that's not all," he said by way of follow-up to his admission of thinking salacious thoughts about her.

"Well, good. Tell me how else you think about me, Roark." She eased closer to him then, and he wanted to scream hallelujah. Her other hand came up to touch his face as well.

"I think about the sound of your voice and the way you smell. It's always like flowers. I don't know what brand of beauty products you use, but I'm ready to invest in their stock."

"You're too funny," she said, rubbing her thumbs along his cheek. "It's a black-owned brand I found in Target."

He nodded. "See, if I invest, it'll be available worldwide. Just give me the name, and I'll take care of the rest."

She continued to smile and to touch him. "I really like being with you, Roark."

He reached out then, putting his hands on her hips, and lifted her off the bench to straddle her on his lap. "That's good, because I like being with you too."

Now her hands were behind his neck, cupping the back of his head. "I think we've been therapeutic to each other during our short time together."

He let his hands run up and down her back, discovering she wore a two-piece and trying desperately not to moan like a horny teenager. "This short time has seemed like months to me," he admitted just as his fingers moved up to find the bow her halter straps were tied into and dismantle it.

The material fell from her neck slowly. She lifted her arms slightly, and it eased down further until he could see her big, dark nipples. The sight made his dick jump. He would've had to be dead for it not to, and she undulated her hips over him.

"Yeah," she said, her voice growing just a little huskier. "I feel like it's been longer too."

Roark found the other tie at her back and eased the top off her completely. "It feels like I've known you all my life but that I've just discovered how much more I want to know about you. If that makes sense."

She pulled her bottom lip between her teeth and sighed when he cupped her breasts. "Yeah, it makes perfect sense," she whispered.

He held the heavy globes in his hands, loving the weight of them, the sight of her nipples puckering at his touch, the way she tilted back to give him full access of her each and every time. "This makes sense. This moment right here, when I can look at you and touch you and think about nothing and nobody else but you." Because that was exactly what Roark was doing at this moment.

He stared down at his hands on her breasts and how natural and alluring they looked on her. When she arched into his touch, offering and waiting for him to take, he did.

Dipping his head, he brought a breast up to meet his open mouth and sucked. Closing his eyes to the burst of pleasure, he gorged on the feel of that taut nipple gliding against his tongue and the hunger inside him blossom to epic proportions.

She moved over him, pumping against his hard dick as if they both weren't wearing bottoms keeping them from going further. He loved that bit of friction; even if it wasn't penetration, her pussy was hot up against his dick. And no, it wasn't the water—it was all her.

He moved to the other breast, never wanting to slight one, and she continued to palm the back of his head. Not necessarily guiding him, but holding him in place as if she never wanted this to end.

Never was a mighty long time.

But he could definitely get on board with how good this was and how much it made him realize he'd been missing.

With a quick move, he released her breasts and eased her off him. She didn't hesitate but immediately stood in the center of the pool and removed the bottom of her bathing suit. He watched her sling the wet material to land somewhere outside of the pool and rushed to do the same with his boxers. Walking to her, Roark bent slightly at the knee and wrapped his arms around her waist, lifting her up into his arms.

She made a little sound of surprise before wrapping and locking her ankles at the base of his back. He took a few steps and was at the bench again. This time when he sat, he guided his dick into her waiting pussy, and they both sighed with pleasure.

"I think about this too much," she said as she lifted her hips and settled down over him once and then twice. "It makes me feel so wanton, like a sex-crazed teenager."

He pumped into her, cupping her ass cheeks in his hands. "Me too. It's so weird and yet so fucking good."

Her hands were planted on his shoulders, blunt-tipped nails digging into his skin. "Definitely good," she said and then moaned. "Very definitely good."

Roark gritted his teeth as he moved inside her, and she rode him with matched vigor. For endless moments, neither of them spoke, just enjoyed the in-and-out pull toward ecstasy.

He moaned abruptly. "All the time. Think about you all the damn time."

"Same," she said, her voice a breathy whisper. "Same. Same. Same."

"Can't stop, and I don't know if I want to." That was true for his thoughts and for the deep strokes he was taking inside her, although he was positive he didn't want to stop pumping.

She shook her head. "No answers. Don't stop. Please, for the love of everything, don't stop."

And he didn't, at least not for long. He stood them up again, this time easing his dick out of her slowly and letting her wet body slide down the length of his. Taking her face in his hands then, Roark kissed her. He dipped his tongue deep into her mouth and stroked it along hers, drenching himself in her taste. She grabbed his biceps, holding them tight as she tilted her head to accept his kiss and offer even more access.

Out of breath and aroused beyond measure, Roark finally tore his mouth away from hers, but for another few seconds he simply stared down at her. She blinked, but stared up at him too. Her eyes weren't quite hazel, but they weren't as dark as his either, and tonight he thought he could see something sparkle in them. Her lips were swollen now after his hungry kiss, parted slightly so he just caught a glimpse of her straight white teeth.

"I could look at you forever." He had no idea where that admission came from. It didn't accurately depict how much he wanted to be inside her again, and yet it seemed true from some far-away place inside him. "You make me feel..." he continued and then stopped to shake his head. "You just make me feel."

She leaned in, resting her forehead against his chest, but didn't speak. After a few seconds, Roark walked them back until she was against the edge of the pool. He dropped another kiss on her lips before turning her away from him and kissing down her spine. He cupped her ass, groaned at how good it felt in his hands and eased her cheeks apart so he could slide his dick into her pussy again.

Tamika gripped the lip of the tub and leaned forward

until he had to take a step back. He held her hips and just stood, buried deep inside her for endless moments, loving how tightly her pussy grabbed his dick every time, as if it'd waited specifically for him. That thought spurred him on, and Roark began to move, at first pumping slowly, but then picking up the pace.

She pumped back, twirling her ass on his dick and then popping her hips so he felt like her pussy would strangle him with how good it felt. He looked down and watched her ass jiggle, and his mouth watered. In the next seconds, he did something he'd never done before, lifted a hand and smacked her ass cheek. It wasn't a hard smack, but the sound echoed over the rumble of the bubbles, and when she moaned, he did that shit again and again. One hand to one cheek, the other hand to the other cheek. In between, her ass moved and he pumped. She arched her back, and he thought he'd explode at that very moment, but Tamika had more to give him, and Roark was there for the taking.

Until there was nothing left for either of them but bliss. She moaned his name, repeating it as his body tensed. "Roark. Roark. Roark."

"Yes. Yes. Yes," he replied as he stiffened behind her and closed his eyes to the intense sensations rippling through him. "Yes, my sweetness. Fuckin' yes!"

Seconds seemed like years as they stood in that water trying to catch their breath. Roark was afraid to move, afraid something inside him might break once they were separated. That feeling bothered him enough that he pulled away and immediately stepped out of the hot tub.

He extended his hands to her, helped her out and when they stood holding hands, he leaned in to kiss her forehead and then her cheek. "I'm sorry."

She shook her head. "For what?"

"For not protecting you." He felt like an ass now for not stopping to think about the condom.

"I'm on birth control," she said, and Roark's mind immediately reverted to their discussion about children. When he didn't speak, she sighed. "It's my fault too. So let's leave the apologies." She eased out of his grasp then and went in search of her bathing suit. Roark found his clothes. He held the wet boxers in his hand after slipping on his pants, shirt and shoes. "You think anybody's still up? I'd love a slice of that rum cake Dorianne made."

Her tone sounded light and when Roark turned, it was to see that she'd put on a robe that came to her knees and flip-flops.

"Probably not. Suri was going over to the manor to see what type of nightly entertainment they had. One of the guards went with her, and he'll bring her back. The others are probably in their rooms for the night."

"I sure hope so," she said and led the way to the door.

Roark followed her, thinking about the things he'd said when inside her and how true they all were. He hadn't come here to get involved with a woman and yet, that was exactly what he'd done.

Now, he had to figure out what he was going to do about that.

CHAPTER 18

It was Sunday morning, and Tamika was dressed for church. It had been years since she'd attended a church service, and she'd never attended one in England.

Standing in front of the floor-length mirror in her room, she surveyed the outfit she'd selected again. She adjusted the waist of the chocolate-brown pleated skirt she'd decided to wear and then tugged on the navy-blue jacket she'd put on over a white top.

"Dressy, but not too dressy. Every body part covered, except my toes, which will need a pedicure pretty soon." She turned one way and looked at her reflection and then another to see the same reflection.

"The shoes are really cute."

Tamika spun around to see Lily walking further into her room. She hadn't heard the woman enter, but she knew her door was open, because her mother had been in here to hurry her along about ten minutes ago. "Thank you, and yes, I agree," Tamika said, extending one foot so she could look down at the strappy brown sandals that had come with the shipment of things from CKDavis Designs. "Oh, and thanks again for recommending the design website. There are some great things on there for plus-size women. You don't see that often."

Lily stood closer to her now. She'd pulled her hair up today, twisting it into a stylish knot that sat at her nape. She was a pretty woman with an American accent, and Tamika wondered if being an assistant concierge was her dream job. It seemed like such an out-of-the-ordinary thought, so she didn't say anything. "I love the clothes there, although I can't afford any." Lily lifted one of Tamika's curls and continued to smile at her.

"Is it too much?" she asked and then looked at her hair in the mirror. "I wanted to do something other than wear it straight or in a ponytail. That's all I've done to it since I've been here. I mean, I am going to church with Roark's family for the first time."

"Yes, it's fine. And I completely understand your being worried about a family outing such as this, but believe me, everything is going to be just fine." Lily's smile was reassuring.

"You're always so helpful," Tamika told her. "And I don't think it's all your job, either."

She shrugged. "I like what I do, so I try to do it well. Anyway, I came up to tell you Roark wanted to see you before everyone got into the cars to leave."

"Oh, okay. I'm ready." Tamika finally moved away from the mirror. She walked over to the chair where she'd put the brown leather purse she'd dumped all her stuff into earlier this morning and picked it up. At the door, she took a deep breath and released it slowly. "I can do this."

Lily chuckled and touched her shoulder, giving her a little nudge out the door. "Of course, you can."

Downstairs, Roark was talking to Jack and two other guards in the foyer. He looked devilishly handsome in a navy-blue suit, light-blue shirt and pink tie. "Good morning," he said when he turned to see her standing just a few feet away from him.

"Mornin'. You look really good in that suit, Mr. Donovan."

He grinned. "You look even better in that skirt, Ms. Rayder."

She picked up the sides of her skirt and did a frilly little turn. "Why thank you, kind sir."

When her gaze rested on him, Tamika admitted she'd never felt as happy and excited in her life. Right now, there was nothing better than standing here being stared at and complimented with obvious appreciation and adoration. It felt good, and she wanted to revel in it forever. In addition to that feeling, there was something else she'd been pushing aside for the past two days since Roark's sister and aunt had arrived. Despite the circumstances, a comfortable feeling had settled over her. Knowing that her mother was safe and healthy just a couple of doors down from her, seeing Tuppence healing and thriving as she enjoyed the gardens, and sitting in the kitchen talking with Dorianne was great. Even listening to Aunt Birdie tell stories about the Donovan Seniors and her brothers before them after dinner each night was enlightening and entertaining. Not to mention the fact that she'd felt like she'd known Roark forever, like they'd been a couple for...a very long time.

"You're going to ride with me," Roark was saying when she snapped herself out of those thoughts. "Suri's going to ride with Aunt Birdie, and your mother and Tuppence will be in the middle truck."

"Trucks? We're not taking limos this time?" Her question was meant as a joke, but Roark answered seriously.

"These are specially equipped tactical vehicles made to look like any other truck on the road. There'll be three guards in the truck with your mother, two in every other vehicle. Once we get to the church, the guards will hang back a bit, but we'll have half a dozen positioned inside the sanctuary and half a dozen outside."

And this right here brought her soundly back to reality. This wasn't a family vacation on the English countryside. It was a dire situation where her mother's life was in danger. "I thought about this all last night, wondering if it was a smart move to let her go to church," she said and then sighed. "But she doesn't want to act like a victim, and I can't blame her. Hiding from a problem has never been my mom's thing, and I get that from her. I like to face my issues head-on."

Roark moved closer to her then, touching her shoulders. "None of us are going to hide from this bastard. We're going to be prepared for him, and we're going to win."

"Watch your mouth, Roark. It's a good thing you're going to the house of the Lord this morning. I'll say a few extra prayers for you." Aunt Birdie walked past them wearing a lavish church hat in royal purple.

Roark never looked away from Tamika. "Good morning, Aunt Birdie."

"Let's get moving—we don't want to be late," was his aunt's reply as she headed for the door.

A few seconds passed, and Tamika grinned. "We'd better get going before she yells for the guards to pick us up and dump us into the vehicles."

"Yeah, you're right," Roark said, laughing. He extended his elbow, and Tamika laced her arm through it before they took the first step toward the door.

Detectives Gibbons and Pennington walked in before they could exit. Gibbons held up a piece of paper. "Search warrant."

That was it—no good morning, no nothing, just back to business.

Roark reached for the document and opened it. While he read, Geoff and Lily appeared.

"Is everything alright, sir?" Geoff asked.

"Yes." Roark's response was terse. "These detectives have a warrant to search the clubhouse."

"Why?" Tamika asked.

Roark refolded the paper and looked at Gibbons. "Because now they think I planted that bomb at Suri's flat."

"I'll stay here to make sure nothing's disturbed, sir," Geoff said immediately.

"And I'll have a guard come into the house as well." Roark handed the warrant to Geoff. "I'm going to call Burrows from the truck."

"Where will you be in case we need to contact you?" Pennington asked.

Roark smirked. "You're the detectives—if you want me, you'll find me."

"They won't find anything," Tamika said ten minutes later when they were seated in the backseat of the truck and on their way to church.

"I know," he replied and continued staring out the window.

The countryside whizzed by, hills and small houses, wooden fences that held back healthy growing gardens, creeks that broke through the landscape. During the time he'd been on the phone with his attorney, she'd stared out the window, wondering how so much chaos could be happening in such a gorgeous place. "It's their job to be thorough, and when they don't find anything, this will further clear your name."

"Whose side are you on?"

"Yours. Always. But I know how it feels to have a job to do, to have to ask the hard questions. I've had family members sic their dogs on me when I showed up to ask them questions. Businesses have banned me from entering their buildings, and I've been cursed out by more than one firefighter who didn't agree when I found something in my investigation that said they'd been negligent on the job."

"But I bet you weren't an asshole about any of that. You weren't rude or disrespectful in any way."

"Um, maybe not all those things all the time, but there were situations where I had to clap back at a few people. That wasn't because I disliked any of them or held a personal grudge, it was just because I had to stand my ground."

"Yes, I understand," she continued. "Gibbons has an ax to grind. He doesn't like rich people."

"Huh. Well, there're a lot of people suffering from that affliction."

"Not you." She looked at him then, saw the sincerity and question in his gaze. "No, not me. I mean, to be honest, you're the first rich person I've known personally. I've had occasion to deal with a few businessmen who were clients of the insurance company, but that was just business."

"Did you judge me by my portfolio before you met me?"

That was a heavy question considering, she had done her research and she'd known just how much Roark Donovan was worth—the man, not the companies he ran. That only added more. But at no point had she considered how that would affect the answers she'd sought. "I didn't plan to become personally involved with you, so there was no need to make any judgments. But if you're talking about now, I can tell you I've never known a family as loyal and dedicated to each other, and your family seems to be. That's why you'll get over people like Gibbons and all the others who think they know you, but really don't."

He reached across the seat to take her hand. "You're good for me. Really good."

They were pulling up along the side of the church now so Tamika didn't have to reply, or rather she took that as a cop-out to replying, because she didn't know how to explain the way Roark's words had made her feel.

Minutes later, they were out of the truck and being seated on a row that'd been reserved for them. Tamika wasn't even surprised the Donovans had called ahead to the church to let them know they'd be coming. It was actually a pretty preemptive move, since they had to have security there as well. She was still thinking about Roark's words and the comfortable feeling she'd noted before the police had shown up at the clubhouse when the choir stood up to sing. On one side of her, Sandra clapped and sang along, and Tamika was instantly taken back to her days as a little girl in church. She remembered the music, the lyrics and felt an entirely different meaning to them now. It was a surreal moment, but she found herself enjoying it throughout the service. She'd also stopped thinking about Kaymen Benedict, mysterious letters, arson and what was going on between her and Roark.

That was until she felt him move beside her. When she looked over at him, she watched him reach into the inside pocket of his jacket and pull out his phone. The screen lit up, and he swiped it to pull up a text message. Tamika looked away then. She refocused on the pastor's sermon and what, if anything, she could take from it that might help her in life this coming week.

~

There's something I need to tell you that I should've told you before. Please call me back, or at least answer when I call.

Roark stared down at the phone screen, reading Katrina's message for the third time.

What the hell was she talking about? There was absolutely nothing else they needed to say to each other. The divorce papers she'd served him four years ago had said it all. She wasn't happy with him, and she'd wanted to leave. He hadn't known what to say at the time, and so he'd said nothing. And frankly, he hadn't felt overly bad about that decision. He stuffed the phone back into his pocket and turned his attention back to the service. Katrina was the last person he planned to deal with today.

The first, when he returned to the clubhouse, would be Detective Gibbons and the ridiculous warrant he'd pursued even after his commanding officer had informed him about the information Pierce and Cade had found. During his call with Ed Burrows on the ride to church, he'd learned that little tidbit and had been even angrier about the search currently going on at the clubhouse.

Roark had instructed Geoff to call him the moment they were gone. That was why he'd answered the vibration of his phone, because he'd thought it was something about the search, not his ex-wife.

Tamika stood beside him, and Roark realized the service was over, so he stood too.

"Is everything alright?" she asked.

Roark nodded. "Yeah. It's fine. I think we'll go out for lunch."

"They're still at the clubhouse."

"Yeah. Let's go out and treat the family to a lovely lunch and not think about that for a while." He knew that was going to be easier said than done, but Roark had to try.

He wanted to try. These fires, the killing, it was all taking a toll on him. Every day he was away from the office, he was playing catch-up. His assistant was great and she was attempting to stay on top of things, but Roark knew it was difficult because he wasn't there.

Putting himself aside, he could see Aunt Birdie was stressed, because she was more irritable than normal. Sandra had moments where she'd cry silently, and Roark knew she was thinking about the secret she and her friends had kept and all that it had led to. Suri seemed to be dealing the best, remaining her upbeat self as she attended to not only Aunt Birdie, but the other two elderly women as well.

So yes, he wanted to treat them all to lunch, to give them a glimpse of normalcy if just for a little while.

Two hours later, after they'd returned to the clubhouse, Roark was in the library checking, as he'd already done with each room in the house, to make sure the police hadn't left anything out of place. Of course, they hadn't found anything to prove he was involved with the fires or the explosion, and Burrows had contacted the chief of the department at the MPD to let him know the detectives' behavior was dangerously close to harassment, which would not be tolerated in the future.

Roark hadn't found anything out of place yet, but he was certain that was because Geoff, Lily and Dorianne had been here and had probably put everything back in place before their return. As far as staff went, those three were the best, and once this was over and they were ready to leave, Roark would have to think of a way to repay them for how helpful and attentive they'd each been in the past weeks.

"You're sleeping with that girl."

He turned at the sound of Aunt Birdie's voice and fought back a frown when he saw her entering the library and going over to take a seat on one of the burgundy leather couches in the center of the room. "Excuse me?"

"Don't try to lie to me. I can tell when two people are having sex. It's in the way you talk to each other and touch each other. Plus, she was in your room in the middle of the night when I arrived." Aunt Birdie waved her hand as she settled back on the couch and then heaved a deep breath.

Roark wanted to be more irritated by her waltzing in here saying these things, but he didn't miss the fact that she'd been looking even more tired lately. "Aunt Birdie, I'm an adult. I think it's okay for me to have sex with a woman." He tried to go back to what he was doing, looking along the bookshelves and on the desk in the corner.

"You're a Donovan man, so you're virile enough. But that doesn't mean I don't have something to say about it." She slapped a hand down on the arm of the chair to get his attention.

"With all due respect——" he began.

"Oh please, don't give me that crap. Anytime somebody says that, it means they're getting ready to disrespect you. And you'd better not even try it. Besides, I'd still keep going until I said what I had to say."

Roark clapped his lips shut, because every word of what she'd just said was correct. It was better and would probably go quicker if he just listened to what she had to say and got it over with.

"Now, she's a nice enough girl. Takes care of her mother, which is always a good thing. Even though I still don't understand why she let that poor woman come all the way over here and live by herself for a year."

"She wasn't actually by herself. Tuppence was with her," he interjected.

"Please, that woman's a little off."

Roark held back a chuckle, because he was almost certain people had said that about Aunt Birdie a time or two.

"But like I said, Tamika's a good enough girl. She's not like Katrina."

For the second time today Roark's mind reluctantly went to his ex-wife. "Katrina and I have been over for a long time, Aunt Birdie."

"And thank the good Lord for that. She wasn't right for you. Maxine and I talked about that. It was one of the few things she and I agreed on. But that's not what I came in here to talk to you about."

Roark walked over to the couch and took a seat beside her.

"I want to know your intentions toward her," Aunt Birdie said simply. "Are you going to just keep sleeping with her, or do you plan to marry this girl?"

"Whoa, Aunt Birdie, slow down. I just got a divorce."

"You also just reminded me that was a long time ago. Don't dilly-dally with me, Roark. Tell me what you have planned."

He'd never answered to anyone before regarding his personal relationships, and Roark didn't plan to now. He also didn't plan to disrespect his aunt for fear she'd carry through on whatever unspoken threat she'd mentioned just a few moments ago. "Tamika and I are just— We're getting to know each other," he said and then swallowed because he hated that he was having this conversation with her.

"In a biblical way," his aunt continued. Of course, this morning's church service was the culprit.

"Yes, ma'am. We're both consenting adults, and we're okay with the status of our relation...I mean, friendship." To his own ears, that word sounded incorrect for what was actually going on between them, but Aunt Birdie didn't need to know he was feeling that way.

"Women aren't to be toyed with, Roark. I've had this conversation with Ridge more times than I can count, but he's as stubborn as a mule, just like my daddy was. Anyway, I always thought you were the smarter, more reasonable of Gabe's boys." There was a compliment in there somewhere, Roark was certain. "If this isn't going to go past the sex stage, you should stop it now."

"Even if she's in agreement?"

"No woman is ever going to agree to be just a sex partner for long. It'll always change. Feelings will grow, expectations will be set and you'll be caught if you're not careful. You've been sleeping with her all during this dilemma, but when it's over, what happens? How do you think she's going to react to being nothing better than your mistress at that point?"

"I wouldn't ever call her a mistress."

"But you'll treat her like one."

"I'm not treating her like a mistress." Hadn't they gone out in public? Well, not on a real date, but this is a different scenario. He'd like to think that if he'd met her on the street, he would've asked her out on a proper date before they'd begun sleeping together.

"Not yet. But mark my words, all of this is going to change."

"My first concern right now is for Sandra's safety, Aunt

Birdie. I want this killer to be caught so we all can get back to some semblance of normalcy. I can finish grieving for my mother, and Tamika can continue grieving for her father. Then we can both move on."

She pointed a finger, pressing it into his arm. "And you'll move on together or apart? That's the question I'm asking you. It's what you need to think long and hard about before the time comes, or mark my words, they'll be confusion and hurt feelings and another big mess you didn't anticipate. Trust me," she said. "I'm an old woman but I've been a mistress before. I know how things can change in the blink of an eye."

Roark didn't know how to respond to her last words. He didn't want to know about his aunt's previous lovers or any who'd broken her heart for fear he might have to hunt down some old guy and beat his ass. No, Roark only wanted Kaymen Benedict to be caught, finally, and for everyone to be safe again. That was all he wanted, or at least that was all he was going to let himself acknowledge that he wanted.

CHAPTER 19

*R*oark awoke with a start. His eyes opened but he didn't move. He was laying on his side so he could see the lighted numbers from the alarm clock on the nightstand. It was two a.m.

He sighed, because for the past nights Tamika had been in his bed, Roark had been sleeping soundly through the night. He'd even dreamed of a calmer, happier time in his sleep. But tonight, he was up.

After a few seconds of going over that fact, he rolled over and reached for her. She was there, and he loved the feel of her softness pressing eagerly against him. Not in a sexual way —of course, that didn't mean he didn't thoroughly enjoy having sex with her—but what he was feeling right now was a heavy dose of comfort.

Roark wrapped his arm tighter around her, snuggling his face into her neck where he inhaled her scent.

He paused and inhaled again, deeper this time.

Roark sat straight up in the bed. It wasn't flowers he smelled.

Tamika sat up right behind him. "Smoke," she whispered, and in the next seconds they were both leaping out of the bed.

Roark paused long enough to slip on shoes; he was bare-chested and wore only basketball shorts, but that would have to be enough. Tamika wore a nightgown and she pushed her feet into her slippers too, but they both made it to the door at the same time.

"Touch it first," she said. "See if it's hot. The door and the handle."

Roark did as she instructed, pressing his palm to the center of the door at the top, then bending down to do the same at the bottom. There was no heat. He stood and reached slowly for the doorknob—again, no heat. In the next second, he yanked the door open and stepped through with Tamika right behind him.

They both looked up and down the hall but didn't see any evidence of smoke. They only smelled it.

"We need to check each room before going downstairs," she told him.

"And call for the guards," he said as an afterthought and then cursed when he ran back to his room to grab his phone off the nightstand. Sure, the phone wouldn't save anyone from a fire, but Roark was acutely aware they weren't just dealing with a fire.

He dialed Jack's number and waited for him to pick up, but after five rings, Roark disconnected. By then, he was at the door to Tuppence's room, because it was the first room next to his. Tamika was already in there waking Tuppence and telling her to get her slippers and robe on.

"There's no fire or smoke in here," Tamika came to him saying.

He nodded, and they both headed to the next room. Sandra's.

Tamika checked the door this time and then hurriedly pushed inside. She flicked on lights as she moved, and Roark looked around the room, his heart sinking as he did.

"She's probably in the bathroom," Tamika said. "She goes a lot at night." She walked toward the closed bathroom door.

As she checked it, Roark knew what she'd find. He reached for his phone again this time dialing Cade.

Tamika came running out of the bathroom, eyes wide, voice cracking as she said, "She's not in here."

Roark went to her then, wrapping an arm around her and hurriedly leading her out of the room as he waited for Cade to pick up. Tuppence was already in the hallway when Cade answered.

"Sandra's gone," Roark told him. "She's gone, and we smell smoke in the house. I'm gonna get everyone out."

"What? We're sitting right outside and we don't see anything," Cade replied.

"Well, she's gone, Cade! She's gone!"

Roark and Tamika walked Tuppence down the steps gently, only to stop the minute they saw the smoke coming from the parlor.

"Why aren't the smoke alarms going off?" Roark asked. "What the hell is wrong with the alarms?" There was a security system connected to the smoke alarms, but nothing was going off, even though something was clearly burning in the house. "Take her back upstairs. I have to get Suri and Aunt Birdie." He was talking to Tamika, who looked at him as if she were getting ready to tell him it was too dangerous to go downstairs. He wasn't going to accept that if she did. "Or just stay right here, and I'll give you a signal if it's clear for you to get her to the doorway."

Roark didn't wait for another reaction from her or a response. He ran down the stairs, using his arm to cover his mouth and nose so he wouldn't inhale too much smoke. There was only a dim glow from the two wall sconces in the foyer, which was how they'd seen the smoke. Other than that, no lights were on down here. It didn't matter—he knew where he was going.

Roark ran past the parlor and the formal living room. He turned down the hallway that led to the bedrooms facing the back of the house. But before he could get to the first one, there was a blast, and a door flew off its hinges. Flames quickly followed blocking his progress. Roark reared back so fast he stumbled and landed on his ass, heat from the flames causing his skin to sweat instantly.

"Fuck!" he yelled. He had to get to Suri and Aunt Birdie. He wasn't going to leave them in here.

There were noises all around now. He thought the front door may have been kicked in or there was more thumping. Smoke was definitely thicker now, and he choked after inhaling quite a bit of it.

"Suri!" he yelled. "Suri!"

Maybe if she heard him, she could at least find Aunt Birdie and lead her out the window or something. There was nothing on this side of the house but bedrooms. Down the opposite hallway was the pool area and the exit to the back veranda.

"Suri! Suri!"

Nothing. All Roark heard was thumping. All he smelled was smoke and just ahead of him, all he could see were the glowing flames licking against the walls and everything else they touched as they traveled. He had to get up, and find them some help. He stood and ran back the way he'd come, but there was even more smoke in that direction now.

Tamika had waited long enough. She had Tuppence remove her robe and nightgown. Then she put the robe back on and zipped it up to her neck. She used the nightgown to wrap around the bottom half of Tuppence's face, protecting her from the smoke.

"We're gonna walk now," she instructed her. "We'll take it slow, one step at a time, but we need to get downstairs and out the front door." Because there was no way Tuppence could jump out of a window. It wasn't Tamika's best idea either, but she would've done it if she had to. What she wasn't going to do was leave Tuppence.

They made their way slowly down the curving staircase until she knew they were on the ground floor because it was covered with smoke. The front door was open, and security guys were filing in.

"Over here! We're here! Get her out!" she yelled.

A guard ran over and lifted Tuppence into his arms. Tamika watched them go toward the door when out of the corner of her eye she saw another guard coming her way.

"Come on, you can get out this way!" he yelled to her.

She was shaking her head, even though she wasn't sure he could see or understand her. "Not without my mother!"

"Ma'am, the Fire Brigade is on their way. We gotta get you out of here." He grabbed for Tamika's arm, but she pulled away from him and ran in the opposite direction.

"Mama! Mama, are you in here?" she screamed and ran

down the hallway until she slammed into something hard and fell back on the floor.

Roark picked her up. "You can't go back there," he was yelling. "There's too much fire. We gotta get help. Let's go out the front door and get help!"

"Not without my mother, Roark. I won't leave this house without her," she said. "The pool, did you check the pool? It doesn't look like the smoke's coming from down there."

She pushed past him and ran down the hall, only to be stopped by a strong arm around her waist. Tamika protested when he lifted her off her feet and carried her back toward the front of the house.

"We've got to get out of here!" he yelled.

She was screaming at him and trying to break free when they were both knocked back by a blast. On their hands and knees now, Roark pointed to a door. She'd pulled her nightshirt up over her face to block the smoke and followed him. Roark kicked the door in and pushed her inside before closing the door behind them.

"Welcome to the party."

They both stopped dead in their tracks when they saw him. Dressed in full firefighter regalia and holding a blowtorch in his right hand was Kaymen Benedict. And strapped to the chair in front of him was her mother.

Tamika screamed and tried to run toward her, but Roark caught her around the waist again as Kaymen lifted the blowtorch and aimed it at her.

"Don't come any closer, or I'll burn your ass too." His voice was a raspy snarl, but she didn't care. All that mattered to her now was getting her mother to safety.

"He's not gonna kill her in front of us."

She heard Roark talking from behind her, but her heart was beating so fast every part of her body was shaking. Why was he talking to him? What did he think that was going to do? The man was obviously a lunatic.

"I don't give a damn about any of you, just her. She's the last one. You were last that night too, weren't you, Sandra? You'd been sitting right next to me, and I felt when your body eased away from mine. You never touched me, never checked to see if I was still breathing." Kaymen moved closer to her mother, putting the torch beside her right ear as he spoke.

Tamika tried to calm herself as Roark spoke. "Why didn't you call out to them? Why didn't you tell them you were alive, Kaymen?"

Okay, he was going to try distracting the psychotic killer. She guessed there were worst things to do, but again she focused on her own breathing. There was gasoline in here. It was all over the place—on the floors, the furniture, probably even the walls. That meant he was planning to burn the place down. The question now was how did he think he was going to get out in time if he'd already started fires in other areas of the house?

She didn't have time to figure that out.

"We thought you were with us," Sandra said, her voice barely a creak amid the sound of the torch.

"Stop lying!" Kaymen shouted into her face. "Stop sitting there telling those lies when you knew I wasn't with you. Not one time during that three-mile walk to the motel did any of you see me and wonder where I was. Or did you just not care?"

Kaymen really didn't seem to care that Tamika and Roark were there, because when Roark heard footsteps, he eased back to the door and opened it so whoever was outside would know they were there. Tamika took those moments to move closer, walking to the other side of the room, opposite of where Kaymen was still yelling at her mother.

"Kaymen, I'm so sorry. If we'd known...if I'd known you weren't with us at first, I would've said something. And when we wanted to go back...we just couldn't," Sandra said.

"Why? Because they told you to leave me, didn't they? Tony and Gabe, they told you to leave the poor no-class Kaymen behind. They never liked me, never accepted me, because I didn't bend down to lick their rich-ass boots."

Sandra was shaking her head now. Her arms and hands were taped to the arms of the chair, her ankles likewise taped to the legs of the chair. "Nobody cared about money, Kaymen. You know that. None of us cared which one of us had what."

"Oh, you cared! All of you cared! That's why Ronnie kept sleeping with Tony. Even until they took their last breath, she was still sleeping with him and not giving a damn about me. You all forgot about me!"

"Kaymen, I need you to step back and put the blowtorch down."

Tamika heard Cade's familiar voice, but she didn't stop moving. She was getting closer.

"Fuck you! Fuck all of you! I'm not putting nothing down, and she's not getting out of this house alive!" He fired up the flame on the blowtorch and held it close to Sandra's face again. "If you were gonna live, you'd have to live looking just like me!" With his free hand Kaymen, flipped off the helmet and hood beneath it.

Tamika paused and gasped at the sight of his completely burned face. What was left of his skin had healed over, and she could tell there'd been attempts at skin grafts, but the result hadn't been good. He looked like a creature.

"If you touch her with that, you're dead, Kaymen. I'll shoot you where you stand," Cade yelled.

Kaymen shook his head. Tamika could see as his eyes

moved and he spared Cade a glance. "You think I give a damn about dying, man? I ain't had no life since that day. There's nothing left for me here. Nothing, and it's all her fault!"

Tamika was just about to lunge toward her mother's chair when Pierce grabbed her this time and pushed her back out of the way. "Stay there!" he yelled at her.

When he pushed her, she fell back into Roark. She hadn't realized either of them had crossed the room with her.

"He's right, stay back and let them handle this," Roark said.

"They're talking, and he's gonna kill her. If I don't get to her, she'll die!"

"She's gonna die anyway. Just like the rest of them. They all deserved to die, just like they thought I did!"

The next seconds passed in a blur as Kaymen touched the torch to Sandra's cheek and gunshots rang out. The blowtorch fell to the floor, and Kaymen's body fell back. Roark left her side at that moment and she followed him, both of them going to her mother. They were ripping away the tape to free her from the chair when the first flames shot up from the floor.

Tamika shook her head as she saw it following the trail of gasoline. "We gotta go now!"

Roark pulled Sandra up from the chair and tossed her over his shoulder, while Pierce wrapped an arm around Tamika's shoulders and hurried her to the door. Cade was behind them, yelling, "Run! Run! Run!"

The next minutes were a blur as Tamika only felt herself running, her lungs burning from the smoke, and the smack of cool night air against her skin when they finally made it out of the house.

～

"How the fuck did he get in there?" Ridge bellowed.

Pierce paced the length of the waiting room and Cade sat in the chair beside Roark.

"That's the million-dollar question," Cade replied.

"It's the only question," Roark said. Damn, he didn't want to be sitting in this hospital again, and he definitely didn't want to be trying to figure out how the clubhouse had been set on fire right beneath their noses. He'd done everything Cade and Pierce had told him to do. Had hired two security teams and personal guards, leased new vehicles, and upgraded the security system throughout the entire Dynasty Manor property. Hell, he'd even had Devlin send him a trunk full of guns to use just in case he came face-to-face with Kaymen Benedict.

Well, that had happened and Roark hadn't had a gun, and Kaymen had gotten part of what he'd wanted—he'd set another fire.

"We were sitting right outside," Cade said again. He'd been repeating that since they'd arrived at the hospital. "Pierce and I were in one truck because we didn't think Kaymen was going to wait too long before striking. We hadn't been able to find him anywhere, but we knew he'd find Sandra, so we waited for him to show up. We had cops added to your security force surrounding the entire house. So how did this motherfucker get in there and have time to grab Sandra out of her room, set a fire in the parlor, one of the back storage rooms and in the sitting room where he'd held her?"

"What was he, a magician and a demented killer?" Ridge snapped. "Because I don't know any other way this could've happened. My sister and my aunt could've died in that house.

My whole fucking family was in that house!" Roark stood then and went to his brother. He clapped a hand on his shoulder until Ridge looked at him. "Suri and Aunt Birdie are gonna be fine. They're in the back being treated for smoke inhalation, and then they'll be discharged. The firefighters were able to get them out," he told him.

"What the hell is happening to us, man?" Ridge said, his voice cracking on the last word.

Roark wrapped his arms around his brother then and pulled him into a hug. If he held on a moment longer than was probably necessary, it was because a part of him was roiling with the fact that he'd almost lost his family in that house tonight too.

"Somebody had to let him in," Pierce said. "That's the only explanation."

"Nobody would've done that," Cade insisted. "And he couldn't have disguised himself enough. Every part of his face was a dead giveaway. None of the guards or anyone inside would've let in someone wearing a mask or even a long dark coat and hoodie. And they especially wouldn't have let him in at that time of night."

"But what if they let him in earlier?" Pierce asked. "What if he'd been in the house since…maybe when the police were there in the morning executing their search warrant. There were at least two dozen cops rummaging around inside and outside of the house for more than three hours. What if someone just walked on in and went unnoticed because everyone was otherwise occupied?"

"If that's how he got in, I'm gonna have the badges of every one of those disorganized cops, and then I'm gonna sue the entire department for negligence," Cade said.

Roark and Ridge were standing side-by-side now, and neither of them said anything to Cade's comment. Mainly because they were behind him one hundred percent in taking down the bastards who'd allowed this to happen.

Pierce headed toward the open doorway.

"Where are you going?" Cade asked him.

"To wake up the police chief so he can wake up his detectives and get to the bottom of this. I don't give a damn what time it is." Pierce not only looked angry, but his voice had a lethal edge to it Roark hadn't heard before. "You stay here with your family. I'll keep you posted."

Cade nodded. "Call me immediately."

"Will do," Pierce said before leaving.

The next person to appear in that doorway was Tamika, and Roark immediately went to her. "How is she?"

"In shock," she said. "He dropped the torch almost instantly after putting it to her face, so it's a second-degree burn, but Dr. Duvall thinks it'll heal nicely. Better than the ones on her arm, obviously. We're just—" Her voice cracked, and she looked up at him with a panicked expression on her face.

"Come on, let's take a walk," he said and grabbed her elbow, leading her down the hall. When they were standing near a bank of elevators, Roark stopped because he felt like she'd had time to catch her breath. "She's going to be alright," he said, wrapping his arms around her and hugging her. "She's going to be alright and this is over. Kaymen's dead."

He wanted to feel tremendous relief at saying those words, but right now all he felt was the pain of Tamika's ragged breaths and the hurt he knew she was feeling at this moment.

"My mother could've died." Her voice was so quiet as her face remained pressed against his chest. "If we hadn't gotten into that room in time, my mother would be dead. Not suffering from second-degree burns for the second time in as many weeks, but dead. For real."

"I know. I know." All he could do right now was repeat the words, because Roark did know. He'd watched Tamika about to risk her own life to save her mother's and while he'd been scared to death of what might happen to her, he knew if he'd been in her position, he would've done the same thing. "But she didn't, and you're going to be able to go back and see her and be with her, and this is going to pass, sweetness. It's going to pass."

Each time he'd fallen or hurt himself in some way when he was younger, or when he'd gotten older and someone had disappointed him or he hadn't gotten the grade he'd expected, his mother would hold him and say, "It's going to pass." So Roark said that to Tamika, believing with all that he and his mother had shared that the words were true.

Her body jerked while he held her, and in the next moment, he heard her first sob. Roark held her tighter.

"I don't cry," she said and lifted a hand to wipe her face. "I try not to cry. When my dad died, I cried a little at the hospital with my mom, but then not again. Not at the funeral when all those people were there staring at me. And not at the cemetery when my legs threatened to buckle beneath me as we left him there. I didn't cry."

But now she was sobbing. Thick, ragged breaths ripped from her, tears came and her entire body shook in his arms.

"It's okay to cry, Tamika. I cried when the paramedics came out of the house and told me Mum was dead. I cried at the funeral and then again when I was home alone. Because it hurt so much, it felt like a part of me was being ripped out of my chest."

And a tear rolled down Roark's cheek now, because he knew Tamika's pain and also because there was a part of him that hurt for each sob that broke free from her. He didn't like seeing her this way, didn't like that she had to suffer at all.

"She's gonna be okay," she said softly when the sobs stopped taking her breath away. "She's gonna be okay."

"We're gonna be okay," he told her. "We're all gonna be okay."

CHAPTER 20

One Week Later

"Aunt Birdie and Suri insisted on having this party tonight."

Tamika brushed her hands over the lapels of Roark's tuxedo jacket. "You look great in a tux."

"You look great in anything," he said and looped an arm around her waist to pull her up against him.

It'd only been a few hours since they'd escaped to his room and had sex for what felt like the billionth time this week. Whoever said relationships that started under intense circumstances didn't work out was a coward. Roark felt closer to Tamika now than he had a week ago, and he knew she was feeling the same way, because whenever she hadn't been with her mother these past seven days, she was with him.

"Stay focused," she said with a grin. "This party means a lot to your aunt. She said the Donovans need to show their resilience under extremely trying circumstances. Suri said she just liked big fancy parties. They're both pretty excited."

"Yes, they are," he agreed. Roark was excited too, but that wasn't because of the party or the beautiful woman he held in his arms. It was more about what was in his front pant pocket. "I don't want to be here long," he confessed.

She eased out of his grasp and took his hand. "Well, we should at least mingle a little, show everyone we're here. I think they invited some people from the media just to make sure there was full coverage."

"That sounds just like Aunt Birdie," Roark said as they started walking through the open glass doors at the back of the Manor.

Since the fire, they'd all relocated to the manor. Work on Sandra's cottage would be completed in a couple of days, and she and Tuppence would be leaving then. Aunt Birdie had a cruise lined up for next week, and Suri mentioned having a big budget meeting in a few days. So this was the best Saturday to have their little party.

A little party that was actually a very big party with two-hundred fifty guests.

They stepped out onto the tiled veranda, a warm evening breeze surrounding them. Above, the sky seemed full of stars, the moon shining extra bright, as if Aunt Birdie had dared them each not to show up. Roark chuckled at his thoughts and continued to look around at all the people moving about. The party stretched from the large veranda down the stairs and into the garden area of the manor.

White tables and chairs had been set up with dainty pink-and-white striped linens. Flowers were everywhere, from the center of each table to along the trellises lining the walkway, and in huge terracotta pots placed strategically throughout the veranda. His mother would've been pleased.

Roark could think about Maxine now without his chest

constricting with pain, because he knew why she'd died and at whose hand. The knowledge didn't make him forgive Kaymen Benedict, but it had given him the closure he needed.

"Hey, man. You clean up well." Ridge was back to his joking self and by the looks of the beautiful woman on his arm, his dating life was also in full swing.

"You don't look bad yourself," Roark said as he noted his brother's tuxedo was almost identical to his.

"Tamika, my dear, you look lovely as always." Ridge released his date long enough to reach for Tamika's hand and lift it to his lips for a quick kiss.

"You're so full of it, Ridge. But thanks, you look really good too," she said.

Ridge chuckled as he released her hand. "This is Yolanda."

The woman with the striking light-brown eyes and high cheekbones smiled and extended her hand to Tamika first and then Roark. They talked for a few minutes, but Roark was glad when they walked away.

"She's stunning," Tamika said when they were gone. "Did you see her dress? And her hair? She looks like a supermodel."

"Yeah, that's usually Ridge's type."

"Oh, really? So, you Donovan guys have a type?"

"No," he said with a shake of his head. "I definitely do not have a type."

"Yeah, right," she said, and Roark sighed with relief as Cade and his date walked up.

"Saved by the cousin," he mumbled under his breath, and she elbowed him playfully.

"Hey man, don't you two look lovely tonight." Cade

leaned in to drop a kiss on Tamika's cheek. Roark hadn't asked his cousin why or how he was still able to be here when his official job was in the US, but he planned to. "This is Miranda." Cade introduced his date, and Roark and Tamika went through the formalities again.

"You should go over and see Aunt Birdie," Roark told Cade when he mentioned he and Miranda weren't going to be there long. Most likely because Cade had other plans for the lovely woman that didn't include partying with two hundred fifty people.

Cade shook his head. "Uh, no, I think I'll pass on that one. Besides, I have one final briefing with the police tomorrow morning that I need to be up early for, so I think I'm going to skip out."

"Still no answers on how he got in?" Tamika asked him.

"Nah. The detectives had a log during the search, and everybody who entered and exited the house signed it. Even the guards vouched for the fact that they were at the only door the cops were allowed to enter or leave through, and they made sure everyone was signing that log."

"Guess we'll never know," she said, her tone softer than it'd been before.

Roark moved closer, putting his arm around her waist. "Let's not talk about this tonight. For weeks, this is all we've talked about. Let's just have one night without it."

Miranda smiled when Cade took her hand. "That's fine by me. Let's go hit up the bar."

When they were gone, Tamika said, "Oh, there's Suri, and she's with a date. Do you know who he is?"

Roark followed Tamika's gaze and saw his sister sitting at a table as a man approached her. She looked surprised and then happy to see him, so Roark tamped down on the overprotective-brother routine about to rear its head. "No, I don't, and I'm not really up to meeting anyone else at the moment."

"Oh, okay. Do you wanna go over to the bar to get a drink? Or do you want to sit and eat first?"

"Actually, I'd rather talk to you about something." Because he couldn't wait a moment longer.

"Roark, we've been together all day. What could you possibly want to talk to me about right now that can't wait until later tonight?"

He stared at her for a few moments. Backtracking? Chickening out? Of course not; that wasn't how Roark rolled. "Just come with me and you'll find out."

With a hand to the small of her back, Roark led her down the steps, but instead of going straight to where everyone was mingling, he turned to the left and walked until they were closer to the stone benches and statues that lined the outside of the garden.

"Have a seat," he said.

When she did, he sat beside her. Then he stood again, reached into his pocket and pulled out what was inside, keeping it tightly closed in his hand so she wouldn't see it. He sat down again and looked at her.

"I've been thinking about this a lot this past week." That wasn't the way he'd planned to start this.

"Thinking about what?" Was that worry he heard in her voice?

Roark cleared his throat. "I enjoy being with you. A lot. I mean, a whole lot."

She laughed nervously. "Okay, I get that."

"And I know you're not working right now and your mother's recuperating, so you'll probably want to be close to her. I want to propose—"

"Wait, what?" She jumped up from the bench. "You're

proposing? To me? Now?"

Roark jumped up too. "No!" The word burst out before he could stop it. "I mean, not in the way you think. I was just going to propose that you stay here. Or rather, in London, with me. It's only an hour and a half drive to Painswick. We could visit with your mum every weekend." He paused and then extended his hand. "I rented you a flat."

She looked down at the key in his hand and then lifted her head up slowly so she could stare at him again. "You rented me a flat so I can stay in London. With you." Her tone wasn't what he'd expected it to be. In fact, it was concerning.

"I don't want what we have to end."

"What do we have, Roark? Are we dating? Because I thought we'd agreed to just sex."

And he'd believed when his aunt had told him women couldn't accept just sex for too long. "I thought we were past that," he admitted. "I know I am."

She nodded and folded her arms over her chest. "You're past just sex. What's after that?"

He'd been asking himself that question all week and as of the moment he'd been getting dressed and had slipped the key to the flat into his pocket, he hadn't come up with an answer. But standing here tonight, with the summer breeze surrounding them and her looking absolutely beautiful in the floor-length emerald-green dress, he knew without a doubt how he felt. "I'm falling in love with you." The admission came and then sat between them like a massive boulder.

She smiled. "Oh, Roark. You have know idea how hard I've fought against this. How with each time you touched me, I wanted to run away and hide, because there was just no way this could work."

"What are you talking about? It can work. All you have to do is say yes."

"Say yes to what? An apartment today. A marriage proposal a year later. And then what? Do we end up like you and Katrina did?"

"That's not fair."

"No," she said, shaking her head. "None of this is fair. I wasn't supposed to like you when we met, let alone be attracted to you. And I damn sure wasn't supposed to fall in love with you in, of all places, Painswick, while we were ensconced in a hunt for a killer." She gave a nervous chuckle. "Do you even realize how preposterous this all sounds? It's almost unfathomable that we would've met, fell in love, caught a killer and lived happily ever after. Nobody does that, Roark. Least of all people like me."

"People like you?"

"Not-rich people," she clarified.

Roark closed his palm and put the key back into his pocket. "So now I'm rich people. I thought you weren't judging me by my portfolio."

"I'm not. I'm judging *us* by my lack of a portfolio. Listen, I don't ever want to feel uneven in a relationship again, and right now that's what I am. I'm unemployed, and you want to put me up in an apartment and pay all my bills so I'll be close for us to go on dates, have sex and what else?"

"Continue to fall in love with each other. You forgot that part."

She was shaking her head now. "No. What I'd be forgetting is myself. Sure, it sounds great: this rich guy is offering to take care of me, so I should hop on that and live the fabulous life. But that's not who I am. It's not what I want for myself. And Roark, before I can love you completely, I have to love me. I have to do what's best for me right now. I hope you can understand that." She hadn't given him a chance to understand, because she walked away, leaving him standing there feeling like a colossal idiot.

"Well, that didn't end well."

Roark knew the voice and he wished like hell he were the one who'd walked away from this spot. "What are you doing here, Katrina?"

"Can't I visit my ex-husband? I mean, I didn't get an invitation to the party, but I'm going to assume that was a mistake." She walked around until she was standing directly in front of him dressed in a white pantsuit.

"You weren't invited because my aunt didn't invite you."

Her lips pursed at his response, and Roark noted she hadn't changed much in four years. She was still just a couple of inches shorter than him when wearing heels, her dark eyes still narrowed when she was annoyed and her tone was still cool and aloof. "You really need to check your staff. All I had to do was ask where you were and they told me." She sighed. "Look, Roark. I really do need to speak to you. We need to clear the air."

"We absolutely do not. Our marriage has been over for a long time."

When he tried to walk away, she grabbed his arm. "I was pregnant," she said. "That first year we were married, I got pregnant."

If Roark thought his conversation with Tamika had rocked him to the core, this admission had just pushed him over the cliff. He yanked his arm out of her grasp. "What the hell are you talking about?"

"By the time I found out it was too late, I'd miscarried. And then there was no point in saying anything. I wanted another baby so badly, but you never seemed to have the time, or that's the way I perceived your actions. In these past weeks I've been really thinking about that and about how much Maxine wanted grandchildren. I should've told you and I should've begged you to let us try again. But I didn't, and I'm so sorry for that."

"What?" He just couldn't wrap his mind around what was happening, now of all times. "Katrina, I don't know what's going on, but I've had enough. I've been through so much in these past weeks, and I can't believe you'd come all the way out here to feed me some bullshit like this."

"It's the truth, Roark!" Katrina was always the one to yell first.

"Okay, fine. It's the truth. What the hell do you expect me to say about it now? What do you want me to do?"

"I want us to try again."

Roark couldn't help it, he laughed. "Are you out of your mind? I mean, really, what on earth is going through your head right now?" He was about to walk away but then he stopped. "It's the money, isn't it? You knew all my mother's stock in the companies would revert to me, Ridge and Suri. That's why you're trying to come back?"

"We could have a beautiful child, Roark. Another Donovan. Perhaps a girl named Maxine. We could continue the legacy for your mother."

"You're insane," he told her. "And you're trespassing. Leave now, and I won't have security drag you out by your designer shoes."

"She doesn't know how to be your wife," she yelled after him. "That's why she really left. Because she knows she can't be what you need. I can give you what you and your mother wanted, Roark."

"You can go to hell," he snapped and continued walking away from her.

~

Tamika had made it to the parking lot when she stopped walking.

What was she doing? Was she really going to just walk away from him? Yes, she was, because she had to. Never in her wildest dreams had she imagined she'd fall in love with a millionaire and stay in a place as luxurious as the Dynasty Manor. She hadn't been one of those girls with the dream of finding and marrying her Prince Charming or of finding a man to take care of her. Tamika had been taught how to take care of herself, how to love herself. Colin had tried to break her down and for a short while she'd let him, but never again. Never, ever again.

Roark would never disrespect her the way Colin had; of that she was certain. But he had a lifestyle, and his family had expectations of him and whoever he married. And she had a life in Arlington. She may not have a job right now, but she had an apartment there and friends.

"You look stunning tonight," Lily said when she stepped out from behind one of the black SUVs Roark had leased.

"Oh." Tamika startled, a hand flying to her chest as if that was supposed to stop her now-thumping heart. "Lily, girl, don't creep up on me like that."

Lily smiled. "I'm sorry. I was just wandering around and saw you walking alone. Is everything alright?"

Dropping her arm back to her side, Tamika shook her head. "Yes. Everything's fine. I was just going to go back inside and spend some time with my mother."

"During a party? Really? You should be out there dancing the night away with Roark."

"No. I'd rather go inside." Tamika moved toward the door, and Lily stepped in front of her.

"No. You should stay out here," Lily insisted.

Tamika had been through a lot these past weeks, staying

in these estates, riding in private cars and limousines, but none of that dulled the street sense she'd honed while growing up. "I'm going inside. Now move out of my way," she told her even though she knew the words weren't going to be enough.

There was something different about Lily tonight. Her hair, for starters, was in one long braid down her back, and instead of wearing some combination of black and white like the rest of the staff, she was wearing jeans and a hoodie.

"I can't do that," Lily said.

"And why not?"

"Because this party was planned especially for you and the rest of the Donovan children. It's my letter of resignation, so to speak."

"What the hell are you talking about?"

Lily moved her arm so it was by her side, and for the first time since they'd been standing here, Tamika noticed there was something in her hand. "Did you think I'd just let you walk away? After all you and Roark have done?"

"We haven't done anything."

"Lies!" Lily screamed and shook her head as if Tamika were still talking and she didn't want to hear what she had to say. "You got in his way."

An icy tendril of dread rolled down Tamika's spine, and then her survival instincts kicked in. She took a step back away from Lily, putting space between them. "We got in whose way?" Keep her talking, that was the plan until she'd cleared those bushes on her left and she could run back toward the party.

"My father's."

Those two words stopped her from taking another step back, and she stared at Lily closely. Of course, there was no physical resemblance, since his face had been burned off. "Kaymen was your father."

Lily smiled brightly. "My mother found him and she took care of him, and he gave her me as a thank-you present."

What kind of insanity ran through that bloodline? Tamika had to focus on the here and now. She took that other step back just as Lily lifted her hand to tuck wayward strands of her hair behind her ear. Tamika couldn't tell what was in her hand, some sort of remote or… Dammit!

"My mother died two years ago and he took it very hard. After that, he said all he wanted to do was to find peace, and I was going to help him. That's why I told Maxine Donovan he was alive. I wanted each one of his former friends to be afraid and wonder when he'd finally come for them. He didn't tell me to do it, but I knew he'd like that they were scared. I knew everything about his accident and once I told Maxine, she knew I was telling the truth."

And Maxine had tried to warn her friends that he'd come back for them.

"Okay, Lily. Well, I'm going to go back to the party now," Tamika said and took another step.

But Lily moved, also closing the distance between them and getting in Tamika's face. "No. You and all the children of the ones who hurt my father are going to die tonight. I think that's only fair since I'm now left alone in this world."

Lily's voice held an eerie calmness, and Tamika wasn't sure how to handle it. She dealt with arsonists for a living, not psychopathic lunatics. It was a risk, because if Lily was holding what Tamika thought she was, doing anything other than trying to kiss up to this crazy heffa was sure to get them all blown up.

"I tried to start with the other girl, Suri, but I didn't make it strong enough. Tonight, it's better, because I had time to work on it after I watched you kill my father. I guess I needed the extra motivation."

"You let him in, didn't you? You let him into the house that night?" Tamika asked the question but she already knew the answer.

Lily laughed as if Tamika had just told a corny joke. "Yes. He's my father. I wanted him to be happy. I told him your mother was there and I left the window open on the pool side of the clubhouse when I went out to feed the guards dinner."

"He was fucking crazy, and so are you!" The rage took over in that moment. Thoughts of her mother being taped to that chair and Kaymen holding that blowtorch in front of her exploded in her mind, and Tamika pulled her arm back and punched Lily in the face.

Lily stumbled back, but she never lost grip of what was in her hand, not even when she charged Tamika. She should've run then, she had that small window of time when Lily had been dazed by the punch, but Tamika didn't move. Instead she stepped to the side and grabbed Lily in a headlock, squeezing so tight she could hear the woman wheeze. "You almost got my mother killed, you and that sick bastard of a father." Tamika wasn't going to kill her, but she'd put that bitch to sleep and then call the cops.

Lily had another plan, one Tamika hadn't seen coming, so when the blade sank into her thigh she cried out in pain and released her hold on Lily.

Lily immediately got the hell away from Tamika, running out into the middle of the parking lot, where she held up her hand. "You can die with the rest of those rich, entitled bitches down there. All of you can join my father in hell!"

Tamika didn't wait another moment but took the adrenaline rush of life versus death and yanked up that gown so she could run back in the direction of the garden. She opened her mouth and screamed for help as loud as she could while she ran, so loud it was almost heard over the blast of the explosion.

Almost.

EPILOGUE

*I*t'd been two months since Roark had left Painswick.

Repairs to the clubhouse had been in full swing, and the repairs to the front of the manor and the parking lot were scheduled to begin in the days following his departure.

The night of the party had been crazy and scary and more emotional than he'd ever wanted to experience again. The explosion had shaken the ground surrounding the manor, sending all the guests into a screaming and running frenzy. Roark had only one person on his mind when the explosion had hit, and he'd run for what seemed like a marathon until he'd found her lying in the grass, blood oozing from her thigh and a gash on her head.

Cade had immediately gone into cop mode, calling the Fire Brigade, the cops and anybody else whose number he had stored in his phone. In moments, the place was pure chaos, and that lasted for at least the next hour. Or rather, that was when Roark had climbed into the back of the ambulance to ride to the hospital with Tamika. Hating that they were once again at the hospital and still feeling guilty as hell for suggesting she be anything like Katrina, he'd only done what she asked him to do. He called her mother and let her speak to her so Sandra would know she was okay. He'd held her hand when the doctor had come in to stitch her thigh and her forehead. Then he'd carried her to her room at the manor after she'd been properly dosed with pain medications.

And then he'd returned to his room, where he'd slept alone.

Lily had died in the explosion, just as her father had died trying to play out his endgame. Roark, Cade and Pierce had been flabbergasted when Tamika had told them Lily was Kaymen's daughter, but when Pierce ran a background search on her under the pretense of notifying the next of kin, he'd indeed found the woman who'd helped Kaymen out of the car crash all those years ago. She'd been homeless at the time and had been living in a tent down under the incline where the car had tumbled. But since it was Tony's car, he'd apparently left a Rolex watch and other expensive jewelry in the glove compartment. The woman had taken it all, and she'd bought food and supplies to nurse Kaymen back to health. By then she'd fallen in love with him, and for a while they'd been happy until two years ago when Lily's mother died and Kaymen had read about the Donovans traveling to Africa for the wedding of Roark's cousin Dane and Zera. The death and mention of the Donovan name had been his stressors, and his plan to kill his former friends had been hatched.

Roark's ringing phone yanked him out of his thoughts, and he answered by pressing the speaker button.

"Where are you? Have you gotten there yet? Was she there? Did you apologize?" Suri rattled questions as fast as Roark drove along the road.

"Pause, take a breath," he said and then chuckled. "I'm not there yet. And it's just dinner."

"There's no such thing as 'just dinner' between two people who obviously love each other and belong together." Suri had been riding his back about him walking away from Tamika ever since he'd arrived back in London.

"She didn't mention anything other than dinner, so that's all I'm assuming it is."

"But you want it to be more, don't you? Come on, Roark, you can tell me. You're still in love with her, aren't you?"

He drummed his fingers on the steering wheel. "I wouldn't be taking this drive if I wasn't. But that's not the point."

"What do you mean, it's not the point? I can't believe you didn't fight for her," Suri snapped.

"Would you want a guy to fight for you, or respect you enough to find what you need for yourself?" That was the question Roark had fought with all these weeks. No, he hadn't wanted to leave Tamika, but he also didn't want to make her feel anything other than satisfied with not only her decision to be with him, but also for herself. She said she needed to love herself and be the woman she knew she could be, and he'd respected the hell out of that admission.

Katrina clearly didn't love herself. There was no way she could've stooped to that last-ditch effort to try and get back in his life if she did.

"Don't toss logic at me right now. I'm living this happy ever after vicariously," Suri said.

Roark chuckled. "I'll call you after dinner, okay?"

Suri sighed. "You'd better, or I'm coming to Painswick and knocking both you and Tamika's heads together until you come to your senses."

"Ah, that sounds painful. Bye, Suri."

"Bye-bye!" she said cheerfully.

With a smile on his face, Roark drove the last ten minutes to the cottage in Painswick. He parked his car and stepped out but didn't immediately go to the door.

He didn't know what to expect by walking in there. Truth be told, he'd hoped it was more than "just dinner" too. He'd dreamed of her every night, especially since he hadn't been able to sleep a solid eight hours since they'd stopped sleeping together. But he'd promised himself he wasn't going to push. And come hell or high water, he was going to abide by that promise.

"Thanks for coming," Tamika said after they'd finished eating the glazed ham, roasted potatoes and asparagus Tuppence had prepared for them. They were outside now, walking along one of the many pathways she'd discovered in the past two months.

"Of course," he said. "I wanted to see how you and your mum were doing, and Tuppence. It's great to hear you're all doing well." He was making a concerted effort to steer clear of any serious talk. He'd been doing that all night, and she appreciated it, but now it was time.

"I didn't go back to the States once my leg healed," she said.

The look on his face said he was shocked to hear that. "I thought you wanted to get back to your life, to look for work and see your friends."

They walked a few more steps before she answered. "I did want all of that. And it made perfect sense to want it at the time I said it."

"It made very good sense, and I'm sorry I didn't realize it before I made my proposal."

That proposal, the one she'd turned down and then kicked herself for weeks later because she'd turned it down. Even her mother had given her the side eye when she'd told her what had happened. Tamika had been more than angry with herself but still prideful about taking a stand until later that night when her mother had come into her room and sat on the edge of her bed. "Always follow your heart, MiMi, because your brain thinks it knows too much."

Those words had replayed in Tamika's mind for weeks after that.

"I got a job," she blurted out when it seemed they'd been silent too long. "At an international insurance company. I'll be supervising their arson investigation unit."

"That's wonderful," Roark said. "Is that what this is? A goodbye dinner? When do you leave?" He'd stopped walking now, just as they came under a gray stone bridge. A few feet behind him there was a stone wall and below that was the creek, the sound of the rustling water soothing.

She cleared her throat and looked up at him. "I'm not leaving. The company's main office is in London."

For a moment, Roark appeared to be speechless and then he looked hopeful. Then his features returned to the stoic and brooding guy she remembered from that first day in the dining room at the manor. "What does that mean?"

"Now, who's being blunt?" she joked, again recalling one of their early conversations.

"I just want to know whether or not I can release this breath I've been holding since walking into that cottage." He gave her a half smile, and it was the sexiest half smile she'd ever seen.

"I'm in love with you, Roark. And if you're not going to say you're still in love with me too, then you can just hold that breath all the way back to your car and drive away from here." There, she'd said it. Sort of.

That wasn't the way she'd rehearsed asking him to take her back. Then again, she wasn't totally sure they'd ever really been together, so she probably didn't need to ask anyway. And she was stalling again instead of getting on with the very important conversation.

"I didn't want you to put me up in a flat, as you call it. If I need a place to live, I'll pay my own rent. At least until we decide to move in together. Then, I'm more than happy to allow you to pay the bulk of the bills. And I didn't want to feel as if you were arranging my life, making decisions only I should make for myself." She paused and took a deep breath. "But I realized none of that stopped me from loving you. Actually, it was the fact that I knew you were a caring and compassionate provider for everyone you loved that made me fall for you in the first place. I know it's in your nature to take care of people, but it's in my nature to stand on my own."

He stepped toward her then, touching a finger to her lips. "Be quiet," he said and gave her that smile again. "Whatever you want, I'll do. However this arrangement plays out in your mind, I'm okay with it. Just so long as you're happy and in my arms."

She tilted her head and made a sound that resembled "awwww." "So we're doing this?" Her words were mumbled over his finger.

Roark chuckled and eased his hand to her cheek. "We're doing this because I can't stop loving you, Tamika Rayder."

She eased her arms around his waist and pulled him closer. "That works for me, because I can't stop loving you either, Roark Donovan."

THE DONOVAN FAMILY TREE

Download the Donovan Family Tree:
http://www.acarthur.net/download/3056/

1ST GENERATION

Elias (d) & Gertrude Donovan (d) – Children: Rowan (m. Adeline) and Charleston (m. Cora)

 Rowan (d) & Adeline Donovan (d) – Children: Isaiah (m. Dorethea), Aaron [d] (m. Sondra), Abraham (never married) and Bridgette a.k.a. Birdie (never married)

 Charleston (d) & Cora Donovan (d) – Children: Cephus (m. MingLee), Joanna (m. Johnathan Bowers), Katherine (d) (m. Myles Denton), Della (m. Robert Sats)

2ND GENERATION

Isaiah "Ike" (d) & Dorethea "Dot" Donovan (d) – Children: Albert (m. Darla[d]), Henry (m. Beverly), Bernard

(m. Jocelyn), Everette (m. Alma), Reginald (m. Carolyn) and Bruce (m. Janean)

> ***Aaron [d] & Sondra*** – Child: Gabriel (m. Maxine)
>
> ***Abraham "Abe" Donovan*** – Child: Margo (m. Klevon Whitfield)
>
> ***Bridgette "Birdie" Donovan*** – No Children

Cephus & Ming Lee – Children: Charles (m. Brenda), Wen (m. Hugo Norton)

> ***Joanna & Johnathan Bowers*** – Children: (twins) Loretta (m. Billy Ringgold), Lorraine (m. Jerry Seavers)
>
> ***Katherine "Kay" (d) & Myles Denton (d)*** – Children: Myles, Jr. (m. Alice)
>
> ***Della & Robert*** – No Children

3RD GENERATION

Albert & Darla – Children: Brock (m. Noelle), Brandon (m. Amber) and Bailey

> ***Henry & Beverly*** – Children: Lincoln (m. Jade), Trenton (m. Tia) and Adam (m. Camille)
>
> ***Bernard & Mary Lee (x)*** – Child: Keysa (m. Ian)
>
> ***Bernard & Jocelyn*** – Child: Brynne
>
> ***Everette & Alma*** – Children: Maxwell (m. Deena) and Benjamin (m. Victoria)
>
> ***Reginald & Carolyn*** – Children: Savian (m. Jenise), Parker (x Jaydon (d)) (Adriana), and Regan (Gavin)
>
> ***Bruce & Janean*** – Children: Dion (m. Lyra) and Sean (m. Tate)
>
> ***Gabriel & Maxine*** – Children: Roark, Ridgely and Suri
>
> ***Margo & Klevon*** – Children: (triplets) Alexis, Adonna and Amelia

Charles & Brenda – Children: Cadence "Cade", Dakota

Wen & Hugo – Child: Xia

Loretta & Billy – Children: Maria, Morganna & Hannah

Lorraine & Jerry – Children: Kendra & Cecile "CeeCee"

Myles Jr. & Alice – Child: Myles, III

4TH GENERATION

Brock & Noelle

    Brandon & Amber – Child: Serene

    Bailey & Devlin

    Lincoln & Jade – Children: Torian & Tamala

    Trenton & Tia – Child: Trevor

    Adam & Camille – Children: Josiah, Jordan

    Dane & Zera

    Keysa & Ian – Child: Madison Lee

    Brynne & Wade

    Maxwell & Deena – Child: Sophia

    Benjamin & Victoria – Child: Aria

    Savian & Jenise

    Parker & Adriana

    Regan & Gavin – Child: Raleigh

    Dion & Lyra – Child: Ilyssa

    Sean & Tate – Child: Briana

******Key: m = married; [d] = deceased; x = divorced

Brynne & Wade — Book 15: DESTINY OF A DONOVAN

* * *

Senior – Everette & Alma Donovan

Maxwell & Deena (Child: Daughter, Sophia) — Book 5: TOUCH OF FATE

Benjamin & Victoria (Child: Daughter, Aria) — Book 9: PLEASURED BY A DONOVAN

* * *

Senior – Reginald & Carolyn Donovan

Parker & Adriana — Book 11: EMBRACED BY A DONOVAN

Savian & Jenise — Book 12: WRAPPED IN A DONOVAN

Regan & Gavin (Child: Son, Raleigh) — Book 10: HEART OF A DONOVAN

* * *

Senior - Bruce & Janean Donovan

Dion & Lyra (Child: Daughter, Ilyssa) — Book 7: DESIRE A DONOVAN

Sean & Tate (Child: Daughter, Briana) — Book 8: SURRENDER TO A DONOVAN

~

THE DONOVAN FRIENDS

The Desdunes

Lucien & Marie Desdune

Lynette & Brice (Child: Son, Jeremy) — A CHRISTMAS WISH, part of the *Under The Mistletoe* Anthology

Cole & Loren — ALWAYS MY VALENTINE

Samuel & Karena (Child: Son, Elijah) — SUMMER HEAT

Sabrina & Lorenzo (Children: Daughters, Delia & Desirae, Son, Daniel) — GUARDING HIS BODY

* * *

The Bennetts

Marvin & Beatriz Bennett

Alexander & Monica — WINTER KISSES

Ricardo & Eva — ALWAYS IN MY HEART

Lorenzo & Sabrina (Children: Daughters, Delia & Desirae, Son, Daniel) — GUARDING HIS BODY

Adriana & Parker — Book 11: EMBRACED BY A DONOVAN

Gabriella & Tyler — FOR ALWAYS

* * *

The Lakefields

Paul & Noreen Lakefield

Monica & Alexander — WINTER KISSES

Karena & Samuel (Child: Son, Elijah) — SUMMER HEAT

Deena & Maxwell (Child: Daughter, Sophia) — Book 5: TOUCH OF FATE

∽

THE DONOVAN SERIES & THE DONOVAN FRIENDS BOOKS IN READING ORDER:

Book 1: LOVE ME LIKE NO OTHER

(Lincoln Donovan & Jade Vincent)

Book 2: A CINDERELLA AFFAIR

(Adam Donovan & Camille Davis)

Donovan Friends #1:

GUARDING HIS BODY

(Lorenzo Bennett & Sabrina Desdune)

Book 3: DEFYING DESIRE

(Trent Donovan & Tia St. Claire)

Book 4: FULL HOUSE SEDUCTION

(Brock Remington & Noelle Vincent)

Book 5: TOUCH OF FATE

(Maxwell Donovan & Deena Lakefield)

Donovan Friends #2:

SUMMER HEAT

(Samuel Desdune & Karena Lakefield)

Donovan Friends #3:

WINTER KISSES

(Alexander Bennett & Monica Lakefield)

Book 6: HOLIDAY HEARTS

(Ian Sanchez & Keysa Donovan)

Book 7: DESIRE A DONOVAN

(Dion Donovan & Lyra Anderson)

Book 8: SURRENDER TO A DONOVAN

(Sean Donovan & Tate Dennison)

Book 9: PLEASURED BY A DONOVAN

(Benjamin Donovan & Victoria Lashley)

Book 10: HEART OF A DONOVAN

(Regan Donovan & Gavin Lucas)

Donovan Friends #4:

A CHRISTMAS WISH

(Brice Wellington & Lynn Desdune),

part of the *Under The Mistletoe* Anthology

Donovan Friends #5:

ALWAYS MY VALENTINE

(Cole Desdune and Loren Knox)

Book 11: EMBRACED BY A DONOVAN

(Parker Donovan & Adriana Bennett)

Book 12: WRAPPED IN A DONOVAN

(Savian Donovan & Jenise Langley)

Donovan Friends #6:

ALWAYS IN MY HEART

(Ricardo "Rico" Bennett & Eva Romaine)

Book 13: IN THE ARMS OF A DONOVAN

(Brandon Donovan & Amber McNair)

Book 14: FALLING FOR A DONOVAN

(Bailey Donovan & Devlin Bonner)

Book 15: DESTINY OF A DONOVAN

(Brynne Donovan & Wade Banks)

Donovan Friends #7:

FOR ALWAYS

(Tyler West & Gabriella Bennett)

Donovan Friends #8:

THE WINTER WEDDING

(Cheyna Dansfield & Logan Williams)

The Donovan Dynasty

Book 1: DANE

Book 2: ROARK

ALSO BY AC ARTHUR

OTHER CONTEMPORARY ROMANCE

After Hours Trilogy

Book 1: OFFICE POLICY

Book 2: CORPORATE SEDUCTION

Book 3: LAWS OF ATTRACTION

Bundle: AFTER HOURS TRILOGY

* * *

The Indecent Series

Book 1: INDECENT PROPOSAL

Book 2: INDECENT EXPOSURE

* * *

Rules of the Game Trilogy

Book 1: RULES OF THE GAME

Book 2: REVELATIONS

Book 3: REDEMPTION

* * *

The Carrington Chronicles

Book 1: WANTING YOU - Part One

Book 2: WANTING YOU - Part Two

Book 3: NEEDING YOU

Book 4: HAVING YOU

* * *

The Rumors Series

Book 1: RUMORS

Book 2: REVEALED

* * *

The Royal Weddings

Book 1: TO MARRY A PRINCE

Book 2: LOVING THE PRINCESS

Book 3: PRINCE EVER AFTER

Book 4: TAMING THE PRINCE

* * *

The Temptation Series

Book 1: ONE MISTLETOE WISH

Book 2: ONE UNFORGETTABLE KISS

Book 3: ONE PERFECT MOMENT

Book 4: ONE CHRISTMAS SONG

* * *

Fashion & Passion

Book 1: A PRIVATE AFFAIR

Book 2: AT YOUR SERVICE

* * *

OBJECT OF HIS DESIRE

UNCONDITIONAL

LOVE ME CAREFULLY

HEART OF THE PHOENIX

SECOND CHANCE, BABY

SING YOUR PLEASURE

DECADENT DREAMS

EVE OF PASSION

PARANORMAL ROMANCE

The Shadow Shifters

Book 1: TEMPTATION RISING

Book 2: SEDUCTION'S SHIFT

Book 3: PASSION'S PREY

Book 4: SHIFTER'S CLAIM

Book 5: HUNGER'S MATE

Book 6: PRIMAL HEAT

Book 7: A LION'S HEART

* * *

The Damaged Hearts Series

(Shadow Shifters Spinoff)

Book 1: MINE TO CLAIM

Book 2: PART OF ME

Book 3: HUNGER FOR YOU

Book 1-3: DAMAGED HEARTS BOX SET

* * *

The Wolf Mates

The Alpha's Woman (Available as part of the GROWL
Anthology and CLAIMED BY THE MATE VOL.1 Duology)

Her Perfect Mates (Available as part of the WILD Anthology and CLAIMED BY THE MATE VOL.2 Duology)

Bound to the Wolf (Available as part of the HUNGER Anthology and CLAIMED BY THE MATE VOL.3 Duology)

* * *

The Legion

Book 1: AWAKEN THE DRAGON

Book 2: CLAIM THE DRAGON

* * *

WICKED: The Desireable Witches

∼

CONTEMPORARY SMALL TOWN ROMANCE (W/A LACEY BAKER)

The Sweetland Series

Book 1: HOMECOMING

Book 2: JUST LIKE HEAVEN

Book 3: SUMMER'S MOON

* * *

A GINGERBREAD ROMANCE

∼

YOUNG ADULT PARANORMAL (W/A ARTIST
ARTHUR)

The Mystyx Series

Book 1: MANIFEST

Book 2: MYSTIFY

Book 3: MAYHEM

A Mystyx Novella: MUTINY

Book 4: MESMERIZE

* * *

Pretty Little Liars Kindle Worlds

THE STRONG SHALL SURVIVE

BE MY SWEETHEART

ABOUT THE AUTHOR

Stay in touch with A.C. on the web!

Be the first to know when A.C. Arthur's next book is available! Follow her at BookBub to get an alert whenever she has a new release, preorder, or discount!

Visit the "Contact" page on her website, www.acarthur.net, to sign up for her monthly newsletter.

"Follow", "Friend" and/or "Like" her on Facebook (AC Arthur's Book Lounge), Twitter (@ACArthur), Book and Main (acarthur22), Pinterest (acarthur22), Instagram (@acarthurbooks), Tumblr (acarthurbooks), and GoodReads.

facebook.com/ACBookLounge

twitter.com/ACArthur

instagram.com/acarthurbooks

pinterest.com/acarthur22

bookbub.com/profile/a-c-arthur

Made in the USA
Middletown, DE
07 July 2024

56991733R00183